The Devil's Pipeline

By the author of ***The Fracking War***
and ***Fracking Justice***

Michael J. Fitzgerald

Subject2Change Media
Point Richmond, California

Copyright © 2018 by Michael J. Fitzgerald
Subject2Change Media

This is a work of fiction. Names, characters, brands, media, and incidents are either the product of the author's imagination or are used factitiously. Any references to historical events, real people, or real locales are used fictitiously. Other names, characters, places and incidents are products of the author's imagination and any resemblance to actual events or locales or persons, living or dead, is coincidental. The author acknowledges the trademarked status and trademark owners of various products referenced in this work of fiction which have been used without permission. The publication/use of these trademarks is not authorized, associated with, sponsored by the trademark owners.

All rights to republication of this work are reserved. No part of this publication may be reproduced, stored in or introduced into a retrieval system, or transmitted, in any form, or by any means (electronic, mechanical, photocopying, recording, or otherwise) without prior written permission of the copyright owner. For permission or information on foreign, audio, or other rights, contact the author at authormichaeljfitzgerald.com

ISBN- 9781730975073
Cover Design by Molly Eckler of California
Published in the United States of America

ACKNOWLEDGMENTS

If it takes a village to raise a child, it takes a cadre of patient people to help a novel go from concept to manuscript to publication.

The leader of my cadre is Sylvia Fox, my wife, best friend and editor. She nudged me when necessary, offered advice at critical junctures, solved innumerable production problems and essentially midwifed *The Devil's Pipeline* from raw ideas and words to a book.

This novel would not be in your hands without hers having helped me through the process as she has done twice before and likely will do again for future planned tomes.

The supporting cadre for this novel included two excellent beta readers, Wrexie Bardaglio of Trumansburg, NY and Elizabeth Claman of Point Richmond, Calif.

Wrexie's name should be familiar to readers of my two previous novels, *The Fracking War* and *Fracking Justice*, for which she was an editor and beta reader. Her expertise was particularly critical on this novel given her knowledge of Native American culture and the Midwest.

Elizabeth Claman's contributions as a beta reader included close editing of dialogue and breaking me of several bad author habits.

Last minute proofreading and editing suggestions by Point Richmond author Rita Gardner puts her firmly in the cadre that brought this book into print.

A special thanks goes to Sebastopol, Calif. artist Molly Eckler who stepped in at the 11th hour to produce a stunning cover for *The Devil's Pipeline* in a dizzyingly short time frame.

And lastly, I thank my four children, Jason, Anne, Dustin and Dylan – and my many friends – who continue to encourage me regularly by asking when the next book is coming out.

Point Richmond, California
November 1, 2018

IOWA

Fifteen-year-old Caleb Osmett adjusted his field glasses just in time to focus on a man in a white gas company uniform cutting the top strand of the five lines of barbed wire at the far edge of the field.

He could see a small knot of men in dark uniforms behind the cutter, carrying rifles.

Caleb was perched in a cupola at the top of his grandfather's farmhouse. He had a commanding view of the remote 1,000-acre Iowa farm he lived on with his grandfather, his mother, and 20 other families scattered on the acreage, all part of a place called *The Redoubt*.

His grandfather had posted him on the platform each morning for the last week with strict instructions to keep a sharp eye out for anyone coming up to the front gate.

Caleb shivered in the early October cold watching men unload equipment from several white pickup trucks. He was too far away to see exactly what was happening but he was *sure* he should ring the alarm bell.

Last month Caleb had helped his grandfather and others string spools of shiny new barbed wire around the entire farm, replacing the rusty metal wire that had broken in dozens of spots. They also replaced the ancient wooden main gate, with a five-foot tall stout metal unit that had barbed wire woven all through the cross pieces and across the top.

Now the uniformed man was cutting through the new wire only a few yards from the metal gate secured with a chain and lock so heavy Caleb's grandfather had grunted when he lifted them out of his truck to wrap it around the post to secure it.

Caleb knew that the man cutting was standing too close to the tightly taut wire as it sprang back, hitting him across the face and knocking him down. Caleb dropped the field glasses, grabbed the bell cord and started pulling hard, sending out a loud clanging peal that could be heard across the farm.

The men with rifles stared, some pointing in Caleb's direction. He kept pulling the cord methodically sounding the bell his grandfather said had been brought from rural upstate New York. "Two hundred years ago, they used it to warn of Indians," his grandfather told him.

People poured out of houses and barns as the bell rang and rang. They hopped into trucks, cars and four-wheelers, all racing toward the main gate and fence line where trucks bearing the bold red letters **DEF** – the symbol of the DeVille Energy Federation – were parked on the gravel road.

Caleb stopped ringing the bell when he saw his grandfather's pickup truck fishtailing on the gravel road toward the gate where the man with the cutting tool was still struggling to cut through a strand of barbed wire.

He picked up the field glasses again and watched. His grandfather had firmly ordered him to stay up in the cupola if something like this happened – unless his mother said to come down. Caleb shouted down the ladder into the house to his mother twice then looked across the fields realizing she had probably been in the pickup truck with his grandfather.

As the farmers started lining up near the fence and gate, they partially blocked Caleb's view. He saw some of them, arms waving in the air. Occasionally he caught a glimpse of the uniformed men with guns who had moved closer to the property line.

Then he heard a voice, sounding like it was coming through a bullhorn.

"Enough of your shouting, you people. Enough! We have the legal right to come on your property. Move it now. All of you. God damn it. I said *move it*. Move it right NOW."

Caleb was about to disobey his grandfather and abandon his post when he saw the line of his neighbors suddenly break. A few of the people turned away from the gate and started running, leaving a big gap. Caleb saw the men with rifles step over the bottom two strands of the barbed wire, pointing their rifles in front of them. Right behind the armed men several men were carrying what to Caleb looked like surveying gear.

Two people, then three – then a fourth dropped to the ground, like dolls tossed down.

Caleb was starting down the ladder when the sound of the gunshots finally reached him.

Chapter 2

Jack Stafford reread a wire service story about the shootings in Iowa again, comparing the national news account to the stories published by his three newspapers, the *Horseheads* (NY) *Clarion*, the *Rockwell Valley* (PA) *Tribune* and his newly launched publication, the *Vashon* (WA) *View*.

He was pretty certain the wire services had all missed a huge piece of historical detail in the story.

Some reporters and editors are going to get chewed out for this one, Jack thought.

He logged off the website of the *Horseheads Clarion*, the flagship of the *Clarion Newspaper Syndicate.*

Outside his office window at the *View*, Jack could see early morning tourists window-shopping at a new art gallery across the street. And the coffee shop/diner where Jack went for tea most mornings was doing a brisk business, too.

He was pleased to see his just-published book, *Saving Pennsylvania: An Environmental and Economic Manual*, on display in the coffee shop window.

The *Vashon View* had become instantly popular with local residents and tourists because of its strong environmental focus and mix of local, national and sometimes even international news. It was an odd combination for a twice-a-week, small town newspaper, but it was a recipe that also worked well in his New York and Pennsylvania newspapers.

And all three newspapers were turning profits in both the print and on-line editions, bucking an industry trend that had many newspapers downsizing – or going bust.

He had just begun to contemplate a topic for his Friday column when *Vashon View* editor Alexandra Potomac burst through the front door of the office, bringing with her a gust of wind, a tan briefcase overstuffed with papers, and a mop of reddish-blonde hair that had clearly lost its battle with the October breeze.

Alexandra's hair, plus a generously freckled face, had prompted Jack's seven-year-old son Noah to nickname her Raggedy Ann the first time he met her.

"Damn," Alexandra said. "I was sure I would beat you into the office today. *Sure* of it. Honestly Jack, do you, like *sleep* here? Am I going to have to sleep here if I want to get to work first?"

She slipped her briefcase off her shoulder onto a corner desk where a cardboard sign had the scrawled sentence "The Editor Sits Here – Not You." She plopped down in her chair, booted up her desktop computer and stared at Jack with her habitual directness that still made him a little uncomfortable.

When he interviewed her for the editor/writer position months before, he finally asked her if she *ever* blinked.

The grin she gave him in response, coupled with a flurry of madly blinking eyes and an eye-popping journalism/environmentalist résumé, landed her the job.

"I don't think my son Noah would like it much if I wasn't there in the morning to make him breakfast," Jack said. "He's in first grade this fall. I drop him off at school – that's why I'm always here so early."

Alexandra turned her attention to her computer then swung back to look at Jack after a moment.

"The wire services are already playing catch up with the Iowa story," she said. "But they credit us, anyway. Well, actually they credit the *Horseheads Clarion*. Nice job, chief. You might be the only person to have made the connection between the Kent State shooting and the people killed in Iowa."

Jack looked back out the window, feeling Alex's eyes on him until he heard her tapping on her keyboard again.

And it's definitely what I'm writing about today, he thought.

Chapter 3

The Clarion Newspaper Syndicate
Column One

Kent State and the Devil's Pipeline

By Jack Stafford

James Albert Osmett was a quiet, gentle man who wanted nothing but to stay clear of all violence, raise his family and grow food on a large Iowa farm he had named The Redoubt when he first took up residence there in late 1970.

The name in Medieval Latin means "place of refuge" – which is what it was for him and many others.

He had been a student and front-row witness to the tragic Kent State shootings that took the lives of four people. Only a few days later he drove west in a battered VW van, eventually settling on an extremely remote patch of Iowa prairie farmland. There, over a period of 40-plus years, he attracted dozens of like-minded, peace-loving people who built small houses in the communal setting on his 1,000-plus acre farm.

The owners of the property deeded the land to Mr. Osmett when they learned he was refugee from Kent State and was looking to live a peaceful life.

I know all about this because I wrote a story about James Albert Osmett more than 20 years ago. In those interviews, his eyes filled with tears as he recalled the smell of cordite in the air, the sounds of the gunshots, the screams of students, and people running as bullets whizzed through the air on the Kent State campus that day.

He was proud of the rural, environmentally conscious community he had founded in Iowa. Long before alternative energy and sustainability became popular buzzwords, The Redoubt was using windmills, early generation solar panels and crops using organic gardening methodologies that are common today.

"Most people wouldn't use the words Iowa and paradise in the same sentence," he told me when I visited. "But I do. Every day."

Mr. Osmett was murdered last week along with three other residents of The Redoubt, killed in a hail of bullets fired by poorly trained security guards in the employ of the DeVille Energy Federation.

Their shooting deaths are eerily similar to what drove Mr. Osmett to seek refuge on the farm.

A court had opened the way for the guards to force their way onto his property by cutting through a barbed-wire fence so DEF could survey the property for a planned massive project that opponents have dubbed "The Devil's Pipeline."

A court order said they had the right to come on to the land.

When The Redoubt residents were slow to move out of the way of the survey team, one of the guards fired his semi-automatic weapon, touching off a chain reaction among the other armed men who likewise began shooting.

The guard who let loose the first volley of bullets claims he fired accidentally.

And the balance of the guards – five in all – claim they thought the sound of gunfire meant that people were shooting at them.

The grim photos of the bloody bodies of Mr. Osmett, two middle-aged women, and a coverall-clad 25-year-old man lying dead on the ground are as emotionally wrenching as the scene that Osmett witnessed at Kent State. Senseless deaths caused by an equally senseless, equally unnecessary confrontation.

The DeVille Energy Federation is refusing to take responsibility for the shootings. If anything, it's blaming the victims who told DEF that they did not want any surveying of their land because The Redoubt was not going to let any pipeline traverse the farm.

No pipelines, period.

A DEF spokesman says the company hired the private security guards to stand by "and keep the peace" while it surveyed the land. The company feared it would meet "armed resistance" based on letters from The Redoubt, and confrontations the company has had in similar situations where residents want no part of the pipeline project.

Had the company bothered to talk directly to Mr. Osmett or others on the farm before launching the assault, it would have known one of the basic tenets of The Redoubt since it was founded in the 1970s is that no guns have ever been allowed on the property.

And it stayed that way, peacefully, until last week.

Jack Stafford is the publisher and editor-in-chief of the Clarion Newspaper Syndicate. He publishes Column One every Friday and can be reached at JJStafford@ClarionNewsSyndicate.com.

Chapter 4

Half of the huge Houston office suite of DeVille Energy Federation President A.G. DeVille was filled with all kinds of miniature, odd mechanical contraptions and small-scale science exhibits like seen in a high school physics laboratory.

The rest of the suite was classic energy-magnate: photos of DeVille with political leaders, a dazzling display of DEF energy projects around the world, maps of proposed (and in-process) DEF endeavors and a shiny maple desk the size of an aircraft carrier.

On the far wall, a framed architectural magazine photo essay featured DeVille and his office headlined: The Playground of the Captain of the Energy Industry.

On this late October day the playground was not a happy place.

The "captain of the energy industry" was contemplating exactly how he would punish the DEF operations manager in Iowa who had responsibility for the survey party where the shootings occurred.

Firing isn't enough for him, DeVille thought. He needs to made an example.

While he brooded and waited for his political/public relations SWAT staff to assemble in the adjacent conference room, his eyes drifted to the only personal photo on his desk.

It was turned so only he could see it from his chair.

He had once nearly fired a vice president for having the temerity to actually pick up the photo from his desk. DeVille still fumed when he thought about that.

Since then, the rare staff member who was allowed into his private office approached DeVille's desk as cautiously and subserviently as if it were the throne of an erratic monarch from the Middle Ages.

The photo had been featured in the Captain of the Energy Industry story, noting that DeVille had never married or ever been linked to any women.

"His work is his life and marriage," the magazine story said. "His personal life is one thing he won't discuss."

DeVille examined the photo closely, something he did nearly every day marveling at how youthful he looked the day he turned 18 and walked out of the Iowa orphanage that raised him. Standing with him in the photo was the Greek janitor who named him on the icy January day he was found on the doorstep in a cardboard box, likely just a week old. The janitor's name was Archimedes, a name he convinced the orphanage to give to DeVille along with his last name – derived from the wheezing Cadillac the orphanage used to ferry its children around.

I suppose I should be happy the orphanage drove a coupe DeVille and didn't own a Toyota, DeVille thought.

In college, some of his classmates took to calling him Archie – short for Archimedes.

But once he began moving through the ranks of the oil and gas industry, he quickly shifted to using his initials only. Very few people knew his middle name was Gabriel, also a gift from Archimedes the janitor.

DeVille capitalized letter 'V' in the middle of his last name to support his claim to French ancestry.

As DeVille put the picture down he saw a line of text had appeared on his glass-top desk, the center of which was a state-of-the-art display system for all types of electronic communications.

At the touch of a button he could adjust the center of the desk from a flat surface to any angle he wanted.

His secretary had written that his staff was assembled in an adjacent conference room with the agenda in front of them as he had ordered.

It only had one word on it:

Iowa.

Chapter 5

The three-way debate among the editors of the *Vashon View, Horseheads Clarion* and *Rockwell Valley Tribune* during their videoconference had started to irritate Jack as he listened to Alexandra arguing with Clarion editor Eli Gupta and Tribune editor Keith Everlight.

"You know, it's a good thing we don't ever record you guys going at it in these meetings," Jack said loudly enough from across the room that it was picked up by the microphone on Alexandra's computer. "Or maybe I should."

Jack's voice stopped all debate about how to follow up on the Iowa shootings. All three editors thought the newspaper group needed boots on the ground there. But each thought they alone should either send someone or go themselves.

Jack moved over from his desk to Alexandra's so he could see Eli and Keith's images projected from their respective offices 2,500 miles to the east.

"Look, I get it," Jack said. "You get it. Yes, we need to follow up. And it is a national story. The thing I want all three of you – and your reporters to do – is to start looking at this not just from the guns-and-bullets angle. We have barely touched this pipeline project. Or whatever it is. Let's not just chase the shiny news object, in this case the shooting. Even as tragic as it is."

He knew that the slight video time delay was accentuating the impact of what he said. But even Alexandra, sitting right next to him, stopped to take a sip of her coffee before speaking.

"I think you need to help us out here, Jack," she said. "Part of the problem is none of us has a budget to send a reporter or go catapulting to Iowa. Plus, Eli knows more about the project than anybody. I nominate him to go."

Before Jack could jump in, Eli spoke up.

"Jack. No one knows details about the pipeline project," Eli said. "Sketchy doesn't even describe it. And you already know all about the feds clamping down again on energy security. We're working a story right now about all the private guards patrolling pipelines. If you think people are pissed about being forced to have a pipeline cross their property, you should talk to them about having armed security guards on motorcycles zooming up and down day and night."

Jack saw that Keith Everlight was patiently waiting for Eli to finish. Eli had been Keith's boss until Jack created the newspaper syndicate when he added the *Rockwell Valley Tribune*. Both had worked well as colleagues at the *Horseheads Clarion* for several years. Even with the somewhat grainy video connection, it looked to Jack like Keith was staying physically fit, though his amateur boxing days in college were getting further and further behind him.

"I don't mean to take over your editors' meeting, guys. Really," Jack said. "But this Iowa thing does need follow-up. I don't know how you want to do it."

Jack waited to hear something from the three editors. He sighed before speaking when they stayed silent. "OK, well, then. I have an idea. I haven't been out of this office for months. I think a trip to Iowa would be good. Plus, I need to pay my respects to James Osmett's family. I met his daughter Janis when I wrote about the farm and her dad. She must be devastated."

His announcement didn't elicit as much as a single groan from the three editors, even though they probably really wanted to go themselves.

"Well Mr. Publisher, I did ask for you to step in, not out," Alexandra said. "And some of your columns coming from Iowa won't hurt."

Jack walked back to his desk, listening with one ear to the chatter about collaboration on other energy-related stories and some local stories planned for each paper that might be suitable for all three publications.

He thought about how lucky he was to have such a great mix of editorial talent: Eli, with amazing computer and research skills, Keith, a fearless editor and reporter, willing to take even physical chances to get the story, and Alexandra, whose analytical skills were almost frightening. Her ability to connect the dots in complicated situations was one of the chief reasons he had hired her.

He was reminded of her ability to sort things out when she came over and sat in the chair next to his desk.

"So, second thoughts?" Jack asked. "Here to plead for an Iowa vacation? The corn crop is already harvested. Might be a little dull for you."

Alexandra gave Jack a stare, then deliberately starting blinking rapidly, which made him laugh.

"Nope, like Spock on Star Trek said? Remember? Only Nixon could go to China. Well, only Stafford can go to Iowa. Your connection to that family cements that."

Jack waited. He knew she had something else and he bet it was about the DeVille pipeline. Something she didn't want to mention to the other two editors yet.

"Well, I started drawing on a map, kind of sketching what we know about the route of that pipeline," she said. "They haven't announced much about approvals or anything. They haven't even admitted it's a pipeline, exactly. Which is so weird it's amazing. But, anyway. I looked at news stories to chart where there have been pockets of opposition. Most of the people protesting were tipped off by obscure legal notices. It's amazing how you can plan a whole project like this and not have to let the public know. Can you believe it? Anyway, I started tracing the protests and even found a couple of pending lawsuits against DeVille working backwards from where The Redoubt farm is in Iowa. It seems like the survey is moving east to west."

Jack looked at Alexandra and congratulated himself – again – grateful for making a good hire for editor of the *Vashon View*.

"The thing is, the eastern end looks like it starts in, well, Milwaukee. I mean, really, Milwaukee?" Alexandra said. "There's no gas or oil near there. Or refineries."

She stood up suddenly and put her hands on top of her head, spinning around twice.

"Oh shit!" she said, her eyes opening wide.

Jack watched her starting to connect the dots on another possibility.

"You're right, Alexandra," Jack said. "I don't think it's for moving energy products west to east. There's nothing on the eastern end to process oil or package natural gas. It's going to be east to west. I doubt it's to ship Milwaukee beer."

"So what the heck are they shipping," Alexandra asked, eyes wide open.

"Water," Jack said. "It's the big new commodity. I think DeVille Energy Federation might be building a pipeline to move water from the Great Lakes."

Chapter 6

The only person happy about Jack's trip to Iowa in the Stafford-Walsh household was Jack.

Seven-year-old Noah, his two aunts, Cass and Anne, and even Jack and Noah's dog Tokanga seemed a little out of sorts that Jack would be gone for a week or more.

It meant Noah would move across the driveway from the small house he and Jack shared into the main house where Cass and Anne lived. Sitting at the dinner table, Noah peppered Jack with questions about Iowa while Cass and Anne exchanged glances. Jack knew he was probably in for a lecture. It was just a matter of when he would get it.

Maybe on the way to the airport tomorrow, he thought. No. After dinner we'll have a family meeting after Noah goes to bed.

When Jack's wife Devon had died in a boating accident in Tonga several years before – and Noah nearly drowned, too – Cass flew to the remote South Pacific island kingdom for the funeral, grieving for the loss of her sister.

She ended up rescuing Jack from a downward spiral of depression. One night, senselessly drunk, he had tried to swim from the island he lived on with Devon to another island – across two miles of open water. Cass had stopped him.

On the island in Tonga, she immediately became attached to little Noah. He quickly latched onto her, too.

Cass tapped her spoon against her wine glass to get everyone's attention.

"You look like you're already in Iowa, Jack," Cass said. "We didn't toast at the beginning of dinner. Tradition, you know. Come on. I have a toast."

They raised their glasses, while they waited for Cass to speak.

Cass, Anne and Jack's wine glasses were filled with Riesling shipped in from the Finger Lakes region of New York. Noah's had a healthy fruit juice-seltzer concoction.

"Here's to safe travels and a safe return," she said. "Oh, and a *quick* return."

Jack leaned over to ensure he could click glasses with everyone. "I know none of you are keen on my leaving so suddenly for Iowa," he said. "But I don't expect to be gone long at all. There's a memorial service for the people who were killed and I'm going to be talking with people about this pipeline project there in Iowa. I think the people working on the pipeline might be telling some of the local folks what's going on. It's an important story."

Jack sat back, feeling defensive as he watched what he said wash over Cass and Anne. Noah had gone back to digging into the vegetable pie Anne had made for their dinner.

Jack marveled at Anne's cooking skills. Her food was always delicious and filling, but he never seemed to gain a pound.

The four of them generally lived in an easy domesticity.

Cass had resumed playwriting and directing at a local playhouse. She was also doing adjunct teaching part time at a private Seattle university.

Anne worked as an accountant and consultant out of her home office. She had clients all over the U.S. and did all of her work via computer links. Anne also was handling a lot of the finances of the three newspapers.

Noah had adopted *both* women as surrogate mothers, causing minor confusion at his school when he insisted that he had two mothers – and a father.

In the year before Jack decided to start the *Vashon View*, he had gone back to Horseheads, NY – the town where he was born, grew up and still owned the flagship newspaper in the small chain. Horseheads was where he and Devon had lived and worked together for several years before going to Tonga for Jack to write his first book.

What was supposed to be a two-to-three-week business trip there had dragged out to more than three months, prompting a flurry of phone calls and emails from Cass and Anne to Jack, urging him to return to Vashon. In the end, the two sisters were right.

"Well, I have an idea, Jack," Cass said. "Anne and I already talked about it."

Uh-oh, Jack thought. *Here it comes.*

Cass covered her mouth as she laughed.

"You should see the look on your face, Jack. Honestly!"

Anne let out a short laugh.

Noah wasn't sure what was going on, but he laughed, too.

"I don't know what you think I'm going to say, but it's no huge thing," Cass said. "I think I should go with you to Iowa. I haven't been away from the West Coast for a long time. A little dose of Middle America in the fall might be just the thing for me. A trip. I don't have any plays for weeks. And you said not long, right?"

Jack leaned back in his chair, trying not to show he was secretly pleased. His sister-in-law Cass was a good traveler and had many of the same journalistic instincts as his late-wife Devon.

"I shouldn't be that surprised, I guess," Jack said. "You'll drag me home if I stay too long, right?"

Cass nodded and raised her glass for another toast, this one for safe travels for both Jack and her.

"By the way," Anne said. "Neither of you has to wake up all that early. I changed your reservation this afternoon when I added Cass to the trip. You and Cass leave at noon from the Seattle Airport."

Jack shook his head and smiled. *Outnumbered,* he thought. *Outnumbered and outflanked.*

Chapter 7

The sketch was a simple drawing, done on a very thin, onion-skin type of paper.

A *Redoubt* shooting survivor – one of the women who narrowly escaped getting hit by a bullet that day – found the drawing on the ground in the aftermath of what news media were calling "The Redoubt Massacre."

Internet memes using altered historical sketches of "The Boston Massacre" were circulating all across social media.

In the confusion of the gunfire, some of the DEF survey workers had run back to the safety of their pickup trucks, dropping instruments, tools and clipboards.

Sheriff's deputies eventually cordoned off the area with yellow crime scene tape. The small space inside the taped area was still littered with some equipment, a few hard hats and other gear the deputies warned not to touch.

The region's news media had proven to be almost as aggressive as the DEF surveyors in wanting to come on *The Redoubt*. They just carried cameras, not guns.

For the first few days after the shooting, a dozen television vans sprouting huge antennas parked across the road day and night, with newscasters doing on-camera standups in front of the gate, often under bright spotlights.

Caleb Osmett watched the media circus from the cupola with his field glasses. He still went up there every morning with his late grandfather's admonishments to keep watch for intruders ringing in his ears.

He knew that he had done *his* job – sounding the bell. But he felt guilty. His mother told him he needed time to grieve and that it would pass.

He wasn't so sure.

Each time he raised the field glasses he found that he replayed the scene of the bodies dropping to the ground.

The other three dead people were like family, too. But his grandfather's death brought tears he mostly kept hidden.

He was starting to feel a boiling anger like nothing he'd ever experienced. His grandfather had raised him from a very young boy when his musician father had abandoned Caleb and his mother. His grandfather's parenting included daily discussions of non-violence and the importance of peaceful, harmonious living.

In the cupola, Caleb had started daydreaming of getting a gun – and protecting *The Redoubt* with it.

In the days after the shooting many of *The Redoubt* residents gathered evenings at the main farmhouse where Caleb's grandfather James had lived with Caleb and Caleb's mother Janis, partly to grieve for the dead, partly to plan.

It was Caleb who first recognized that the pipeline that DEF wanted to push through *The Redoubt* property – at least if the drawing was accurate – seemed bigger than any oil and gas pipeline he had seen in news photos.

"You could drive a pickup truck through that thing," Caleb said, looking at the drawing. "Maybe two, side by side."

Chapter 8

The name "DeVille Energy Federation" obscured the fact that DEF was actually a multi-national corporate conglomerate that included companies of all kinds, ranging from energy to equipment to resource acquisition. In the last few years DEF had even started acquiring some food manufacturing and processing businesses. And in the process, one division was quietly getting control of water rights all over the U.S.

"Food and water are where the money and power will be," A.G. DeVille told his executive staff nearly every time they met. "Oil and gas? They're small potatoes in the big picture. Especially with energy prices right now."

But DeVille was well aware he needed to avoid the kind of overt moves that would draw unwanted media attention. He often used the example of the young hedge fund manager who raised the price of a drug used by cancer patients, ending up becoming a late-night comedy punch line – and briefly one of the most hated people on the planet.

"What an ass," DeVille would tell his staff, "to let himself be the lightning rod like that. Stupid, stupid, stupid."

It was DeVille's philosophy to keep business dealings low-key which made him deeply upset by all the attention surrounding the Iowa shootings. *Journalists, federal regulators and crackpot environmentalists,* DeVille thought. *Damn them all.*

He kept the company insulated from liability through a series of subcontractors for nearly everything. If there was an accident on an oil or gas-drilling rig, the responsibility fell on the shoulders of companies that were hired to do that specific job – and who signed a hold harmless clause for DEF.

But in Iowa, the DEF manager involved in the surveying project incomprehensibly opted to take clearly recognizable DEF employees and equipment to the site. The only thing he did right was hire a private security firm – at least from a liability standpoint.

Now sitting in a staff meeting with his best people, DeVille fumed over the mistake. "I know. I know it would look bad to fire him," DeVille said. "I'd like to have him publicly flogged. Whipped right outside this building. What a jackass to expose us like this. We're looking at potentially billions of dollars – federal subsidy dollars. It could be the golden goose on steroids. And this guy hires clowns who can't even face down a bunch of unarmed farmers. All right. Where are we with this?"

DeVille looked over at Rod Mayenlyn, a survivor of the Rockwell Valley, Pennsylvania gas explosions from several years before that had prompted federal hearings and proposals for safety standards.

Mayenlyn had spent months after the explosions in a wheelchair and only in the last few months had begun to walk with crutches, then canes and most recently short stretches without any aids.

Mayenlyn had testified to federal investigators about his work with the energy company responsible for the twin blasts. One explosion was the result of a huge liquid propane gas spill that fanned out on the surface of the lake near town. The other was triggered when natural gas leaking from an underwater pipeline ignited right in front of an historic hotel.

Civil lawsuits had finally bankrupted Grand Energy Services, where Mayenlyn had been a vice president of public relations, a job that included occasional dirty jobs at the behest of the CEO. His demeanor and answers in televised hearings had earned DeVille's respect.

"The only way this could have been worse is if some children had been killed," Mayenlyn said. "I suppose it's obvious. But of all the goddamn farmers in Iowa, we had to pick one to shoot who was at Kent State the day those four college students were killed. You think God doesn't have a sense of irony? The women and the young guy who died aren't getting much attention. The media only cares about Osmett."

DeVille looked around the table, reading the faces of the other six vice presidents and managers. He called the group the Seven Dwarfs. They always laughed nervously when he said it.

"All right," DeVille said. "So the consensus is just to sit tight? I don't want delays or any goddamn federal investigations."

Mayenlyn waited for any of the other vice presidents to speak. When they didn't he said, "The federal investigations we're working on. As in heading them off. If we can contain this to Iowa, the national media will lose interest pretty soon. Someone at the State Department told me Syria is about to boil over again."

DeVille gave a tiny smile at the first good news he had heard.

"Second, one of the whiz kids in engineering has come up with a way to use drones to do some of the survey work," Mayenlyn said. "Why they didn't come up with that before, I don't know."

DeVille nodded and looked around the table again, settling back on Mayenlyn.

"And one more thing," Mayenlyn added. The manager who sent in the uniformed DEF staff? Why don't we send him to one our sites in Thailand? Who knows what could happen to him there. We can backdate the paperwork to show this was planned for months."

DeVille smiled broadly at that idea and stood, igniting a flurry of people pushing their chairs back to stand.

"All right gentlemen," DeVille said. "Let's get back to work. And Rod, make sure when you send that clown to Thailand he flies coach. The cargo hold would be even better."

Chapter 9

The small knot of *The Redoubt* residents gathered at the main farmhouse was unhappy Jack Stafford didn't think the sketch was as significant as they did.

Jack knew he should be more encouraging. But a thunderstorm over the Rockies had taken its toll on him. It shook the plane so violently that one of the flight attendants fell and badly bruised her forehead on the back of a seat.

He and Cass had gripped the arm rests on their seats so hard they had imprints on their hands that didn't fade completely until after they landed.

Now in the farmhouse living room as the sun was going down, Jack was uncomfortable being the center of attention. He had come to ask questions, not hold court. But the people gathered had been staying on the farm, barely venturing off to even visit 50-miles distant Boyette, the town and county seat that had the only grocery/hardware/farm supply stores of any size.

In the corner, Jack could see that Cass was having an intense private discussion with Caleb's mother, Janis. After her father was killed, Janis had reluctantly assumed the mantle of leadership.

Jack was ringed by a group of farm residents, including Caleb who was the one most intent on getting Jack to make some sense out of the drawing.

"I know you don't want to say," Caleb said. "But my grandpa told me you know a lot about these energy companies. He used to read your newspaper column online. He didn't like to use the computer much. I had to find the column for him sometimes."

Jack smiled and thought back to when he had interviewed James Osmett for a magazine story that turned out to be part paean to rural life, part glimpse of true pacifism at work and part personal history about dealing with witnessing the violent deaths at Kent State.

He was surprised Osmett would even use a computer. When Jack had interviewed him, he was plowing his fields using huge farm horses, just like the Amish.

Caleb was still waiting for Jack's answer when Cass and Janis broke their huddle and came across the room.

Both smiling, that's a good sign, Jack thought.

As soon as they arrived, Janis had insisted they stay in a one of the many spare bedrooms in the huge house. She was slightly embarrassed when Cass told her they really needed separate bedrooms.

"I'm sorry. I thought. Well. Two rooms is no problem," Janis said "Good thing, too, the hotels in Boyette have rats the size of small dogs."

Jack suddenly remembered that her father said she was named after singer Janis Joplin. She even faintly resembled her.

Cass picked up the drawing and looked at it carefully while Jack and Janis sat and chatted about her father and how much he had liked the magazine story Jack had written. Caleb looked bored. The rest of the people weren't sure whether to keep sitting or leave.

"Well, for one thing, this doesn't look like a circle," Cass said aloud. "It looks more oval to me. The other thing is this is tracing paper. It's just tracing paper. We use this paper designing stage sets. We trace over some fancy photo to help make the bones of a set plan. This isn't a sketch. This is somebody's trace of a drawing. Or maybe a construction plan?"

Cass suddenly had the attention of everyone in the room.

"You know, there might be more detail in this. I mean, now it's just a circle that looks like the width could be 24 or 34 feet. The numbers are hard to read. But I bet we can tease more out of it. Maybe something that would even get Jack to pay attention."

Jack smiled at her jibe. And as he looked at Cass holding the paper, he realized he should send a copy of it to Eli Gupta at the *Horseheads Clarion*. Eli would launch a computer search and ask for an analysis from a circle of media friends. It might give some answers about what DEF was building.

If there is anything other than just a huge gas or oil pipeline, Jack thought. *We might be looking for something that isn't there.*

"Jack, I'm reading your mind," Cass said. "But before you send this anywhere, does anybody have a light table? You know like photographers use to use in the old days."

A middle-aged man sitting near the fireplace raised hand.

"Old days?" he said. "Hell, I still have a 35 millimeter Pentax. And I still shoot with film. I just developed some stuff I shot of the massacre. Ouch. Sorry Janis. I didn't mean to use that word. I know we agreed not to."

Janis walked to the fireplace and put her arms around the man who was still sitting.

"Let's find some flashlights to get Jack and Cass over to Roger's house and the light table. They have no idea how dark it gets out here at night."

Chapter 10

Rockwell Valley Tribune editor Keith Everlight looked out the newspaper's large front office window onto Rockwell Valley's Main Street, sipping his second cup of coffee as he waited for his staff of three reporters to come in.

He had a commanding view of the reconstructed downtown area that had been mostly leveled three years before by natural gas and liquid propane gas explosions. Even before 8 a.m., business owners were already sweeping the sidewalks and greeting each other.

In the years since the disaster that killed several dozen people, Rockwell Valley had been the recipient of an astounding amount of state and federal disaster aid, along with money from the energy company responsible for the explosions – Grand Energy Services.

The GES money abruptly stopped flowing when the company declared bankruptcy, buried under an avalanche of civil lawsuits, federal probes into violations of safety protocols and a grand jury investigation into their criminal activity.

But what was equally astounding to Everlight was how local politics shifted from classic, small-town conservative to progressive in the wake of the tragedy.

Even as the reconstruction was just getting underway, people started moving into Rockwell Valley to open small businesses and revive the crushed tourist industry. Town government meetings were full of new ideas for utilizing alternative energy, encouraging sustainable agriculture and boosting education. One group of recent arrivals had gotten a local farmer to donate land for a university agricultural station. And a community college had taken over the former offices of GES, the first step towards offering classes.

It was the reverse of what was happening in most Pennsylvania communities where hydrofracking and oil pipeline spills were creating industrial wastelands.

Within a year of the explosions, Jack Stafford opened the newspaper and installed Keith as editor, giving him a clear mandate to operate as a regional journalistic watchdog, but one that also did everything possible to help the community get back on its municipal feet.

The toll of hydrofracking – contaminated water wells, air pollution, burdensome truck traffic and strange illnesses – was still taking up much of the news space.

Keith looked over the news lineup for the next two issues, a smattering of local news items and a few state reports. He decided to allocate two full pages for the *Tribune's* free classified advertisements for anyone looking for a job or employers seeking to hire. *The Tribune's* online version was booming, too.

Besides the normal news, he was pretty sure that all three newspapers in the *Clarion Newspaper Syndicate* would be publishing a follow-up story about the Iowa shootings. And there might also be a story about the mysterious drawing that Jack had sent to Eli and him to examine.

If it's a pipeline, it's the mother of all pipelines, Keith thought.

Keith had printed out the emailed copy of the drawing he had received and tried to compare it to pipelines already in service or planned.

Looks more like a conduit or a tunnel, he thought.

Keith had started systematically tracking pipeline construction across the United States, winning an environmental group award for his reporting on illegal construction of oil pipelines through national forests.

He had drained the last of his coffee when he saw a message pop up on his computer screen from Eli at the *Horseheads Clarion.*

All it contained were two grainy blown-up photos of a tunnel under construction in China. One photo showed a normal tunnel structure - a semi-circle. The second photo, taken at the other end, where the work was still underway, showed the full diameter of the circular tunnel. Below the roadway level, it looked to Keith like there were a series of pipes or conduits.

Eli, we need to work on your communication skills, Keith thought, as he reached for the telephone.

Then he looked more closely at the full-diameter photo in which he could barely make out a series of smaller circles below the surface of the roadway.

Eli, I take it back. Good grief!

Chapter 11

The Clarion Newspaper Syndicate
Column One

Who will control food, water – and energy?

By Jack Stafford

The recent shooting deaths of James Albert Osmett and three of his neighbors in Iowa were certainly tragic for their families, friends and neighbors.

It was a personal tragedy for me, as I have known the Osmett family for years.

The brutal shootings – despite claims the hail of bullets let loose by security guards was an accident - brought into sharp focus the ruthlessness of some corporations.

Mr. Osmett's shooting shined a light on efforts by major corporations – including DeVille Energy Federation – to snatch all manner of ownership rights for natural AND manufactured resources to create monopoly ownerships which can be devastating to communities.

Most people are familiar with the gold rush mentality energy companies have towards natural gas and oil, particularly since the federal government exempted them from environmental laws governing clean water.

Less familiar is an emerging pattern in which some of these same firms acquire rights to municipal water systems along with subsurface water rights. Corporate conglomerates are also purchasing – and controlling through leasing – large tracts of productive agricultural land formerly in private hands.

Legally, they have every right to do so.

But do we really want private corporations controlling our supplies of water and food, especially if they have been able to secure a monopoly in a particular market?

Despite the 2010 U.S. Supreme Court's Citizens' United decision and what failed GOP presidential candidate Mitt Romney said in 2012, corporations are not people.

Corporations are money-making enterprises, designed to limit the liability of their corporate officers and workers while maximizing profits for shareholders.

The corporate/financial goal is to grow as fast as possible, garnering more and more economic power.

If a corporation – like DEF for example – controls enough of the water and food supplies of any community (or state, or nation), that economic power quickly can turn into the power of life and death over the people living there. By simply creating an artificial scarcity, corporate profits could explode.

A popular science fiction writer published a story some years ago in which the earth's air became so foul everyone was forced to move into huge city-like domes so they could breathe air cleaned by special filters to scrub out the pollution. But – you guessed it – the air in the domes was the property of a private corporation that supplied it. If a citizen didn't pay – or couldn't pay – their "air fee," they were banished from the dome out into the open.

And in this bit of frightening science fiction, it was all quite legal.

Most formerly powerful federal anti-trust laws have been amended to the point of being all but toothless, causing the increased concentration of resources into a few hands that has become not only legally possible, but quite likely given the possibility of great profits.

An alarm bell needs to be rung loud and clear. Just like the alarm bell rung in Iowa to warn James Albert Osmett of danger when DEF cut through his fence.

Jack Stafford is the publisher and editor-in-chief of the Clarion Newspaper Syndicate. He publishes Column One every Friday and can be reached at JJStafford@ClarionNewsSyndicate.com.

Chapter 12

Most of the attention of the drought in the Western United States was focused on California – with good reason.

Between the normal water needs of 39 million people and a voracious agriculture industry that required ever-increasing amounts of fresh irrigation water to survive, California's five years of drought had been devastating.

But we're dry here, too, Alexandra thought, *looking out at a brown patch of grass across the street from the Vashon View office. Right here in the rainy northwest.*

Alexandra looked at the weather forecast – no rain on the horizon in a year that had seen only 20 percent of normal precipitation.

Then she reread Jack's column about corporations grabbing water rights, logged onto the *Vashon View* website and scrolled through a handful national stories that Eli Gupta had posted just moments before.

The three newspapers shared a server, which allowed them to post complementary stories in their own section of the website. State and national stories usually came out of the *Horseheads Clarion* office.

Alexandra had been lobbying Jack to let her have access to post national stories, too, but understood that duplication of effort needed to be avoided. But then she saw a California story about farmers using water from hydrofracking operations for irrigating crops that made her gasp.

A coalition of health professionals had issued a national report about the health risks to the public from hydrofracking. While much of the piece rehashed old claims about air pollution and water pollution, several paragraphs talked about the state's almond farmers – whose trees were often painted in the media as thirsty villains hogging water resources. Now they were reportedly using tankers of water recovered from hydrofracking operations in the Central Valley to keep their trees from dying.

A water purification company near Bakersfield claimed that it was testing the water and only shipping water to farmers that was considered by state regulators to be "within acceptable limits."

Acceptable my butt, Alexandra thought. *Did they test every gallon or just take a tiny sample. God!*

Alexandra also made a note to see if anyone knew how much that fracking water was costing the farmers.

She was so agitated that she started to call Jack's cell phone to make sure he read the story. Then she remembered that Jack had asked her not to call him while he was in Iowa unless it was an emergency.

So she called Eli, instead.

"Fracking water! Eli, how can they use that water? It isn't safe," she said as Eli came onto the phone.

"Alexandra, most people say 'good morning,' or 'hello', something like that," Eli said. "'Fracking water' is a funny way to start the conversation."

Alexandra held her tongue for a heartbeat before hissing at Eli.

"Jerk!" she said, drawing a laugh from him.

"Well, at least you didn't call me a 'fracking asshole,'" Eli said. "But I'm glad you're reading the national reports I'm posting on the website. And that's a beauty. I didn't have time to have anyone track down some of the obvious questions. But I do have somebody calling the group today. Unless you want to do it?"

Alexandra was theoretically on an equal level to Eli, as editor of the *Vashon View*. But she usually bowed to Eli's experience, particularly in writing about energy issues and hydrofracking.

"I think I'll let you East Coast people handle it," she said. "But I'm remembering a story I saw maybe a year ago about fracking waste water. It was about the Bakken oil fields in North Dakota. The headline was something like 'All recovered water was not created equal.'"

She heard a computer keyboard clicking, then a chuckle from Eli.

"Good memory," Eli said. "You were only off by one word. It's "All recovered water is not created equal.'

"You want to call Jack? It sounds like a column. He has one due tomorrow and I think he's written all he wants to about Iowa."

Chapter 13

The media relations department at DEF had watched Jack Stafford repeatedly pummel Grand Energy Services for years with his newspaper column, and far-reaching website. DeVille's media staff worked hard to keep DEF's public profile so low it was barely visible.

Through the GES-pummeling by Stafford, A.G. DeVille had come to have a grudging respect for Stafford's fearless attitude and powers of analysis – even if he was far too green for DeVille's taste.

Those GES idiots did it to themselves anyway, DeVille thought. *All that investment in hardware and political support blown to pieces because they were too stupid to invest in basic safety stuff. Basic. Idiots.*

DeVille's media staff – and particularly Rod Mayenlyn – was even more wary of Stafford now that he controlled three newspapers, websites and a concomitant increase in news staff, many of whom were focusing on the energy and resource industries.

"We should never underestimate Stafford and his people," Mayenlyn had told DeVille in their first conversation. "I worked for two CEOs at Grand Energy who did. And we paid for it."

The Iowa shooting of James Osmett had pushed DEF into the national spotlight, right at the very time DeVille wanted the company to be even more obscure than it had been.

The national media was already losing interest in Iowa, starting to simply chalk up the shootings as an "unfortunate accident." The arrests of some anti-pipeline activists in Nebraska, who were armed when police broke up their protest, had shifted the nation's attention.

And right back to the eco-terrorist narrative, DeVille thought.

DeVille was particularly unhappy that Stafford had started hammering DEF for cross ownership of natural resources.

A text message from DeVille's secretary popped up on his desk screen as he started to scan a just-prepared DEF financial feasibility report on buying a huge tract of California desert land that had water reportedly buried very deep in a hard-to-reach aquifer.

But not too deep for us, he thought.

He read the text from his secretary a second time, then called her on his intercom.

"Tell Mayenlyn this is a good enough time to meet. Tell him I can see him and this Mr. Boviné right now."

Chapter 14

The residents of *The Redoubt* – and Jack – first learned that no charges would be filed against the men who shot and killed James Albert Osmett and three other people when a beefy-looking Boyette County Sheriff's Deputy drove up and started removing the yellow crime scene tape.

The deputy was cordial, though wary, as a contingent of about 20 people – led by Jack and Caleb – hustled to the gate.

"I got orders to pull this tape down," he said. "And I'm not supposed to say anything, officially. But it looks like the DA isn't going to file charges against the guys who did the shooting. It's being ruled an accident. I'm really sorry. You have to talk to the DA."

A few minutes later Caleb's mother Janis pulled up in the battered pickup truck that James Osmett had driven for 20 years.

She burst into tears when Jack told her what the deputy had said.

Caleb watched his mother bury her face in Jack's shoulder. The woman who had arrived with Jack – his sister-in-law Cass, Caleb remembered – put both hands on the hood of the truck and started pushing herself back and forth like she was doing pushups.

After a few moments she came over to Caleb's mother and Jack, gently pulling Caleb's mother to her shoulder. Both women were openly weeping, as were some of the other people who had rushed to the gate.

Those guards murdered them, Caleb thought. *They should go to jail.*

Caleb had only seen his mother cry once, very briefly, since his grandfather had been killed. It was when she gave a short graveside eulogy.

The sound of raised voices behind Caleb made him spin around. The one voice he knew was Jack Stafford. The other voice he guessed was the deputy. Caleb could see that Jack's face was bright red, matched by a similar – fast-blossoming shade on the deputy's face.

At first Caleb thought it had something to do with the things still sitting on the ground where the crime scene tape had been. The deputy had been methodically picking things up and putting them in a box.

But then Jack's voice was clear.

"Next week? This is bullshit. These people watched four of their own get murdered right here, right in front of them. Some of them almost got killed, too. And you're telling me the surveyors are back next week? No. No. **NO**. This is not fair."

The voices of the deputy and Jack alternated, both getting louder and louder, almost to the point of screaming.

Finally the deputy put the box down on the ground.

"All right. I'm leaving. I could arrest you right now for interfering with a police officer. But I respect these people out here. And I respect the grief that you all have. I knew Osmett. He was a good man."

The deputy picked up the box and started to walk away, then turned and walked back up to Jack.

He held the box in one arm while he poked Jack in the chest with a finger.

"He was a good man and that's the only goddamn reason you're not taking a ride in my patrol car. I'm not the bad guy here, buster."

Caleb saw Cass leave his mother and quickly move to Jack's side, slipping her arm around his waist.

"Officer, thank you. My husband is pretty distraught," Cass said. She felt Jack struggling slightly.

She squeezed him hard enough to stop him that he gave out a tiny grunt of "ow."

The deputy turned and walked back to his patrol car with the box, looking back at Jack one more time before closing the door and driving off.

"Your husband?" Jack said. "I've been promoted."

Cass untangled her arm and poked Jack in the chest harder than the deputy had.

"This is exactly why I came on this trip, Jack Stafford. This isn't just another news story about some pipeline or something. Your emotions are tight as a violin string. Whatever it is. I want you to be careful. I'm supposed to get you home safe, in case you didn't figure that out.

Anne and Noah are already asking when we are coming home."

After Cass and Jack had a brief staring contest, Jack looked away and Cass added a softly "Please, Jack."

When they made eye contact again, Cass saw that Jack had forced a smile, obviously holding back tears.

"Ok, Mrs. Stafford. You're right," he said.

"We need to get everybody together back at the main house. I think these people need to figure out what to do next. The devil's coming back to the door."

Chapter 15

As complicated and obscure as federal and state laws and energy regulations could be, Keith Everlight was sure there had to be some official document with details about what DEF was surveying.

And the harder he looked and the more blind alleys he went down, the more frustrated he got.

Phone calls to DEF either went unanswered, or were met with public relations gibberish about "proprietary information." Pleas to other DEF staff – that he was simply searching for issued government permits – were met with quick retorts that if he wanted government information, he needed to talk with the government.

In the corner of his office where Keith kept a heavy punching bag, he had taped the letters DEF near the top, just below where he would punch for exercise.

He weighed whether to go pound on the heavy bag – or keep looking for the DEF details.

A six-foot by eight-foot map of the United States overlaid with lines representing major existing and proposed pipelines took up an entire wall of the office. With the vast quantities of oil and natural gas being produced through hydrofracking and new wells being drilled, companies were rushing to complete new pipelines to get their product to market.

And to hell with anyone standing in their way, Keith thought.

In the eastern U.S. Keith had been closely following the controversies over the Atlantic Sunrise Pipeline, the Constitution Pipeline and the PennEast project, all problematic because so many people in the path of construction didn't want the pipelines crossing their land.

Many were trying to block survey teams – just like Iowa – and struggling to fend off attempts to take their land through eminent domain.

The Atlantic Sunrise was planned to hook up to the proposed – and also-controversial – Cove Point, Maryland export terminal.

Keith mused about both projects, wondering if both could be connected to DEF's project and hidden off the books.

They wouldn't be doing all this surveying without having filed some official documents or applications someplace. Somewhere. It doesn't make sense, Keith thought.

He was about to get up and hit the heavy bag a few times when he noticed a U.S. Army-issue truck drive down the main street, filled with soldiers.

Weekend warriors? Keith wondered.

He sat back down and sent an email message to Jack, Eli and Alexandra.

> *I'm still searching for some documentation of DEF's plans – plans plural. But I wonder if the reason I'm not finding anything is because this is a government-backed project. Feds maybe?*
>
> *Any thoughts? Ideas?*

He sent the email and headed for the heavy bag.

He counted three more U.S. Army trucks rolling through town in the next 15 minutes while he pounded his fists against the punching bag, occasionally raising his aim to throw a looping overhand hook at the letters DEF.

He got into the rhythm of it, careful not to work up a real sweat.

He glanced out the window and saw a tall, bulky man walking across the street pause, look directly at the *Rockwell Valley Tribune* office, then move on quickly.

It couldn't be, Keith thought. *They sent him to prison.*

He took one more solid hit at the bag and went to the front door.

Whoever it was had disappeared.

Keith headed to his telephone.

If Calvin Boviné was *not* in jail, people needed to know.

Right away.

Chapter 16

The email from Keith provided Eli with just the kind of challenge he loved. As a reporter - and now editor of the *Horseheads Clarion* – his real love was web surfing.

And he was a master.

When Eli was doing searches – or almost anytime his slender fingers worked a keyboard – it was like watching a piano virtuoso, the action of his hands so controlled, so smooth, yet constantly moving.

Eli sometimes even sang in a low voice as he bounced across the Internet landscape, finding information and making connections between sources that would end up as news stories in his newspaper and often in the other two Jack Stafford publications.

His skills were such that large newspapers – and many web-based publications – had been trying to hire him away from Jack for years. But he wasn't interested.

Jack gave him free rein and encouraged Eli to use his skills to make the *Clarion* – and the other newspapers – solid sources of information far beyond what would normally be expected of a small-town, twice-a-week newspaper. And Eli generally shared his finds with the other two editors.

As good as they were, they often deferred to Eli when it came time for serious computer digging.

They rightly believed if he couldn't find it, it probably didn't exist.

Eli had already probed the DEF website, trying to squeeze inside the firewall set up to keep people looking solely at the front of the system where all the glossy public relations stuff was featured.

What he really wanted was to hack into the DEF system to get a look at internal documents.

The legality of what he was attempting to do was, at best fuzzy. But he had learned early in his journalism career, if you find a *big enough* smoking gun, it won't matter how you found it.

And then it hit him. *I shouldn't be looking at DEF. I should be looking at their subcontractors*, he thought. *They might be less secretive about DEFs plans. For sure, they won't have such rock-solid computer systems.*

An hour later Eli received an email from an activist group in Iowa that had been monitoring the surveying by DEF and the protests everywhere DEF tried to step onto private land.

A small portion of the DEF survey record-keeping and analysis had been jobbed out to an engineering firm in Sioux City where the college-aged daughter of the activist group's leader was working as an intern.

Chapter 17

The air over Bakersfield, California was a putrid yellow-brown mélange of smog, the result of too many cars and industrial exhaust from the oil and gas industry.

Even at 3,000 feet, the smog swirled around the commercial jet carrying Rod Mayenlyn and two DEF staff members.

It's ugly smog, but it's our smog, Rod Mayenlyn thought.

The haze was so thick the smell of it began to permeate the cabin of the jet heading for a landing at Bakersfield's Meadows Field.

Mayenlyn and his traveling companions were set to meet with the DEF's district supervisor, Petro Rashad, whose actual employer was listed as a distant subsidiary of DEF, many corporate steps removed from the main parent group.

Rashad was in charge of a thriving enterprise that sold truckloads of recovered hydrofracking water to farmers with thirsty trees. It was tricky business because if the water was too chemically laced, it could damage the trees and there were environmental issues at play because each truckload of water – and its contaminants – was different.

"All waste water is not created equal," Rashad told DEF when it got into the business of marketing the water.

Just the week before, a truck destined for the Central Valley had to divert and dump its load into a deep injection well because the water had too a high level of arsenic.

And on the way out of the drilling site, another truck with a load of recovered water set off the radiation alarm at a testing station. The truck's driver had gotten in a row with Rashad, claiming it was unsafe for him to drive the vehicle.

Lucky the driver didn't speak English, Mayenlyn thought. *He might have gone to the press.*

The California press was generally either ignorant of – or disinterested in – most of the issues surrounding hydrofracking in the Central Valley. The farms were too far from metropolitan areas that had newspapers and media big enough to study the issue. Small town newspapers – the few left – shied away from stories critical of most agricultural practices, doing more cheerleading than investigation.

It was only when the drought became more severe – and farmers were pulling more and more water out of underground aquifers – that these communities started paying more attention.

Although activists were screaming that the aquifers were being compromised by fracking chemicals and the injection wells, most state agencies were not particularly eager to condemn the water as unsafe for irrigation.

They don't want to cause a panic, Mayenlyn thought. *Good for them. And really good for us.*

The jet hit an air pocket as it dropped down for its final approach, the land below still barely visible.

Mayenlyn's leg injuries from the Rockwell Valley explosions gave him the excuse to fly first class, but the DEF staff with him had been relegated to the coach area.

Although he still sometimes used a wheelchair, his physical therapist had finally brought him along to the point where he could walk unassisted, though he sometimes still used a cane. It made air travel much easier, not having to wait for some airline dolt to bring a wheelchair.

The DEF staff members with him were both water specialists. Their job was to review the testing equipment, the truck logs and security protocols Rashad was using. Two weeks before some California activists had gotten ahold of a sample from a truckload of water delivered to a farmer.

At least they claim it was from a truck of our water, Mayenlyn thought.

It contained a toxically high level of benzene, high enough that it drew local press attention, but no statewide coverage. Luckily for DEF, the benzene incident had been eclipsed by a cloudburst that same day over Southern California causing millions of dollars of damage from flash flooding.

And it all washed right out into the ocean, Mayenlyn thought.

The plane hit the tarmac with a jolt, the pilot's voice coming on a moment later as they taxied to the terminal.

He spoke with the familiar Texas-drawl that nearly all pilots seem to affect after years of service.

"Welcome to Bakersfield," he said. "The local time is exactly 12 noon. We just got official word that the valley air quality index says you should limit your outside activities. If you looked out the ports on our descent you probably figured that out for yourself. Have good day and fly with us again, y'hear?"

Chapter 18

The Clarion Newspaper Syndicate
Column One

The pipeline mania and citizens' property rights

By Jack Stafford

There is a madcap race across the nation to construct pipelines to transport oil and natural gas.

Madcap might be too tame a word to describe it.

Already the nation is crisscrossed with many thousands of miles of poorly regulated pipelines. Even a casual glance at the headlines about spills and explosions gives plenty of evidence of problems.

And beyond large-scale pipelines, there are pipelines called 'gathering lines' solely under the control of drillers and not federal or state-regulated.

These smaller pipelines are the source of many oil spills and natural gas leaks doing significant damage to the environment. But such leaks barely make headlines.

It's certainly understandable that energy corporations want to get their products to markets and vendors. But in the process, they have also been systematically stomping on people's private property rights with the full cooperation – and sometimes encouragement – of government at all levels.

Perhaps the biggest culprit in all this is the Federal Energy Regulatory Commission that oversees pipeline approvals.

FERC got a tremendous boost in power and authority via the same 2005 federal law that gave us the Halliburton Loophole, a development that shouldn't surprise anyone. But that boost in power is clearly being abused.

The not-very-funny joke among people tracking energy development is that FERC has never seen a pipeline it didn't fall in love with.

The record number of their approvals – almost always over the strident objections of sometimes thousands of citizens – says it's no joke, too.

These pipelines are damaging not only the environment but the social and legal fabrics of communities.

On the environment side, we know that it's not a matter of whether a natural gas or oil pipeline will leak, it's when it will leak.

And on the social and legal side of things, property owners have lost the right to say 'no' to pipelines. The companies first try to buy rights. But if that doesn't work, the companies invoke eminent domain, claiming the pipeline is being built for the good of the community – like a road, school, fire station or public building.

It's textbook corruption.

And maybe it would be different if that natural gas or oil flowing past people's homes, pastures or through clear-cut swaths of forest were for the benefit of the people who lived along the pipeline's route.

It's not. Not at all.

Much of this natural gas or oil is destined for export to markets all over the world.

When hydrofracking first started to boom, early proponents talked about how it would boost U.S. energy independence. It was a very patriotic cover story that hid the real profit-driven motive.

Even as the industry was waving the American flag, corporate officers had an endgame of exporting the gas and oil – which is why so many export terminals are planned around the nation.

U.S. citizens are already paying a price through environmental degradation, as one pipeline failure after another has been reported.

As these pipelines are completed and export terminals come online, we will all start paying a second time, when the price of both oil and natural gas start rising quickly.

Jack Stafford is the publisher and editor in chief of the Clarion Newspaper Syndicate. He publishes Column One every Friday and can be reached at JJStafford@ClarionNewsSyndicate.com.

Chapter 19

The Friday evening debate in the main house of *The Redoubt* would have horrified James Albert Osmett if he had still been alive to listen.

And horrified with his daughter and grandson, Jack Stafford thought.

A letter had been hand-delivered to the front gate at 5 p.m. by an off-duty Sheriff's Deputy in uniform, driving a Sheriff's Department patrol car. The letter, signed by the county attorney, said surveyors from the DeVille Energy Federation would be arriving sometime after 9 a.m. Monday at *The Redoubt* gates.

It cited an earlier court order saying DEF had the legal right to survey. The letter also said the surveyors would be accompanied by private security officers.

"What did my grandfather die for?" Caleb Osmett kept asking. "What?"

Caleb had driven his grandfather's truck down to the front gate while the sheriff's deputy was taping the letter to the farm's combination mailbox/message board.

After they exchanged words – including Caleb calling the deputy a "corporate Nazi" – Caleb drove back home, climbed up in the cupola and rang the alarm bell until he was sure nearly everyone was coming.

And now he has an angry mob in his grandfather's house, Jack thought. *Jesus. Never piss off a pacifist.*

The people of *The Redoubt* had known for most of the week that the DEF surveyors would be coming back. But Janis and the residents were working feverishly with an attorney in Des Moines, preparing a series of motions to try to stop the survey.

"The 5 p.m. delivery of the letter was no accident," Jack said, speaking for the first time since everyone had arrived. "The company knows damn well that there's no way to get to a court – or a judge – over the weekend."

Jack and Cass had met with Janis and a small group of *The Redoubt* residents three days before, convincing them to seek an injunction and to involve the ACLU.

Now in front of the full group, Jack took a breath before talking.

"Before James and the other people were killed, you were one of hundreds of groups and people across the country trying to stop pipelines," he said. "The thing is, your case now has the attention of the public. And for the company to try to ramrod a survey through the property so soon after the shooting? It could be as galvanizing as what James witnessed in 1970."

Ideas for fighting – real fighting, not fighting in court – started bouncing around the room. They escalated from throwing up a picket line of people linking arms to using tractors to push up huge berms of dirt topped with fresh cow manure.

Caleb took the floor again.

"We can dig some trenches, too. Cover them with leaves and stuff," Caleb said. "Let them fall in the holes."

Jack wished for a moment that he wasn't even in the room.

He held his tongue until a bearded Vietnam veteran stood up and starting talking about making punji sticks to put into trenches. His face was red as he described dealing with the Viet Cong and the elaborate booby traps they set for American and South Vietnamese soldiers. Finally Jack couldn't listen anymore.

"I'm not a member of your community," Jack said. "But I am a friend of this family and was a friend of James. I think what you are talking about is understandable. Completely. But the James I knew – the James you knew even better – would not want you to resort to violence. Ever. If you think about it, you know that."

The group got very quiet while Caleb turned bright red, unhappy at Jack's intervention. His mother, Janis, pushed away from the wall and walked to the center of the room.

"I am as crushed as anyone here," she said. "I was raised with non-violence. But I will tell you that I am so close to wanting to get a gun myself it's frightening me. This anger. But I think Jack is right. To honor my father we have to stick with the non-violence he preached. That non-violence he asked all of us to live."

Janis looked around the room, then smiled. "I have to admit though, I do like the idea of spreading cow manure for the surveyors to step in."

Her joke drew a nervous laugh, breaking the angry spell that had been woven.

"Might I speak?" Cass asked.

A low growl of agreement went through the group.

"I have an idea," she said. "It's not a clever as some things I've heard, but it might help.

Janis motioned for Cass to stand with her.

Cass paused in the center of the room standing next to Janis, waiting for some of the minor conversations and low murmurs to stop.

Jack smiled broadly enough that Janis looked at him quizzically.

I've seen her do this in theaters, in plays, Jack thought. *She's doing her dramatic pause to get everyone's curiosity up. In a moment they'll be dying to hear what she has to say.*

"Thank you," Cass said. "All of you. And it's good that you had time to vent like this. Now it's time to do something. I suggest a three-pronged approach for this weekend. Three divisions, if you would like to make it sound military. A non-violent military."

As she spoke, she swiveled her gaze around the room, even turning slightly so the people who were mostly looking at her back saw her face in profile.

"Division one gets the ACLU people to call every judge in the state of Iowa and ask for an injunction," she said. "How many can there be? We can give them a list. Track them down at their favorite restaurant. Or bar. One judge, one order and we stop them in their tracks, at least until we can get a full court hearing."

She paused to let it sink in. After seeing a dozen affirmative nods, she continued. "Division two – with Jack's and my help – starts with contacting all the state media and out-of-state media, too. We can tell them that Monday there will be another confrontation. Tell them to bring their cameras. Tell them it will be epic.

"And Division three? Well, how much cow manure could we spread and disguise with straw all along the route you think they will be surveying? We're a farm, right? And throw in a few potholes. Not so deep they break an ankle, but maybe fill their boots? Fill the potholes with nice clean fresh poop. That would be within acceptable non-violent limits, right? And it would make for some great film."

Jack watched as the people in the room started talking, weighing what Cass had said, agreeing. A few people started laughing while they talked about constructing a manure minefield.

Within a few minutes, Janis and Cass were dividing people into the three groups. The most enthusiastic seemed to be the men who wanted to booby trap the property near the fence with cow droppings.

The mood gradually shifted from angry and helpless to purposeful and mildly hopeful.

Jack saw that the only person in the room still wearing an angry scowl was Caleb.

And his scowl – and angry eyes – were aimed directly at Cass.

Chapter 20

Rockwell Valley residents often treated *Rockwell Valley Tribune* editor Keith Everlight like he was a rock star.

Before the twin gas explosions nearly leveled the town, they had already been entranced by his hard-hitting stories published in the *Horseheads Clarion* in the year leading up to the blasts.

In the wake of the destruction, he was the newsman who most doggedly reported about the fiscal malfeasance and environmental shortcuts taken by Grand Energy Services that contributed to the tragedy.

And local residents were pretty sure he had a lot to do with *The Clarion*'s support of the community after the blasts and during the rebuilding. The *Clarion* encouraged its New York readers to help with the rebuilding effort. The newspaper even helped convince a big box store to locate in Rockwell Valley by promising a huge discount for any print or online advertising for as long as the store had more than 75 percent local employees and offered special discounts to Rockwell Valley residents.

When the *Clarion* announced it was opening a newspaper in town – and that included Keith becoming the editor – the town council donated city land for a new newspaper building, a portion of the property where Rockwell Valley City Hall had stood before it was destroyed in the explosions.

After Keith thought he spotted Calvin Boviné walking across the street from the newspaper office, it was no surprise that local merchants were almost fawningly helpful when he asked them to be on the lookout for his former nemesis. Several remembered Boviné, including the day he was taken away by police, arrested for a variety of crimes while in the employ of Grand Energy Services.

Surely, they said, he was still in jail for assaulting Keith in addition to a long string of crimes?

But sitting in the *Rockwell Valley Tribune* office on Sunday afternoon, waiting for a call from Jack, Keith scanned the street after ensuring the front and back doors of the newspaper were locked. A phone call to the Rockwell Valley district attorney Friday had confirmed that Boviné was out of jail after winning an appeal in a downstate county – an appeal the press in *that* area hadn't written about.

The DA was apologetic, Keith should have been notified both as a victim and newsman about Boviné's release.

Is he here to pound on me, or is he working for someone, Keith wondered. *And who would hire him?*

As these thoughts drifted through his mind, he looked up and saw Calvin Boviné's football lineman-sized body standing across the street. He was wearing a long coat. His head covered in a slouch hat, like something from a 1930s gangster movie. Even at that distance, Keith could see that Boviné was staring into the office at Keith. But it was difficult to read his expression.

They stayed locked in a staring contest for a moment, until Boviné stepped off the curb and began walking across the street.

I better call for backup, Keith thought, reaching for telephone.

But when he looked up, Boviné was gone again.

Chapter 21

A nervous energy pulsed through the conference room at the DeVille Energy Federation's office where key DEF staff members and execs were sitting anxiously, waiting for A.G. DeVille to come in.

The chatter while they waited centered on stories they all had read earlier that day in Sunday metropolitan newspapers about the DEF surveying in Iowa.

The stories were similar in tone – the residents of *The Redoubt*, after seeing four of their community members shot and killed – had convinced a Boyette County judge to issue an injunction halting DEF's planned surveying Monday morning.

The judge, with the unlikely name of Roy Bean, had approved the injunction Saturday afternoon, just in time to make the deadlines for the Sunday daily newspapers and television newscasts. "There are sufficient irregularities in the way the original order was issued for me to call a halt – for the moment – to the surveying," Bean wrote in a statement accompanying his order. "And I am not swayed by the arguments of the federal government about this project at this point."

His comment about the federal government sent reporters scrambling to contact him to clarify his ruling. But Bean was at an out-of-state hunting camp, beyond the reach of the media.

In the DEF conference room, a teleconference video connection with Rod Mayenlyn in California was open though no one dared discuss actual company business until DeVille arrived.

The meeting had no formal, announced agenda. But when the staff had been called in by DeVille's executive secretary, everyone knew there was no excuse for not attending. One staff member drove 150 miles to make the meeting.

In his office next door, DeVille watched the staff on a surveillance camera and listened to their chatter.

He hit the touch screen and cut the video feed of Rod Mayenlyn into the conference room, setting it so he could have a private conversation with him.

Mayenlyn looked surprised when DeVille's face suddenly loomed on his computer screen in California. Mayenlyn was sitting in a DEF subsidiary's office near the oil fields, enjoying the filtration system's clean air.

"A.G., I thought we were having an emergency staff meeting," Mayenlyn said. "In fact, I was eavesdropping a minute ago."

DeVille smiled, a thin smile a newspaper columnist once compared in a magazine profile of him to the grin of the devilish cartoon boss Mr. Burns from a television program called *The Simpsons.*

"I was doing a little listening myself," DeVille said, impressed that Mayenlyn was willing to be honest about his lurking in on the conversation.

"What do you think? Where are we with all this?"

Mayenlyn adjusted his computer screen and camera slightly.

"Well, it's done," Mayenlyn said. "The delay is unfortunate. But that comment in the injunction about the federal government? Christ. That's going to get those damn reporters asking questions. And I don't think they'll buy that he was talking about FERC's approvals. I've been trying to get to the judge but he's way off the grid. I did find his court clerk. She said he might not be back until the middle of next week."

DeVille watched a monitor of the activity in the conference room, noting that a couple of staff members were playing Scrabble. Another was carefully folding a sheet of paper to make a paper airplane.

Enjoy your leisure, DeVille thought. *It's about to end.*

"Maybe it's time to roll it out," DeVille said. "Not all of it, of course. But enough to get us out from under the shooting."

Mayenlyn was glad he was in California. If DeVille went ahead with making an announcement about the pipeline Monday, it meant the staff would be working the rest of Sunday and probably all night to make sure that what got released was *exactly* what A.G. wanted – and not one pissant-sized detail more.

"I will have the California piece all ready," Mayenlyn said.

DeVille reconnected Mayenlyn to the conference room monitor, then walked into the conference room, pleased that the men all stood up quickly when he entered.

"Gentlemen, sit. Sit please. And get comfortable. I have decided that tomorrow morning we are going to announce the water element of the pipeline project. That should turn the bad press into good press and let us get on with this."

A series of involuntary groans began, then quickly stopped.

"I'm aware of what this means for all of your divisions and what you have to do to prepare. Remember that after tomorrow, we won't be viewed as the villains anymore. People won't think of DEF just as an energy company," he said.

"We will be the water people."

Welcome to Mars

Chapter 1

The news that the DeVille Energy Federation was planning a massive pipeline project to bring water to the southwestern U.S. and California – and that it apparently had the blessing and some hazy financial backing of the federal government – prompted so much gushing praise that one Southern California newspaper ran a headline that said, "DeVille Walks On Water."

"DEF has for years watched with concern the suffering and negative economic consequences of the drought in the west," DEF spokesman Rod Mayenlyn told the press in Los Angeles. "Granted, it will be several years before water reaches the area. But engineers, economists and even environmentalists agree this plan will work and will help our nation. For security reasons, many of the details about this project can't be released, except in general terms. But water will be flowing west as soon as possible. Count on it."

The announcement caught the nation's press flatfooted, prompting a flurry of speculative stories, most coming from California news outlets, the state that would benefit the most from a gusher of fresh water for agriculture.

Alarming news stories about the use of tainted hydrofracking water for irrigation were pushed off the news pages entirely, since the shady practice was now just a temporary, emergency measure to get the state through the crisis, until DEF saved the day with its pipeline.

Also gone were stories about how polluted several major aquifers were from injection wells that California regulators had allowed to be used as dumps for the fracking waste.

Jack Stafford was one a handful of journalists who didn't believe DEF's attempt to don the mantle of savior.

But the political impact of the statement was undeniable.

"This announcement is going to make stopping the surveying of your land – or anybody else's land – damn near impossible," Jack told Janis and the other *Redoubt* residents.

"It's one thing to argue against the energy companies bringing gas and oil across the land for profit. But water? For thirsty people and farms? Right now, I think it's unstoppable."

Within an hour of the announcement, Jack and Cass had made travel arrangements to get back to Vashon Island, with a second set of plans for Jack to go to California and reconnect with journalist friends in the northern half of the state.

Most of Jack Stafford's friends and contacts in the California press corps had moved on to jobs in government, public relations or simply retired in the years since Jack had worked in the state as an environmental reporter.

But most were still journalists at heart and willing to share information with Jack and his three newspapers.

He was hoping that they would be privy to some of the background information on the pipeline that DEF was holding back.

Jack had been so busy emailing his California contacts that he didn't see an urgent text message from Alexandra until he was in a car on the way to the airport.

> *Keith didn't join the editor's video meeting this morning. We've tried to call him, but he's not answering his telephone. The receptionist at the*

newspaper says she hasn't seen him. Something is weird. This isn't like Keith. I want to call the Rockwell Valley police. Eli said ask you first.

Chapter 2

The last time Keith had seen Calvin Boviné this close up, Keith had thrown three quick punches to Boviné's head after a tussle in the ballroom of the Rockwell Valley Lakeside Hotel, less than an hour before the hotel was leveled by twin gas explosions – one natural gas, the other liquid propane gas.

Boviné was taken away in handcuffs that night, eventually tried and convicted of assault on both Keith and an elderly college professor.

Christ, I think he's even bigger than he was then, Keith now thought, looking at Boviné sitting in a booth at a country-style diner on the outskirts of Rockwell Valley, where most of the breakfast crowd had come and gone, leaving the place nearly empty.

Prison weight lifting, I bet.

When Keith had opened the front door of his house to walk to the newspaper office that morning, Boviné had been standing on the walkway.

He put his hands up in the air immediately to show he meant no harm. "I need to talk to you," Boviné said. "Some place away from a lot of people. I came by your office, but there were always people around."

A very wary Keith suggested they take separate cars out to the diner.

Keith was already sitting in the booth before he realized he had left his cell phone at home.

A waitress came by and refilled their coffee mugs, asking for the third time if they wanted any food.

On this pass through, Boviné ordered enough food for three people: Eggs, bacon, sausage, potatoes, French toast and a separate platter of various types of bread and rolls.

"Calvin, I have to ask you. What do you tip the scales at?" Keith asked.

For the first time in their conversation that morning, Boviné offered up a slight grin.

"I was 325 when I went into jail. But I'm about 290 right now." he said. "Even my BMI is good. Prison can keep you pretty fit in some ways."

Keith did a quick calculation in his head – his own body mass index being something he kept track of.

"I put you at about 6' 8". Am I close?

Boviné actually grinned this time.

"Close. I'm 6' 9" in bare feet."

Sitting across from Boviné, Keith had to look up so much he was beginning to get a slight pain in his neck. Keith was barely 5 feet 6 inches – unless wearing his trademark cowboy boots with two-inch heels.

I suppose a booster chair for me is out of the question, he thought.

When they first sat down, Keith kept one hand below the table, solidly in a fist, his body tense.

But as Boviné talked, Keith relaxed. He wanted to fill Keith in on some things about the DeVille Energy Federation.

This isn't the same guy I remember, Keith thought. *He's apologizing for what he did before.*

"We'll talk about what DEF is up to in a minute," Keith said.

"But first tell me more about this whole Buddhist thing you discovered in jail."

Chapter 3

The Clarion Newspaper Syndicate
Column One

**More details needed
about DEF's water plans**

By Jack Stafford

The laudatory comments being lavishly heaped on the DeVille Energy Federation's plan to create a water transit system from the Great Lakes to the southwestern U.S. and California should come as no surprise.
- There is no arguing that the West desperately needs water.
- There is no arguing that continued drought spells disaster for the people of the West and the economy of the nation.
- There is no arguing that something radical needs to be done.

But is the project announced by DEF that something?

It's hard to answer that because the details made public so far are so sketchy and leave so many unanswered questions it's difficult to make a reasoned judgment.

Questions?

The following come to mind quickly:

How much money is the federal government kicking in to this project?

Have environmental impact studies been done to assess the effects on the Great Lakes?

What is the actual route the pipeline will take?

What will the cost of this water be to end users across the nation?

Who ultimately will control the allocation of the water?

What's alarming is that questions like these are unlikely to be answered anytime soon because DEF claims that the federal government's involvement – and even national security – requires details to be kept secret.

How many times have we heard that before?

And how many times have we found out later that details kept secret were simply hiding profiteering, criminal activities and often actions clearly not in the best interest of the public.

This is essentially a public works project, being built by a private corporation – not some CIA black-ops endeavor.

It needs a bright light shining on it.

It should not be given a pass on transparency simply because it may be doing a lot of good when completed.

Beyond that, the liberal use of eminent domain in the survey process – and probably even more in the actual construction phase – would seem to overrule the need to keep details from public view.

There is one thing about this cloak of secrecy that is good, however. It encourages citizens – and the press – to remain skeptical. We all need to keep asking questions, keep dogging those in charge, and keep up pressure to find out sufficient detail to ensure that whatever is being proposed is truly beneficial.

And by beneficial, I mean not just to the bottom line of a mega-corporation like DEF, but to the people the project is supposed to help.

There are plenty of technical and engineering hurdles involved, to be sure. And so far, most of the news accounts and commentary have been focused on the concept of moving and storing water as it works its way from east to west.

When it was first announced, many skeptics actually laughed at the idea, thinking it is too far-fetched to be believable.

But after reviewing the thin details about the project that have been released, most of those same skeptics have changed their tune.

It's do-able – maybe.

Admittedly, the science-engineering aspect is fascinating. And because of that, political, environmental and social concerns are being ignored for the moment.

One detail that has been leaked – perhaps deliberately simply as a publicity-garnering stunt – has science writers scratching their heads: in parts of the envisioned water system a 2000-plus year old technology called the Archimedes Screw will be utilized to lift water and to keep it flowing west. The technology is still in use all over the planet, its principle one of the bedrocks of low-tech irrigation and water moving.

Perhaps it's a coincidence that the name of the chief executive of the DeVille

Energy Federation building the structure is Archimedes Gabriel DeVille.

No matter, the nation is waiting for more details.

Jack Stafford is the publisher and editor in chief of the Clarion Newspaper Syndicate. He publishes Column One every Friday and can be reached at JJStafford@ClarionNewsSyndicate.com.

Chapter 4

A stiff west wind had blown out enough of the foul air in Bakersfield to allow Rod Mayenlyn to sit poolside at his hotel. His suitcase and computer bag were on the concrete next to him. His wingtip shoes and three-piece suit were drawing stares from other hotel patrons who had come down to sunbathe or swim.

Almost escaped this hell-hole, he thought. *Almost.*

Mayenlyn had made it as far as the limousine DEF had sent to take him to the airport when he received an urgent text message from A.G. DeVille's secretary, asking him to delay his return.

A phone call to her had yielded no details about the delay. The only thing she would say was that Mayenlyn was to "sit tight."

And so he was, starting to bake under the haze-hidden sun, the limousine driver inside having coffee and waiting to see if he would be going to the airport or not.

In the last few days Mayenlyn had been able to walk without his cane, though his legs still hurt. His doctors warned him that at the first signs of knee or hip pain he should use some support or he would end up in a wheelchair again.

Mayenlyn's work in California would be finished as soon as DEF made the announcement about the pipeline bringing water west.

He only had to give some instructions to DEF oil-rig supervisors and staff about handling press inquiries relating to continued use of hydrofracking wastewater for irrigation. He expected those questions to tail off to zero very quickly, even though it would be years before a drop of water made it to California via any DEF pipeline.

He decided to get out of the increasingly hot sun. The breeze was beginning to smell faintly of petrochemicals and smog again when a young female hotel desk clerk came out waving a room key.

"Um, Mr. Mayenlyn?" the clerk said. "Your office just called and said to give you a room again. I know you just checked out. But. Well. I gave you a suite, just like before? And it's ready. Anytime you want to go up."

Mayenlyn frowned at the key as he took it from the woman's hand.

She gave a practiced, faked smile and headed back inside.

Christ, even the hotel clerk knows more than I do, Mayenlen thought.

Irritated, he called A.G. DeVille's secretary again, explaining to her that he knew he was staying, but wondered if he needed to get back to the Bakersfield DEF facility.

He waited on hold, some hideous elevator music playing in the background.

"Mr. DeVille said to wait at the hotel for right now," the secretary said as she came back online. "He's busy in a meeting. But he said to tell you that you should read the newspaper column by someone named Jack Stafford as soon as possible. He will talk with you directly later."

Mayenlyn stood, juggling the phone at his ear, his suitcase and computer bag. "Fine, fine," he said, his voice irritated.

"Good," the secretary said. "Um, the other thing is that he wants you to find someone named Calvin? Calvin Boviné? Mr. DeVille said this Mr. Boviné left a message that he won't being doing any work for DEF anymore. That's all Mr. DeVille said. He was pretty emphatic when he said 'find him.'"

Mayenlyn sat back on the chair, putting down the suitcase and computer bag.

His knees were starting to hurt again, a lot.

Chapter 5

When the DEF surveyors finally arrived at *The Redoubt* at noon, the gate was wide open.

A dozen farm residents – including Caleb and his mother Janis – were chopping field grass with scythes in the area where the people had been shot.

Three-foot high stone cairns were set in place where each of the four people killed had fallen.

At a farm-wide meeting the night before at the main farmhouse, the consensus was to allow the surveying to take place without confrontation.

The Redoubt's sympathetic judge, Roy Bean, said he could leave his injunction in place, but he knew higher courts would overturn it.

And it wouldn't be worth the cost of appeals, he counseled.

"What we *will* do is work with other groups on a legal strategy to stop the pipeline from crossing our land," Janis had said. "I don't care if it *is* carrying water. I don't like the idea of our land being chopped up by it."

A survey team of six men came through the gate accompanied by just two armed security guards. The guards only wore side arms in holsters on their hips.

Several of the surveyors peered at a GPS screen, occasionally pointing in the distance or behind them. The others took photographs. As they walked on the farm property inside the gate, they tread as carefully as someone might entering a house when they knew their boots were muddy.

The men were chatting in hushed tones.

After a few minutes of looking at clipboards and pointing, one of the surveyors walked up to the farm residents, his eyes searching for someone to tell or ask something.

The two security guards stood close behind him.

Janis stepped forward from the knot of people, struggling to contain her anger.

"Um, ma'am. I just wanted to let you know we need to *drive* onto the property, set up a line of sight for our gear. You know?" he said. "If you could point out where you don't want us driving. Where you still have crops, you know. We'll avoid them. Or try anyway."

Janis stared at the surveyor for a moment then gave him a quick rundown of where they should drive.

"I'd stick close on the roads," she said, her voice shaking slightly. "It's been raining and the fields are bogs. Your trucks will get stuck."

She turned quickly leaving the surveyor, the security guards and the rest of the DEF people staring at her back as she returned to the farm residents already back to cutting and raking.

No one paid any attention to Caleb when he slipped around to the opposite side of the DEF vehicles and the security guards' truck.

Chapter 6

The flight from Iowa back to Vashon Island in Washington state was uneventful, weather-wise.

But somewhere over the Rockies, Cass had launched into the familiar conversation she, Jack and Anne frequently had about Noah and the need for Jack to be home on Vashon.

"I know this story is important to you. And, honestly, I find myself as tied to those people as you do," Cass said. "Maybe more. What a horrible thing. But damn it, Jack, you can't just go running off again to California after changing your shirt at home."

Jack tried to keep his eyes focused ahead and not set his jaw – a dead giveaway he didn't like what he was hearing. He never liked being lectured – particularly when he knew the lecture was so on target.

He had winced at the "shirt" remark because it was a replay of what Cass had said at *The Redoubt* as they were packing before leaving to go to the airport. "You're not a nomadic newspaperman without responsibilities, Jack," she had said. "I'm sorry to sound harsh. But really, you need to be home with Noah. This whole business has you like a horse in full gallop. You have good staff to do this stuff. You're a general now, right? Isn't that what a publisher really is? You have troops to send into the field."

Jack brooded without responding. Cass was certainly correct. The problem was he liked chasing stories and tracking down news, even though most he handed off to his staff members. Sometimes his leads worked their way into his weekly columns. But it was always fun, thrilling even.

The plane hit a small air pocket, prompting the pilot to turn on the seatbelt sign again.

"I know you were thinking about getting up and using the restroom," Cass said. "You're stuck here now."

Jack heard a smile in her voice and reached over and put his hand on hers.

"There are worse places to get stuck. And I'm sorry I'm being so obtuse. No, you would probably say 'stubborn.' Please don't misunderstand this, but you and Anne are doing such a great job with Noah, I never worry for a moment about him. He loves both of you so much. He's a lucky kid. I can't imagine what his life would have been like, well…"

Jack let his thought go without finishing it. Nasty images of his drunken rages on Tonga after his wife Devon had drowned jolted him. Anne and Cass – and their love for Noah – kept him balanced.

Cass squeezed his hand to bring him back to the present. "Anne and I want Noah *and* you around, Jack. We love being aunts and moms to Noah. But without you it doesn't feel like a full family. We all need you. But Noah especially."

Jack felt a small smile creeping across his face as Cass looked at him and then threw her head back against the seatback.

"God!!! All *right*. Tell me when you think you're leaving for California. You might have me going with you again. If you keep this up, you might have a staff of Anne and Noah traveling with you on your adventures, too. That will be interesting to explain to Noah's first grade teacher."

Jack looked up at the sound of bell, signifying that the seatbelt sign was turned off.

"If you say 'saved by the bell' I will tell Noah you didn't bring him a present from Iowa," Cass said, smiling as the puzzled look on Jack's face made clear he hadn't even considered it.

"Don't worry. I bought him a cute T-shirt at the airport. But you should have thought of it Jack. I rest my case."

Chapter 7

The news that Calvin Boviné was out of jail – and was talking with Keith Everlight about the DeVille Energy Federation – had Alexandra Potomac scrambling to refresh her memory about what had happened several years before in Rockwell Valley.

She had been working for a newspaper in the San Francisco Bay Area at the time. And gas industry doings in Pennsylvania were not high on her editor's radar.

He called Pennsylvania "Pennsyltucky." And it wasn't a compliment.

What made Alexandra particularly curious was Keith's brief comments earlier that morning during their editors' meeting that Boviné might provide the window they needed to get a better idea of what DEF was up to with the pipeline. He said that Boviné apparently was no longer the thug he had been when he went into prison.

But Alexandra was more worried about some of Eli's comments about Jack.

The two had had a long telephone conversation the night before. Of the three editors, Eli was closest to Jack. Eli, his wife Shania and their daughter Nikki had flown from New York to vacation on Vashon Island several times, so Alexandra had gotten to know him well.

"He's been like this before," Eli said. "He says he's worried about our reach exceeding our grasp. This DeVille project has links all over the place. Big money, big political players. Some nasty people, too. Plus, with three newspapers now, it's actually more complicated than when it was just the *Clarion*."

Alexandra knew something was up when Jack had not come into the office, even though he'd been back on the island for two days.

She and Jack had talked on the telephone several times. He sounded tired. Plus, he had gotten a ton of hate mail – both electronic and via the USPS – for his recent columns critical of DeVille. Usually the criticisms from the wing nuts didn't bother him, but this time it did.

"We just need to give him a little time. And keep on banging away on the research," Eli had said in their meeting.

"When Jack came to the *Clarion* from California he and Walter Nagle, the publisher, used to go round and round about the same thing. Walter couldn't believe that his small newspaper in Horseheads, New York could play hardball on a national scale. Jack proved him wrong. We just need to keep working. Jack will come around."

Alexandra looked across the street as someone walked out the door of the coffee shop, carrying in his hands a copy of Jack's just-published book, *Saving Pennsylvania: An Environmental and Economic Manual*. He was reading it so intently he nearly collided with a trash can just outside the shop door.

When he did collide with a woman walking on the sidewalk – still reading intently – she got an idea how to get Jack back on track.

A quick exchange of texts with Eli cemented the idea.

Chapter 8

The ground shook sufficiently – and for long enough – that Rod Mayenlyn realized he was experiencing his first California earthquake. The wine glass he had carelessly left close to the edge of the table in his Bakersfield hotel room danced a slight jig, the Merlot left in it sloshing until the glass and wine tumbled to the floor.

The beige carpet saved the glass from breaking. It also soaked up the wine nicely.

The temblor lasted about 30 seconds, long enough for Mayenlyn to wonder how well the hotel had been constructed.

California buildings generally could handle all but the most ferocious earthquakes. He was glad he wasn't in Oklahoma where more than 900 quakes had hit the state the year before. Nearly all of them were blamed on injection wells into which the DeVille Energy Federation and other companies were pushing water recovered from hydrofracking operations.

Prior to the introduction of hydrofracking technology, Oklahoma had an average of 3 to 5 measurable quakes per year. But Mayenlyn and other oil and gas industry execs jumped in front of television cameras with the regularity of figures on a Swiss Cuckoo clock, each time denying the injection wells had any connection to the shaking.

And the idiots never push it, Mayenlyn thought as he watched the Merlot fan out to create a three-inch stain.

Mayenlyn had been waiting for several days in Bakersfield for someone A.G. DeVille said would help as a "consultant" with difficult situations now that Calvin Boviné had dropped off the radar.

Boviné's disappearance troubled Mayenlyn. He had told DeVille that Boviné could be very useful at convincing people to sign leases to let DEF pipelines cross their properties. Plus, just his hulking presence often cowed people into submission no matter what the issue.

A prior three-way conversation among Boviné, Mayenlyn and DeVille in DeVille's office when Boviné first got out had been cordial, even though Boviné barely spoke, a silence Mayenlyn attributed to his recent release from prison.

Mayenlyn remembered that Boviné had often previously disappeared for days at a time when working for the now defunct Grand Energy Services.

And that's why I am worried, Mayenlyn thought. *When he takes initiative, people usually get hurt.*

Mayenlyn scanned the list of issues that DeVille wanted the new consultant to work on with him. He frowned when he saw Jack Stafford's name and the names of his three newspapers.

DEF's announcement about its pipeline bringing water from the east to California and other dry western states had mostly insulated DEF from media criticisms. And when some reporters did get aggressive about wanting more details, DEF would make vague reference to "national security" issues.

The only reporters who persisted worked for Jack Stafford at the *Horseheads Clarion*, *Vashon View* and *Rockwell Valley Tribune*.

Mayenlyn was staring at the Merlot rug stain, thinking that it reminded him of some impressionist painting when his newly arrived DEF company cell phone rang.

DeVille had ordered all the vice presidents to use the new preloaded smart phones – and only for DEF communications. Mayenlyn was sure there was some encryption program written in the phone, along with some system for recording all conversations. Plus the history of a numbers dialed, calls received and voice mail messages were supposedly wiped off the phone every 24 hours.

Except the records are probably stored at DEF headquarters, Mayenlyn thought.

He swore as he tried to quickly type in his numeric password. He hadn't bothered to set up the fingerprint touch unlock function yet.

He mistyped the number a second time just as the phone rolled over to show a missed call.

He took a closer look at the long face that nearly filled the screen. Even with the relatively poor resolution of the photo, it was impossible to overlook the deadness in the man's eyes and a dour, borderline-evil expression that made Mayenlyn shiver slightly. The man's sloping forehead made him look like close relative to the Neanderthals.

A moment later, the phone rang again, bringing up the photo on the screen. This time the name "Mars" was covering up part of the downturned smear of the man's mouth.

Mayenlyn hesitated to answer.

Then the phone connected all by itself and Mars started speaking.

Chapter 9

The Clarion Newspaper Syndicate
Column One

Send in the trolls

By Jack Stafford

In the media business, criticism is just part of professional life.

Good media outlets listen to critics and weigh their words carefully. Sometimes media adjust coverage and even the basic mission – when truly warranted.

The Clarion Newspaper Syndicate has been doing some of that weighing as the ongoing saga about the DeVille Energy Federation's plans for a trans-national pipeline have trickled out.

The three newspapers that make up the CNS – the New York Horseheads Clarion, Washington state Vashon View and Pennsylvania's Rockwell Valley Tribune have been collectively trying to shed light on what DEF is really planning.

If that sounds like skepticism on the part of these newspapers – and this columnist – it is. That's our job.

But the clamor from a number of directions has been unusually loud, saying that our newspapers need to stop trying to provide coverage of a project of this magnitude. The critics – who some journalists dismiss by using the unflattering term trolls – say that to try to cover a major national story is beyond our capability.

We've heard this before.

Similar criticism has been leveled since the late Walter Nagle, publisher of the Horseheads Clarion, declared that his small, twice-a-week newspaper would take on the role of documenting what was really going on with hydrofracking for natural gas and oil.

It was under his direction that the newspaper broke the story that some natural gas exploration companies were using gas wells as illegal dumps for toxic chemicals.

And that was just one story, a story that won great acclaim for the newspaper.

This past week I had a dialog with a thoughtful critic who I would never brand with the pejorative label of troll.

He's a movie buff who contacts CNS often – usually trying to cajole one of CNS newspapers into doing more film reviews.

But talking about CNS and our investigative efforts, he said he likens our situation to a classic 1965 movie, starring James Stewart. (Not the remake in 2004, which he said should never had been filmed.)

In the 1965 film, a group of men are stranded in the Sahara Desert after their plane crashes. The Sahara, of course, is a hostile environment in which to be stranded – boiling hot by day, freezing by night. And food and water? Forget it.

One member of the group says he is an airplane designer. He directs the construction of an aircraft made from parts of the wrecked plane. But just before the rickety craft is to lift off, the men learn the airplane designer was keeping a secret. He is an aircraft designer, but only toy airplanes.

At that point the men, understandably, want to tear him apart. But he convinces them that the scientific, aeronautical principles of a toy aircraft are no different from a full-size airplane.

Their bubble-gum and baling wire aircraft eventually does lift off and get them out of the desert to safety.

If you haven't guessed the title by now, the name of the film is The Flight of the Phoenix.

It's an inspiring movie on many levels and it fits with conversations my staff and I have been having in recent days.

The principles of good journalism, solid investigative reporting and the courage to tell stories that trouble the powerful (be they corporations, the government, or individuals) are the same whether the name on the publication is New York Times or any CNS newspaper or website.

It's a good lesson for everyone to remember.

My pledge as publisher today is that we will keep on flying – and keep you informed.

No matter what the trolls say about it.

Jack Stafford is the publisher and editor in chief of the Clarion Newspaper Syndicate. He publishes Column One every Friday and can be reached at JJStafford@ClarionNewsSyndicate.com.

Chapter 10

Caleb Osmett pulled the small gray backpack out of the closet in his bedroom on the top floor of the farmhouse.

He dropped it on the bed then went to the window to be sure his mother was still outside somewhere near where the DeVille Energy Federation surveyors were working.

He saw her standing near his grandfather's pickup truck, a half-mile from the house.

It was the third day of surveying by DEF, hampered by two men falling into pits dug by farm residents.

Both had injured themselves sufficiently they had to be replaced by other workers the next day.

Caleb's mother had convinced a sputtering DEF supervisor the pits were naturally occurring – including the fresh cow manure in the bottom.

He dumped the backpack on the bed, spilling out a pistol, a box of .38 caliber bullets, a clip with bullets in it, along with a knife, a pair of cheap binoculars, handcuffs, and a clipboard.

Caleb couldn't remember if it was the fourth or fifth time he'd pulled the backpack out of his closet and looked at the contents. *No one has said anything*, he thought as he picked up the pistol, noting how heavy it seemed.

On the day he had reached into the truck bed and grabbed the backpack, Caleb had only wanted to strike back at DEF and the men who had killed his grandfather and friends. He intended to simply take the backpack and throw it in a ditch somewhere, creating an inconvenience for the DEF surveyors and the guard who likely was the owner.

Just basic vandalism.

Then he found the gun and the bullets.

Everyone at the farm had been so focused on the surveyors and the guards that no one saw him lift the backpack out of the truck bed or take it to a culvert a few yards away. He stashed it until that night, then spirited it up to his bedroom.

The gun felt strange in his hand. Not even toy guys were allowed in the house or anywhere on *The Redoubt*. He remembered his grandfather arguing with other families when a toy gun would show up on the property.

"We're here because of guns. And we will not have them. Period," Caleb's grandfather said enough times that Caleb could hear the words ringing in his ears.

He understood on one level. On another, he couldn't erase the image of his grandfather and others dropping to the ground when they were shot. He had *seen* it that day with the binoculars.

He stood up and aimed the gun at a nearby tree. It was heavy and it took both hands to hold it steady. He put the gun down quickly on the bed, years of lectures about the danger of guns roiling around in his mind like water in a boiling pot.

Since he had brought the backpack and the gun into the house, he still hadn't figured out how to unload the clip of bullets from it.

Every time he had gone on the one computer he had access to in the house – in the small office downstairs – his mother or someone else was lurking too close for him to go online and find about the pistol.

The night before when his mother left for a short walk just at sunset he was typing in the name of the gun when she returned suddenly.

If she was suspicious of his scrambling when she walked in, she didn't say anything.

He hefted the gun up again, drawing a bead on the tree a second time.

"Pow," he said aloud. "Pow."

Caleb looked out the window and saw his mother had gotten into the pickup truck and was heading out the front gate, possibly into town.

He had the gun, bullets and all the contents back in the backpack and hidden in the corner of his closet before Janis made the turn out of *The Redoubt*. Then he took the stairs three at a time to get to the computer.

Chapter 11

The debate over whether Jack should go to California or not simmered quietly at the Stafford-Walsh Vashon Island household. After taking a few days at home, Jack had gone back into the *Vashon View* office, where Alexandra was busy keeping up with local news, simultaneously tracking the DeVille Energy Federation.

On this morning, he and Alexandra entered the office at precisely the same time, heading to their respective spaces, computers whirring within a moment. Alexandra filled her ever-present coffee mug when the office coffee maker signaled. Jack sipped a cup of hot tea he'd gotten from the shop across the street.

"Alex, I'm not sure I ever said thanks for the pep talk," he said. "I've been battling these energy corporations so much, that when DeVille shifted gears, it caught me by surprise. It's a whole new commodity and a whole new kind of story, really."

Alex looked at Jack, her eyes flitting back and forth to her screen.

"You're welcome. Like you said in your column, oil, gas, water – it's all reporting. The principles are the same," she said, her eyes glued now to her computer. "Oh, yeah. I forgot to add, corporate greed is corporate greed. You following this thing in the Mojave Desert?"

Jack searched his brain, faintly remembering a story from months back about a company's scheme to get at groundwater buried deep below California's Mojave Desert. The company had been at it for some years, losing a lot of money. But the drought across the western states had revived interest in it.

"I am following it, but I bet you have something new right in front of you," Jack said.

She tapped her keyboard and moved her lips slightly while she read, then turned to Jack. "Well, Eli found the story – actually a part of a story – that I thought we should follow up on."

Jack waited. Then he broke the silence. "It's too early for me to play 20 questions. The story?"

She made an I-am-sorry face, then turned and tapped on her keyboard.

"Sorry. It's early for me, too. Plus, I swear one of our reporters has slipped decaf into that machine.

"Anyway, Eli has been checking into who's buying water rights and where they're buying them. I think he has all of his staff helping, too. I just sent you his message so you can read it yourself. But the short version is he's pretty sure DeVille is using its subsidiaries to buy ground water rights all over the place. The Mojave Desert story is what made him start to look."

Jack turned to his computer to check the message. He also made a mental note to double-check the recently published contents of the *Horseheads Clarion*. As much as the *CNS* chased national stories like DeVille, it was important to keep the local communities happy, too.

"I see he's made a little progress, but I don't see proof in any of these examples."

Alexandra tapped on her keyboard again.

"Okay, here's the story. It's about Nebraska. There are groups talking about how valuable their water is and how vulnerable they are to outside interests raiding it. It's the Ogallala Aquifer. It's like an ocean. And it's shrinking."

Jack glanced at the story as it popped up on his screen. "I've been reading about the aquifer for several years. It's a problem. And I'm sure California is looking everywhere. But where's DeVille in all this?" he asked.

She swung back to her keyboard and pulled up a blog posting from a Nebraska environmentalist group. The headline said, "Investment group makes bid for Ogallala water rights."

"Somebody is offering ten times what the water is supposedly worth," she said.

Jack frowned then motioned for her to keep going.

"Oh, did I forget to mention that Eli says one of the corporate officers listed is named C. Boviné? With the accent on the 'e' and all."

Calvin Boviné? Jack thought. *And where is DEF getting all that money to buy up these water rights?*

Chapter 12

Keith Everlight re-read the string of three emails from his high school friend Harvey Weilbruner.

Weilbruner – nicknamed Wallbanger (often shortened to Wally) after the popular Harvey Wallbanger cocktail – was working in an office in Williston, North Dakota doing accounting and record-keeping for several energy companies.

The first email had been sent in the middle of the day, North Dakota time, followed by two others in the space of an hour.

> *Hey Keith. I saw your name and contact info on the class website and thought I would give you a shout. Plus, I did a quick search and figured out that you're a newspaper editor in Pennsylvania. And a hero! Holy shit! That was some blast that leveled your town a few years ago. I had no idea you were there. I'm out here in the middle of frack world North Dakota, crunching numbers for a couple of different energy companies. Are you going to make it to the reunion next summer? Let me know. Wally Wallbanger*

Keith had received similar chatty emails from a half-dozen other classmates in recent weeks, all triggered by his email being prominently listed on the high school reunion website. But except for one old flame's request that they hook up, those email messages stuck to the upcoming class reunion.

He was deciding whether or not to respond to Wally, when a second email popped up.

> *Hey Keith. I was just reading a story you wrote awhile back about the DeVille pipeline project. I was kind of stunned when I read that crazy asshole DeVille wants to ship water from the Great Lakes to California. But maybe it isn't that crazy. We have water problems, here, too. Good story, man. There's a lot more that*

The second email, sent 15 minutes after the first one, tweaked Keith's curiosity enough that he had started to compose a response to Wally, just a mild inquiry to see if he really knew anything about DeVille plan or was just trying to impress Keith.

> *Hey Keith. Sorry I had to cut that last email short. My boss walked in and I had to swap screens really fast. Kind of like when we were in French class. Remember that? My boss is like the Gestapo, but has to pee every 15 minutes. Ha! Prostate trouble.*
> *I think you'd be interested in some stuff I've been running across. But email's not good. Maybe we can talk on the telephone? Tonight maybe. Let me know. Hey, you still boxing? I should've learned how. It would come in handy with all oil jerks around here.*
> *Wally*

Keith composed a short email to Wally, suggesting that they talk soon, possibly via Skype if Wally had a good connection.

Then Keith wrote a second email to Eli at the *Horseheads Clarion*, asking if he knew anything about DeVille's connections to the Williston oil fields. Keith knew that Wally could just be peddling rumors. He had been a gossip in high school, but his rumors always had *some* grain of truth.

And he mentioned DeVille by name, Keith thought. *And water.*

Chapter 13

The media coverage so far of the DeVille pipeline project had been overwhelmingly gushing, a fact that made A.G. DeVille almost smile.

But his entire staff would watch his face drop when the issue of protesters or nosy journalists came up.

And it always seemed to slip into their conversations. *Fucking protesters. Fucking investigative journalists,* DeVille would think.

The negative coverage was prompted by small knots of very vocal protesters along the proposed route of the pipeline through farmlands – or too close to residences who learned how to get media attention. In press conferences, they would assail the project, saying that the pipeline would disrupt wildlife and be a blight on the landscape. Native American groups in Nebraska likened the pipeline to the 19th century building of the transcontinental railway that bisected the nation, causing problems for the then-amazing numbers of American Bison wandering the Great Plains.

In Iowa and Nebraska inbred stubbornness coupled with decades of dealing with water issues created an odd coalition of people trying to slow down DeVille's plans.

He had called his staff into the conference room for a conversation about surveying progress and a report from their California subsidiary about diluting fracking wastewater to make it acceptable – according to federal and state water rules – for agricultural use.

A new university study just published was damning when it talked about the chemicals in recovered water – so damning that it made front pages all over the country and was costing DeVille and other energy companies a fortune to refute.

A small army of paid energy company public relations professionals were busy telling media outlets that the study was unscientific and poorly done. If that didn't work, they would say the study had been funded by environmental wackos who had a clear anti-fossil fuel political agenda. And if that failed, they would go through the backdoor and subtly threaten publishers and TV news directors with a loss of advertising revenues if they didn't publish "fair and balanced" reports.

Currently researchers had made progress putting the pieces together on what chemicals were being used in the fracking process, a trade secret. Then they followed that thread to determine what chemicals were in the recovered water.

It was a complicated analysis that had been done before. But this time the researchers were a lot sharper than previously. They had better access to data about what was being forced down the fracked wells and were able to test samples of what was coming back up.

After doing so, they concluded that the recovered water – at least from the handful of wells they tested – was up to 10 times more toxic than the actual cocktail of water and chemicals that was used to hydrofrack.

When this was reported, the conference room got ominously silent.

"All right, all right," DeVille said. "Rod Mayenlyn is still out in California but coming back here tomorrow. I've told him to put together a group to make sure this study gets discredited right into the ground. Some of you will be tapped for that."

Then he noticed that two of the engineers at the far end of the conference table had their heads close and were whispering, looking at the screen of a tablet computer propped up in front of them.

He stopped talking and stared until one of the men – who had previously worked for the now-defunct Grand Energy Services – looked up, a horrified expression on his face. He flipped his tablet down on the table so hard it let out a solid bang.

"Sorry A.G.," he said, quickly amending his statement. "I *mean* sorry Mr. DeVille. We were talking about that newspaper columnist Jack Stafford and the column published this morning."

DeVille stared at the engineer for a long moment, making everyone around the table uncomfortable.

"Enlighten us will you, *Wilshire*, isn't it? Oh, yes, Herman Wilshire. I remember now."

Wilshire looked around the table. The faces of the other men reflected a combination of fear and relief that they weren't in the sights of A.G. DeVille.

"Well, sir. Um, Mr. DeVille, the column is all about using recovered water for crops and how it can't be made safe. I mean he claims it can't be made safe."

DeVille looked disgusted.

"That claim is hardly news Wilshire, certainly not enough for you to be disruptive when I'm trying to get us to focus, God damn it," DeVille said. "We have a bunch of Indian protesters in Nebraska, at least that's what my morning news digest from Mayenlyn said. They're led by some young woman. We'll need to deal with that quickly before it gets too much attention."

DeVille looked over at his executive secretary, then swung his head back.

"Wilshire, what's the headline on that Stafford column?"

Wilshire flipped his tablet computer back upright and touched the screen to wake it up.

"It's a quote from one of the people he cites in the column," Wilshire said.

"Dilution is not a solution."

Archimedes Gabriel DeVille's face turned a crimson color *so* bright that his executive secretary reached and touched his hand – a taboo that DeVille didn't even notice in his rage.

"This meeting is over," he said in a flat voice.

As his staff filed out, he sat very still, the color gradually fading. He looked down at his secretary's hand, which she was slowly withdrawing.

"Mayenlyn," he whispered, barely audible. "Mayenlyn and Mars. I want to talk to them the minute they arrive."

Chapter 14

The Clarion Newspaper Syndicate
Column One

Dilution is NOT a solution

By Jack Stafford

Everything always seems to come back to water.

Most of the water news recently has been in the form of published or broadcast bouquets thrown in the direction of the DeVille Energy Federation for its proposed pipeline to bring water from the Great Lakes west to the arid Southwest and California.

As we noted, the whole project is so wrapped in secrecy, it's hard to know much about it. We're continuing to ask hard questions about funding, the route the pipeline will take and what the costs to consumers will be.

While this hazy project has the spotlight, the world's water woes are stacking up quickly and in ugly ways.

In Flint, Michigan, an entire city has been poisoned by municipal officials. They gambled with citizen safety and lost catastrophically. In a bumbling attempt to save tax monies, they tapped a new water source and ended up setting toxic levels of lead loose in the city water system.

People are sick.

People are dying.

Around the globe, fresh water sources are being polluted so badly the water is unfit for human, animal or plant consumption.

There are plenty of culprits at which to point: hydrofracking for natural gas and oil, mining, and almost all industrial chemical processes where careless corporations take only the minimal of precautions to ensure water safety.

But among the many remedies being attempted, there is a common theme.

If water is polluted, no matter how badly, many polluters peddle the idea that simply adding a sufficient volume of clean water can make the problem go away.

Just add clean water and poof!

That particular theory has even been applied to a catastrophic iron mine water spill in Brazil – one that polluted a 400-mile stretch of a river so badly it won't recover for decades, if ever.

And as a toxic plume raced toward the ocean, most news reports reflected the official attitude of the Brazilian government (and the mining industry) that the crisis would be over just as soon as the mud slurry of toxic wastewater reached the coast and the deep waters of the Atlantic.

The ocean would dilute the many millions of gallons of water so that it would no longer be toxic, a notion that on one level may seem reasonable.

Except in the big picture it's false.

Toxic chemicals in water don't go away when mixed with clean water. The concentrations are simply lower.

So what? Isn't' that good enough?

No, no, no! It's not good enough.

Over time the toxic chemicals begin to add up, concentrating in mud, in animals and even humans using the water. That's why the Brazilian river that was filled with toxic waste is for all intent, dead. At least in our lifetimes.

That water in Brazil might pass some government analysis that says the toxic chemicals are below a threshold that some arbitrary standard declares as "safe."

But is it safe?

Not at all.

And the mud in the river will now be the repository for those toxic chemicals. The same can be said for any living thing that survived the initial onslaught. And if it is small animals, when predators eat them they will be ingesting not just a meal, but a dose of toxic chemicals.

Dilution is not a solution, water experts say. The only solution is to keep the toxic chemicals out of the water in the first place, a kind of an environmental zero-tolerance policy.

But that concept is categorically dismissed as unreasonable by industries of all stripes. That's hardly surprising as it threatens their continued dumping of chemicals into water sources and water supplies.

Industry has been treating our waterways and oceans as sewers for hundreds of years, all tied to the idea that they could absorb basically anything.

We won't even bother discussing the ongoing radioactive water traveling from Japan's Fukushima nuclear power plant into the Northern Pacific Ocean.

The idea that dilution is not a solution remains an issue in California and other parts of the nation because of the continued shortage of water.

The need for water – any water – has people turning to hydrofracking wastewater as a source for irrigation of crops – sufficiently diluted, of course.

The western U.S. water shortage has been somewhat eased by El Niño weather systems. But so far it's not enough.

And water experts are saying it's easy to envision a time – even in the next year or two – when water-starved communities will look at diluted fracking wastewater for domestic uses, too.

What a nightmare.

In the meantime, a university study released last week included an avalanche of data showing that wastewater from hydrofracking operations is many times more toxic and dangerous to living things than previously thought.

Among the conclusions of the researchers is this bit of grim news:

"A spill of a few thousand gallons in a creek, for example, was once thought to be an annoyance, even as it killed much aquatic life. Now we know it has much greater potential for harm, including to humans."

Knowing that, it's clear: Dilution is not a solution.

Jack Stafford is the publisher and editor in chief of the Clarion Newspaper Syndicate. He publishes Column One every Friday and can be reached at JJStafford@ClarionNewsSyndicate.com.

Chapter 15

Rod Mayenlen shifted in his seat, aware that the female flight attendant at the front of the cabin could not take her eyes off his huge first-class seat mate, Marsden Weesley who was looking out the window at the clouds, his head bent way down so he could peer out.

Christ, Mayenlyn thought, *she's staring, but I can barely look at him.*

When Weesley showed up at Mayenlyn's hotel in Bakersfield he almost caused a panic in the lobby.

He was as tall as Calvin Boviné, with broad-shoulders and disproportionately long arms that hung down nearly to his knees.

He didn't share Boviné's resemblance to an NFL football player. He appeared more gangly. But he was still an imposing sight to any average sized person.

But what had the flight attendant staring – and what had scared the hell out of the hotel desk clerk – was Weesley's sloped forehead leading across a nearly bald head where small tufts of fiercely black hair popped up in a half-dozen spots, like sagebrush.

Plus, he had an overbite so dramatic it made it seem as if his lower jaw belonged to someone else and had been grafted onto his skull.

He looks like the love child of Quasimodo and the bride of Frankenstein, Mayenlyn thought.

Mayenlyn liked that phrase so well that he chuckled silently to himself, thinking he really needed to remember to use it sometime later.

He leaned back and closed his eyes, a slight grin on his face. Then he felt pressure on his left forearm, a steady pressure that startled him at first, and then hurt as the pressure went up.

It started to hurt a lot.

"Something funny?" Weesley asked, putting even more pressure on Mayenlyn's forearm.

He leaned down, putting his face next to Mayenlyn's, examining Mayenlyn's face closely like it was something exotic, or a puzzle to solve. Mayenlyn stared straight ahead, watching Weesley out of the corner of his eye and trying not to show any fear.

But when Weesley rolled his eyes slightly, making them look like loose marbles, it was just too much.

"Mars, back off will you?" Mayenlyn said, hearing a slight quaver in his voice. "Let me go. Just get some sleep, will you. DeVille wants to see us early."

Weesley's hand stayed on Mayenlyn's forearm, but the pressure lightened. He turned his face forward, slowly, almost like an animatronic figure. Mayenlyn saw that the flight attendant had stopped staring and was talking with a male flight attendant, waving her arms around and occasionally glancing towards him and Weesley.

"I know people make fun of me," Weesley said, his face now looking straight ahead.

He squeezed Mayenlyn's arm hard again. "Most of the time I let them."

Then Weesley swung his head quickly, putting his huge front teeth up against Mayenlyn's right ear.

Mayenlyn fought the idea that Weesley might be about to bite him.

Weesley pulled back an inch so his horse-like teeth weren't making contact with Mayenlyn's ear and hissed. "But sometimes I *don't* let them make fun of me," Weesley said, his voice a light whisper. "You better remember that. *Rodney.*"

Chapter 16

The 6 a.m. Monday morning videoconference was problematic for Jack and Alexandra in Washington state, but even more so for Eli and Keith at their newspapers in New York and Pennsylvania, even though for them, it was 9 a.m.

Jack and Alexandra were half-asleep from rising early to get into the office. Eli and Keith were stressed because Monday was deadline day for the Tuesday edition of all three newspapers.

Eli and Keith had already been working for two hours on editing, page layouts and adjustments to their next editions by the time Jack and Alexandra buzzed to start the meeting.

"Sorry everyone," Jack said. "But over the weekend I had a dream. Really."

Alexandra, sitting next to Jack, Eli in Horseheads, NY and Keith in Rockwell Valley, PA didn't crack even the slightest of smiles.

"Ok, it's too early for subtlety and humor," Jack said. "But honest, I did have kind of dream of sorts. Or nightmare, more accurately."

Alexandra sipped her coffee and Jack noticed that both of his east coast editors were leaning forward in their chairs, their finger no doubt itching to get back to their newspapers.

"I know all three of you are thinking we could have done this Tuesday when the deadline for print had past," Jack said. "But honestly, with the way you three are pumping out fresh stories for the websites, I don't see anybody having any down time, any day."

Keith jumped in first. "You are absolutely right about no down time, Jack. So now is fine… Plus I did some thinking about how get more organized about the DeVille pipeline coverage. We've been getting distracted."

The distractions included the seizure of a bird sanctuary in Oregon, the oil glut's impacts on local economies and the wild swings in the U.S. stock market.

A new video software package Eli had just installed in their system allowed the screens on the computers to be divided neatly into four quadrants, with the three newspaper offices displayed and a fourth accessible for any of the editors to put something up for the others to see.

A photo of a man in camouflage, cradling what looked like a semi-automatic assault weapon, popped up with the *Horsehead Clarion*'s signature logo above it.

"This is one of our fine upstate NY citizens who says he wants to go to Oregon to 'fight for freedom'," Eli said. "We're doing a story today about a local group of militant wing nuts. Hold the jokes about sending snacks with him, OK?"

Keith and Alexandra both laughed at a second photo that showed the man loading the back of his pickup truck with some gear for the drive 2,500-mile drive across country.

The mid 1980s model pickup truck had rusty fenders, pockmarked with holes. A wire was holding up a sketchy-looking muffler. And the tailgate was held in place with rope.

"That's what's going into print," Eli said. "Tomorrow afternoon I'll put up the full package of photos and video online. And I am not kidding, I had to use captioning on the screen whenever he spoke into the camera. He was talking in some kind of woodchuck dialect."

This time Jack laughed the hardest. That odd speech pattern was very familiar to him from his years growing up in New York and going to high school in Horseheads. And chewing tobacco – the vice of so many of the rural men in that part of the state – made it worse.

"We can do show-and-tell in a few minutes for your regular editors' meeting. But right now, I want your thoughts," Jack said. "That dream I had? DeVille Energy was pulling a fast one on the whole nation. I don't believe that much thinking has gone into this idea of taking water from the Great Lakes. Environmental thinking anyway. Where is the analysis of this project? And the B.S. about national security?"

The photo of the deteriorating pickup truck was replaced by a black-and-white studio shot of a thin-faced young man in a coat and tie. His face was screwed up into a forced smile. A classic high school yearbook shot.

"This is from 20 years ago," Keith said. "I went to high school with this guy – Harvey Weilbruner. I won't bore you with the details, but we called him Harvey Wallbanger in high school. The interesting part about him is he works in Williston, North Dakota. He's an accountant I think. Some kind of number cruncher for several oil and gas outfits doing work in the area."

Alexandra looked at the photo closely.

"He's kind of cute. Or was anyway," she said.

Keith laughed and flipped up another shot, this one a more current one of Weilbruner from his Facebook page.

The thin-faced boy with the forced smile now had a wide grin on a puffy face, a beer can in his hand and a protruding belly that made it look like he enjoyed brewed beverages often.

"He's single, Alex, too … Go for it," Keith said.

When the editors all got done laughing, a photo of the DeVille Energy Federation President A.G. DeVille popped up, drawing boos all around.

"I'm not sure how we are going to divvy up this coverage of the pipeline," Keith said. "But I want to pursue this one piece, particularly because I think Wally – Weilbruner, I mean – will help us."

Jack looked at the clock and realized they were already pushing into the time needed for Eli and Keith to finish their pages.

"OK, done," Jack said. "And while we've been talking, I realized I should ask Alexandra to put together a master document online for coverage. Let's all look at that later today – after deadline – and comment or put in what you want. But Keith, before we all start the deadline dance again. What do you think Wally knows?"

The yearbook photo popped up again.

"We had a very quick conversation on the telephone yesterday," Keith said. "He said DeVille is talking very quietly to some of the big players here about water and a pipeline."

Jack leaned into the computer.

"You think he wants to provide water way up there for fracking?" Jack said.

This time a map of the Midwestern U.S. popped up in the corner showing the vast spaghetti-like maze of pipelines already in existence.

"That's what I thought at first," Keith said. "And maybe it is. But Wally said he thinks DeVille might be offering something else. "A way to get rid of fracking wastewater."

Jack's hand slapped down on the desk next to Alexandra so hard, she spilled some of her coffee on her keyboard and swore.

Jack grabbed some paper towels and apologized profusely while Eli and Keith watched amused.

Then Jack's cell phone rang.

It was an Iowa phone number he didn't recognized.

"Jack Stafford, can I help you?"

The voice on the other end was sobbing at first, then a female voice came through. "Sorry Jack. This is Janis, Janis Osmett. I didn't know if I should call. But I thought you should know.

"Caleb's been arrested. I'm on my way to the sheriff's office right now."

Drums along the Ogallala

Chapter 1

Growing up in Horseheads, New York, Sheode Walker hated her name.

The teachers pronounced it *She-owed*, instead of *Shay-o-day*, the proper Pawnee way – at least according to her mother.

The name supposedly was that of her great-great-grandmother, a Pawnee woman who had learned to speak English and French from traders in Nebraska.

Sheode was not completely convinced of the origin of her supposed Native American name. She had tried to track it down many times finding only names with somewhat similar spellings.

And there were no Pawnee living anywhere near Horseheads.

But her jet-black hair and strong resemblance to young Pawnee and Sioux women she had viewed in historical photos made it clear her predominately English ancestors were only partly responsible for her genes.

Sheode had tried using a simple "Shay" as a nickname, but a boy who was in all of her junior high classes was named Shea and it only caused confusion.

Her pique over the proper pronunciation of her name came flooding back as she carefully explained how to pronounce it to her seatmate on a Greyhound bus rumbling through eastern Iowa on its way to Nebraska and points west of the Rockies.

But she felt better at the end of her lecture when her young, very athletic-looking seatmate introduced herself and said *her* name was Amber – but spelled *Amburr*. That spelling that caused Amburr plenty of her own angst growing up.

Amburr had jumped on the bus right at the Illinois-Iowa border, explaining that she was on her way to Mancos, Colorado, where a relative had a job waiting for her at a dude ranch near Mesa Verde National Park.

"*Soooooo* we both have kind of, well, weird names," Amburr said. "But where are you from? Where are you going?"

Sheode looked at her seatmate and decided to say Ithaca instead of the lesser known town of Horseheads.

Then she launched into a short history of the last couple of years.

"I've been rehearsing answers to those two questions ever since got I on this bus," Sheode said.

She explained she had just dropped out of an Ithaca-area college after several semesters of environmental studies, political science and journalism.

She was an A student and had gravitated towards activist students, most of whom were forever marching around the Ithaca Commons, a revitalized downtown center of upscale stores, restaurants, college bars and a few head shops with hash pipes displayed in the windows.

Although the chanting and colorful sign-making was amusing, Sheode decided that writing about issues – particularly important environmental ones – was more her style than standard-issue protesting.

"My dad was a writer," Sheode told Amburr. "I was the only kid I knew growing up who read newspapers all the time. I had to. My dad would quiz me at the dinner table."

Sheode paused.

"My dad died about 5 years ago. It was cancer."

Amburr leaned back in her seat, with the quiet that envelopes some people when a death is mentioned.

She turned to face Sheode. "I am sooooo sorry about your dad. My parents are both still around and not very happy I'm going to Colorado. They wanted me to keep going to junior college. But my grades were so shitty it was embarrassing."

She paused for a moment, a slight grin on her face.

"Actually, I flunked out. No shit! I flunked out of a junior college. Can you fucking believe it?"

The two women starting laughing so hard a few people poked their heads up from their seats to see what the ruckus was about.

"Anyway, that's my story," Amburr said. "Where are you going?"

Sheode reached into her backpack and rifled through a sheaf of newspapers finally finding the one she wanted.

"Oh my God," Amburr said, reading the front page of the *Horseheads Clarion*. "You're going to that farm where the people were killed? Holy shit! Why?"

Sheode took the newspaper back and stuck it in her backpack.

"For right now I'm just going there," Sheode said. "And that column I just showed you? My dad knew the guy who wrote it. They were friends in high school. That was before Jack Stafford left our little town for California. Now he's a publisher and lives in Washington most of the time. Washington the state. But he was just in Iowa. Right there with those people."

Amburr frowned, then her eyes opened really wide. "We read a book he wrote in one of my classes! It was called *Hope and Solutions*, or something like that." Amburr said. "Of course, I flunked the damn class. The teacher was nuts about Stafford and his crusading columns."

Sheode smiled and leaned back in her seat. "I am, too," she said. "I think I'm going to ask him for a job."

Chapter 2

The emails and messages between Alexandra and Eli had been flying back and forth all day, culminating in a video call between the two of them.

Alexandra had been the one to first figure out the supposed starting point of the Devil's Pipeline, while Eli continued to try to map its route across the country to California.

"It could go through Canada or Mexico for all I know and what the official documents I can find say," Eli said. "Something just is wrong about this. Plus the pipeline itself. Usually the companies blast it right out there."

The week before all three newspapers in the *Clarion Newspaper Syndicate* had published a cheerleading opinion piece by a Wall Street financial analyst who applauded DEF's insistence on keeping the company's plans private.

> *It is very early in this development game. And DeVille is smart to keep the exact routes and details about the project confidential. The amount of property DEF will be leasing is huge and people in the pipeline's path will be doing everything they can to boost the price to DeVille.*
>
> *Plus there are all the national security implications to consider as well as each state's particular process for approving routes.*
>
> *Company sources have also hinted that the exact route hasn't even been*

established and will depend on financial and political factors that are still evolving.

"Political and financial factors my butt," Alexandra said. "Did you see what happened with DEF stock this week? They got a big bounce thanks to this guy's piece. The TV stations were even quoting from it.

"National security, my butt, too," she said.

Alexandra watched as Eli tapped furiously on his keys.

He had opened a window on their videoconference screen so that one quarter of Alexandra's screen was taken up with a direct screen image of what Eli was doing.

The pages opened and closed so fast she had trouble keeping up as he whizzed through county records in Wisconsin, Iowa and Nebraska.

"Eli! Yoo-hoo!" she said. "Hey, we agreed to talk – not have a database search Olympics."

He stopped typing. "Sorry. It's just that since we talked with Keith about the fracking water, I've been trying to track *that* down, too. Those wells in North Dakota are producing a lot of wastewater, even with the slowdown in drilling. I think most of the companies are keeping their records about their recovered water offline. I know they spread some of it on the roads. That was in some North Dakota newspapers. The towns were so proud that they saved some money."

Alexandra let out a snort.

"They should go talk to the people in Flint about saving money," she said.

"We are making progress though. We know where they've been surveying in Iowa, near Milwaukee and maybe in Nebraska. It's hard to stay hidden in Nebraska because anybody with a tripod who even looks remotely like a surveyor for a gas or oil company is likely to get shot at."

When Eli stared at the screen and shook his head, she revised her hyperbole.

"OK, maybe not shot at. But the tribal nations, the Native Americans? They have been riled up ever since the Keystone Pipeline debacle where the oil companies wanted to run tar sands bitumen across the reservations."

After comparing notes for a few minutes more, they talked about a message from Jack telling all three editors to hold the story about the arrest of Caleb Osmett until he gave the go ahead. And they were to coordinate with him on what was published.

Caleb's being a minor had kept it off the police blotter, temporarily.

"I hope he gives us the green light soon," Eli said. "It's big news that the grandson of a pacifist Kent State shooting survivor was caught with a gun and threatening a DEF worker. Somebody is going to get the story soon. We should be the ones to do it."

As Alexandra called up her notes on Caleb, a message from Jack popped up simultaneously on her screen and Eli's.

> *In addition to what you already know, I've confirmed something that you need to include in the story about Caleb. Let's do one master story that runs on all three websites. Caleb's mother Janis said the police are going to make his arrest public in about three hours. Here's what to include, attributed to Janis Osmett:*
>
> *When he was arrested, Caleb was in the middle of attempting a citizen's arrest of someone he says is a DeVille Energy Federation employee. Caleb said the*

> *DEF employee was alone and trespassing in a wooded section of The Redoubt property near the highway when Caleb confronted him.*

Eli shot a message to Keith so they could have a three-way conversation about who would write the story for the website.

Before Keith could reply, a second message popped up from Jack.

> *Please be sure to attribute the DEF employee part to Caleb believing that's who the man works for. We have no evidence, but Janis said she talked with Caleb. And we can't print this yet, but it appears the maybe-DEF employee – if he is one – used his cell phone to dial 911 when he saw Caleb coming towards him, waving a pistol at him.*

Chapter 3

The Greyhound bus dropped Sheode off in an empty parking lot at a crossroads convenience store and gas station near Boyette, the county seat and nearest big town to *The Redoubt*, 50 miles away.

The sun was quickly nearing the flat horizon.

A teenage male clerk wearing a baseball cap bearing the logo of an Iowa tractor dealer looked Sheode up and down when she walked in to the counter where he was perched on a stool.

Sheode sized him up, too, thinking that whatever teen fantasies he might have boosting his hormonal flow, her college self-defense classes – plus three years of Tae Kwon Do in high school – more than made her a match to drop his skinny ass on the floor if need be.

When she saw his plastic nametag said "Lester" she almost burst out laughing.

Lester the molester, she thought. *Boy, I'm a long way from Horseheads.*

"Can I help ya Miss?" Lester said, his eyes still wandering while a big grin filled his face.

Sheode lowered her backpack to the floor – her one piece of luggage.

"You might be able to help," she said. "I'm going to the farm called *The Redoubt*. I think it's near here. Is there a bus that goes there maybe? Or is there a taxi service or something?"

Lester's grin dropped along with his jaw, revealing for Sheode that he had some bad dental work – or maybe *no* dental work. The scowl that replaced his leering grin made Sheode happy the counter separated the two of them, whether she could thrash him or not.

"Why you going there? Just a bunch old hippies and radicals out on that place," Lester said. He reached beneath the counter and produced a tin of chewing tobacco and a stained piece of paper that looked like some kind of timetable.

He opened the tobacco tin and pulled out a pinch, dropping it expertly into his cheek, staring at Sheode the whole time.

That explains the teeth, she thought.

After a moment, he broke off his gaze and looked down at the piece of paper, Sheode guessed it might be a bus schedule. He studied it as carefully as if it was a treasure map, tracing his finger across it several times.

He finally shook his head.

"Nope," he said, looking up at her.

"Nope," he said again.

"Only one bus a day going towards Hippie Town," he said. "It came by hours ago. Thought I seen it."

He leaned his head down behind the counter spitting into something below. He lifted his head back up, renewing his leering smile. Sheode knew he was within a moment or two of offering her a ride in whatever his vehicle was.

And that's why I always walk when I need to, she thought. *Thank God I read those* Jack Reacher *novels about traveling light. Reacher wouldn't even have a backpack.*

Lester turned and looked over his shoulder, smiling at the sunset before turning around to look at Sheode.

But before he could speak, a bell rang twice in quick succession, a sound Sheode recognized as one of the old air hose-tripped bells that gas stations used so they would know when customers pulled in needing gasoline.

Lester turned looked out the window, muttering a barely audible "shit" under his breath before looking back at Sheode.

"Fer fuck's sake, you maybe got yourself a ride, I bet. That there is a woman named Janis who lives out there with them other hippies on that farm. She'll probably give you a lift after she gets gas."

Sheode picked up her backpack and headed for the door, stopping to turn before she opened it.

"Lester, did you ever see a movie called *Deliverance*?"

From the quizzical look on his face, Sheode was pretty sure he hadn't.

Chapter 4

The conference room chair Marsden Weesley was sitting in was going to break. Rod Mayenlyn was sure of it.

He looked like an adult stuffed in a chair made for a child.

A very ugly, very big, very scary adult, Mayenlyn thought.

And if it did break, it would be about the only thing that made much sense.

Gravity I understand. But Mars and DeVille?

Weesley, Mayenlyn and A.G. DeVille were in a hotel suite about 10 miles from the DeVille Energy Federation offices, a suite that DEF had on permanent retainer in a non-descript Houston suburb consisting of mostly strip malls, auto repair shops and the occasional used furniture store.

Outside the hotel, A.G. DeVille's Cadillac limousine was parked, his chauffeur waiting. A separate unmarked DEF car and driver was waiting after bringing Mars and Mayenlyn from their hotel that was even further from DEF headquarters where the two men had been waiting in another DEF paid-for suite until DeVille summoned them an hour before.

Mayenlyn's former employer, the bankrupt Grand Energy Services, had a few places like this set up, too, away from all prying corporate rivals and media eyes.

But those hotel rooms GES kept on retainer mostly so there was a private place to entertain male customers with young women. They weren't used for conferences or meetings. *Or for keeping a hired gorilla out of sight*, Mayenlyn thought.

Gorilla was what Mayenlyn had finally settled on as his working image of Mars – a really big ape that could talk.

This three-room hotel suite was stripped of standard hotel furniture but had an assortment of desks, white boards, computers and a small conference table with a dozen chairs. Mayenlyn had not been to this place in the short time since he joined DEF, though several vice presidents had quietly mentioned its existence to him.

When he first heard of the place, the vice president who had whispered it to him called the suburban hotel suite *Black Ops*. He didn't smile when he said it.

Mayenlyn had spent years in the energy industry working for CEOs who had outsized personalities and weird quirks, most of which were close to the surface and pretty easy to assess. But DeVille was proving to be full of surprises. Like his relationship to Mars.

When he joined the DEF staff, one of Mayenlyn's jobs was to promote DeVille's image as a captain of industry, someone who had come up from humble beginnings as an orphan, while keeping details about his private life shielded.

Since getting an avalanche of favorable publicity, DeVille seemed to crave it more and more.

It's like cancer of the ego, Mayenlyn thought.

When Mayenlyn and Mars first walked in, Mayenlyn quickly realized there was a lot left out of DeVille's official biography.

Mayenlyn nearly gasped when he and Mars entered the hotel suite and Mars lumbered quickly towards DeVille, then bent over and wrapped his arms around DeVille, tenderly pulling him to his chest.

Jesus! DeVille is the guy who rarely even shakes hands, Mayenlyn thought.

DeVille disappeared behind Mars' bulk in the embrace with his hands and wrists visible wrapped around Mars. It looked to Mayenlyn like DeVille was clutching Mars just as tightly, in return.

They stood in the embrace long enough that Mayenlyn began to get very uncomfortable. Then he heard a series of muffled words from DeVille that sounded like "Enough. Now sit, Mars. Sit. Yes. Yes. Good boy."

Mars stood up straight and walked to the nearest chair along the wall by the conference table, gingerly sitting down like a man who knows his size is tough on furniture.

Mayenlyn sat down two chairs away, while DeVille continued to stand.

"Rod, I'm going to tell you a story about Marsden – and me – that can never be repeated. But I'm telling you because it's important and I trust you. Do you understand?"

Mayenlyn felt his stomach go sour, knowing that whatever this story was he probably really didn't want to hear it. But there was no way *not* to listen or *not* to know whatever DeVille was about to say.

He looked at Mars who was still focused on DeVille, looking almost enraptured. Mars' face was as close to a smile as his massive overbite and sloped head allowed.

When Mayenlyn didn't reply to DeVille, Mars swiveled his head slowly towards Mayenlyn, the smile disappearing.

"A.G., you *know* I can keep a secret," Mayenlyn said, staring at Mars. "I've been in this industry a long time and worked for lots of people. I know secrets I'll take with me to the grave. You know that."

Then Mayenlyn turned his attention to DeVille, whose arms were now folded across his chest, his lips pursed slightly.

"I was sure you would say that, Rod," DeVille said. "I'm counting on it. So is Mars."

Mayenlyn shivered involuntarily when Mars tried to grin.

Chapter 5

The flight from Seattle to Iowa over the Rockies was less bumpy than the one Jack had taken when he flew in to visit *The Redoubt* in the wake of James Osmett's death.

But the night before had been very bumpy at the dinner table with Cass, Anne and Noah.

He had offhandedly announced that he would be leaving in the morning to fly back to Iowa because of Caleb's arrest. "I talked with Janis today. I need to go back there and help," he had said. "Plus, I think I'm going to write more about the irony of all this because of the Kent State connection."

His sudden pronouncement drew such daggers from his sisters-in-law that he quickly realized his gaffe.

"I'm sorry," he said. "I'm assuming that you two can take care of Noah while I'm gone. I should have started with *asking* if you can do it."

After the short apology Jack had held up his hands in mock surrender, prompting Noah to raise his hands, too. He thought it was a funny game.

But Noah wondered why Aunt Cass and Aunt Anne weren't joining the game.

Noah's hands in the air, along with Jack's, took the steam out of Cass and Anne. Their expressions softened, though they both shook their heads.

"I think we have had this conversation before, Jack," Anne said. "More than once, right? Of *course*, we love having Noah stay with us. Our little compound of houses is your home and Noah's home and *always* will be. When I see Noah playing in the yard, he reminds me of Devon. And he's a gem – most of the time."

Jack nodded to Noah and they lowered their hands.

"I apologize again," Jack said. "And I'm hoping this will be a short trip. I have to sort out things on the ground there."

Jack noticed that Cass hadn't said anything in the exchange. Her expression was hard to read.

Sad? Jack wondered. *Or disappointed.*

Cass pushed the food around on her plate for a moment while they all ate in silence.

Then she spoke without looking up.

"Jack, did Janis ask you to come to Iowa to help?" Cass asked.

Jack looked at Anne, then Cass before answering. "Actually, she did," he said. "She said Caleb asked when I was coming back. He's in a juvenile detention center. She seems to think some on-the-ground media might get the judge to spring him without having to pay a huge bail bond."

Jack watched Cass and Anne exchange a look Jack had come to think of as "Sister-Com" in which they seemed to read each other thoughts.

Crisis looks over, Jack thought. *They're both smiling now.*

"OK, Noah," Anne said. "Let's walk over to your house and get your pajamas. I don't think we have any clean ones since you stayed here when your Aunt Cass and your dad went away. You better bring your school bag, too."

Jack squirmed in his seat and took a sip of wine.

"That's not really necessary, Anne," he said. "Um ... I brought his PJs and school bag with us when we walked over for dinner. I, um, left them in the hallway when we walked in."

Anne and Cass exchanged another look. But much to Jack's relief, they kept smiling.

Chapter 6

Jack Stafford's return to *The Redoubt* – even if planned to be very brief – was welcome news to everyone in the community.

And Sheode Walker couldn't believe her luck when Janis told her that the man she was hoping to meet – and maybe work for – was on his way to *The Redoubt*'s doorstep.

She had been overwhelmed with the welcome she received from Janis, who insisted that she stay at the rambling main farmhouse.

"Since my father died we've been kind of regrouping and re-forming the whole community," Janis told her. "He was the center of everything. And the way he died along with our friends? It was such a shock. Everyone is still struggling with it, mostly with grief and mourning. But a few people are angry – like Caleb. Thank God he didn't fire the gun."

Although there were only a handful of single 20-something males scattered in the homes around *The Redoubt*, every one of them seemed to find an excuse to stop by Janis' house the day after Sheode arrived.

By the time the third fellow had stopped by to ask Janis if she needed anything – and by the way, how is Caleb? – Janis started calling Sheode to the front door when she saw any male figure approaching under the age of 40.

"You're the new girl in very small town," Janis said. "And the fact that you're cute as a bug? It throws a pretty big rock in this tiny pond."

In high school in Horseheads and then college, Sheode drew lots of admiring glances.

She had a perfectly symmetrical face that always appeared smiling, a clear, slightly tan complexion – a gift from her Pawnee ancestors, her mother said – and a slender but athletic build.

"I bet you are one of those young women who doesn't realize she's gorgeous," Janis said. "Watch out for these farm boys. They are going to be coming around here like dogs chasing a female in heat."

Sheode blushed. She generally laughed when Janis would talk about the young men on *The Redoubt*, but she was secretly quite pleased. Her high school romances had been few, short and unmemorable. The young men in college seemed smart and interesting at first.

But she discovered they were actually very interested in themselves. And too many were spending too much time with drugs.

On the bus trip and now at *The Redoubt*, Sheode was fantasizing about Jack Stafford and what working with him might be like. She had become deeply concerned about the environment and thought journalism – as practiced by Jack Stafford's newspapers – was key to making a difference.

She had followed his career closely, his marriage to Devon Walsh – and the tragedy of Devon's drowning all documented through his columns and news stories.

In the late afternoon, Sheode heard Janis talking on the house phone, thinking by her tone that it might be Caleb. He was allowed to make phone calls twice a day from the juvenile detention facility.

But then she heard Janis say "Jack."

After she hung up Janis said Jack Stafford was calling from his rental car on his way to *The Redoubt*. "He said he should get here in an hour or so – if the GPS in the car is accurate," Janis said.

"I guess I better change out of these dirty farm clothes."

Me, too, Sheode thought.

Chapter 7

The three editors of the *Clarion Newspaper Syndicate* debated whether to nickname Jack Stafford "RR" – for Roving Reporter – just a few days after he had landed in Iowa.

After only two days at *The Redoubt*, he had announced he would be flying to Southern California to check out the catastrophic Porter Ranch gas leak – and that he was considering hiring a recent New York college student to be a reporter for the syndicate.

As Jack had predicted, it only took a few phone calls to the district attorney's office – and the juvenile court judge – to get Caleb quietly let out of the juvenile hall. His no-bail release came with a caveat that he was under a court order of house arrest. He was not allowed to leave *The Redoubt* property.

The order was no hardship. Caleb and several of the other teenagers at *The Redoubt* were homeschooled, also gathering as a group every day for at least two hours to work on farm or academic projects together.

The homeschooling program James had set up was so good that children raised on *The Redoubt*, were referred to at Iowa colleges as "Osmett" kids, a reference to *The Redoubt* founder.

The morning after Jack arrived, Caleb followed his mother in the house with his head down. He looked exhausted. And while it was hard to say what the shower facilities were like at the juvenile lockup, it looked to Jack like Caleb hadn't bathed for a long time. *But at least he doesn't seem defiant or angry*, Jack thought, watching him come in, avoiding eye contact.

Janis had asked Jack to talk with Caleb right away, a man-to-man conversation like the ones he had so often with his grandfather. Janis told Jack that Caleb admired his pluck in taking on the energy companies.

At first Jack wasn't too sure about it, until he thought about Noah home on Vashon Island and whom Noah might need if something happened to Jack.

It won't be that long and he won't be a little boy anymore, Jack thought.

His stomach tightened at the thought of raising a teenager – remembering what a handful he had been for his parents in Horseheads.

Thank God for Anne and Cass, he thought.

Jack had taken over a card table in one corner of the living room for his laptop computer and papers – a small mobile office. There were several bedrooms available upstairs where he kept a lot of the papers he had brought along. But being downstairs felt like being in the hub of a newsroom.

He was sitting at the table immersed in memories from his teens waiting for Caleb to come downstairs. *Probably good for him to know everyone makes mistakes*, Jack thought. *But I have to be careful with that. He had a gun. A loaded gun.*

The thought of the gun and how to talk about it was on Jack's mind when a freshly showered Caleb walked in and sat down in a folding chair by Jack's table, his head still in a hangdog attitude.

"Caleb, you don't go to a high school – which by the way I think is a good thing. But if you did, the way you look right now is like someone who has been sent to the principal's office," Jack said. "But I'm no principal, believe me. OK?"

Caleb raised his head and turned to meet Jack's eyes. His eyes were red and watery, but Jack could see he was trying to pull it together and even force a smile.

"I know what a principal is," Caleb said. Then he turned his face away from Jack and took deep breath. His words poured out in a cascade of staccato phrases that came so fast that Jack could barely keep up.

"My chest hurts all the time... I'm mad at everything... I feel like crying whenever I think about my grandfather... I get sick to my stomach when I think about the shooting... Sometimes I think crazy stuff. You know? Like not being able to live like this."

He paused, putting his head down into his hands. A full minute went by before Caleb spoke again.

"That's why I had that gun out in the woods. I didn't want to shoot somebody else. I was thinking of me."

Caleb paused again. He raised his head and looked straight at Jack, his eyes full of tears.

"I don't know what to do anymore. I don't."

And I don't either, Jack thought. *This is way above my pay grade.*

They both sat silently for a moment. Then Jack reached out and put his hand on Caleb's shoulder.

"We'll get through this," Jack said.

Chapter 8

It was difficult, but Mayenlyn held back his urge to vomit as DeVille told his story about how he and Mars had come to terrorize the orphanage where DeVille and he had been raised. And how they had been terrorized, too.

Mars was an infant when he had been deposited on the same orphanage doorstep where DeVille had been dropped off. Their arrivals were only a few months apart. In Mars' case, his name was written on the outside of a cardboard beer carton he arrived in, wrapped in a dirty towel.

His physical deformity – or as DeVille cruelly put it – his "Goddamned-ugly Neanderthal head" – prompted the staff to isolate Mars.

"He was hard to look at from the beginning," DeVille said. "Not as handsome as today."

As Mars grew up he was kept out of sight most of the time, a fast-growing hulking phantom figure to the other boys. He was a presence they would see in the distance, working in the orphanage gardens, around the buildings or out in the fields with farm equipment.

He didn't attend the nearby public school and ate alone in the kitchen where the cooks put him to work. As he grew up, Mars loved the knives and his favorite job was to keep them razor sharp.

One day DeVille snuck into the kitchen to look for food and discovered Mars sharpening knives. Mars was eager to show DeVille where the hidden tasty snacks were – the ones the cooks kept for themselves.

"I was the only boy who ever spoke to him," DeVille said. "His only friend. The staff used him like servant. More like a slave, really. And we all had strict orders to stay away from him. They dressed Mars in bulky sweat clothes."

I wasn't that far off with thinking of him like Quasimodo, locked in the bell tower, Mayenlyn thought.

"The mistake everyone made was thinking that he was *stupid*," DeVille said. "He's not. He's a genius wrapped in an unfortunate body. All that time he wasn't going to school he was reading things from the orphanage library. I taught him to read."

DeVille paused, letting this all sink in for Mayenlyn. Mars rolled his eyes up into his head, then made a snorting sound.

"When we were 13, eight older boys cornered me outside in the woods," DeVille said. "I was used to being picked on. I was small and skinny. The food was shit. They pulled my pants down, calling me a queer and started punching me. Why me? I was small and weak. I knew what was going to happen. I fought. But there were too many of them."

Mayenlyn looked over at Mars, sitting with his eyes now closed tight. But Mayenlyn could see blotches of red rising in his ghastly pale neck, moving towards his ears.

Mars' hands were gripping the arms of the chair tightly enough that Mayenlyn thought he might break them.

"Mars had filled out pretty much. He was huge and strong even at 13," DeVille said. "I was on the ground, on my stomach with my pants down around my knees. You can fill in the blanks. They were all in a circle around me. I can still hear their voices. They were laughing. Cheering.

"Mars came and pulled the kid on top of me off. He flung him into a tree. Hard. The other boys swarmed Mars, jumping up on him, punching and kicking. But he shook them off one by one, tossing them around like sacks of grain. After a few minutes, the ones that could, ran away."

Mayenlyn sat transfixed, uncomfortable – not only because of the story – but because DeVille was staring at him with a look that felt like it was piercing his skull.

Mars' face was beet-red and it didn't take a lot of Mayenlyn's imagination to conjure up an image of an avenging giant with a Neanderthal head throwing boys through the air to help DeVille.

"The boy Mars heaved into the tree first was badly hurt. A broken arm, broken rib, and a nasty slice on his face that turned into a moon-shaped scar. In fact, they starting calling him Moon after that. The orphanage tried to blame everything on Mars. After all, it was just my word and his word against the other boys. Plus Mars was an easy, ugly target. And they were used to using him as a scapegoat," DeVille said. "The staff didn't believe me, or care a bit. So Mars and I had some conversations with those little raping bastards. One at a time, whenever we could catch them alone."

Mayenlyn's tried to keep a blank expression as DeVille finished.

"So you see Rod, Mars and I are very much connected. His loyalty to me is absolute. As is my loyalty to *him*. We're family. He's been very helpful to me over the years. And I take good care of him."

Mars stood up and for a moment Mayenlyn thought they were going to hug again.

But Mars lumbered over to the conference table to take a file folder from DeVille's hand.

"Rod, that folder has information about a fellow up in North Dakota. I'd like you to pay him a visit to convince him to be more discreet in who he talks with about our business. It's all in there," DeVille said.

"And take Mars. In case our loose-lipped North Dakota accountant needs some help seeing our point of view."

Chapter 9

The Clarion Newspaper Syndicate
Column One

Trust industry and government – really?

By Jack Stafford

The horrific Porter Ranch, California natural gas leak and the poisoning of the water in Flint, Michigan have people wondering how much they can trust any corporation or government agency.

In Porter Ranch, a for-profit corporation made the decision to cut a corner on safety decades ago, resulting in thousands of families being forced to move from their homes.

A broken safety valve was removed – and not replaced. Had it been in place and working, officials say the gas leak would not have happened.

Now state regulators – suddenly paying attention to this catastrophe – are worried about the possibility of an explosion of the methane pouring from an out-of-control natural gas well.

An explosion of that type nearly leveled the town of Rockwell Valley, Pennsylvania several years ago, killing many people, injuring hundreds and resulting in the bankruptcy of a large corporation known as Grand Energy Services.

At Porter Ranch, investigators are looking into the possibility that the leak might have been caused by hydrofracking too close to the underground gas storage field.

That any drilling of that type is allowed in earthquake-prone California is mind-boggling, let alone in an area honeycombed with defunct oil wells holding natural gas under pressure.

In Flint, government officials also cut corners to save money, taking water from an untrustworthy source and neglecting to treat it properly. They managed to poison an entire city's water supply with lead.

The tale gets even more sordid because Flint is mostly populated by low income residents with little political clout. It's clear the people in charge – including the governor of the state – weren't proactive in dealing with the bad water.

Expect indictments.

Both situations bear close scrutiny as the nation continues to rush pell-mell with the expansion of hydrofracking for natural gas and oil and a controversial plan to shift water from the Great Lakes in the east to the arid western states.

The water is to run through the mysterious pipeline project of the DeVille Energy Federation.

Hidden behind the twin mantles of corporate proprietary information and alleged national security concerns, the DeVille project – dubbed The Devil's

Pipeline by opponents – supposedly will ship water from the Great Lakes to the Southwest.

It is an amazingly bold plan in concept. It is so bold that it has water conveyance engineers, water supply experts, state government officials and planners all scratching their heads because details – even the route – are still sketchy.

And there is a growing number of skeptics who say what DEF is proposing simply can't be done – at least not in any reasonable, cost-effective way.

Added to that are concerns raised by environmentalists about the wisdom of moving any substantial volume of water from the Great Lakes watershed to the West.

DEF spokesmen say the company has studied the issue and there are no problems. Of course, they also refuse to disclose a single bit of data to prove that conclusion,

If the crises in Porter Ranch, California and Flint, Michigan have taught the public anything, it's to be skeptical of such cavalier pronouncements.

It's time for the DeVille Energy Federation to stop hiding behind federal skirts about the planned Devil's Pipeline.

The public needs to know whether the project can hold water or not.

Jack Stafford is the publisher and editor in chief of the Clarion Newspaper Syndicate. He publishes Column One every Friday and can be reached at JJStafford@ClarionNewsSyndicate.com.

Chapter 10

It was difficult for Eli to be so far from the action, a sentiment shared by Keith and Alexandra.

Although all three were contributing to the ongoing news coverage of the Devil's Pipeline, they felt office-bound, running their small town, twice-a-week newspapers even though their respective websites were filled with national and international news, particularly as it related to the environment and energy.

The three were busy directing their newsroom staffs in the reporting of local and regional news every day. But the intriguing pipeline story was *the* major national story that they each really would have liked to take on full time.

They believed – as did Jack Stafford – that it was an important piece in the puzzle about the effects of climate change.

Somehow.

Climate change – and the resultant drought blamed for it – was being cited by many scientists as the reason California and the Southwest were so desperate for the water the pipeline promised to deliver.

The three editors – all of whom were excellent street reporters as well as newsroom leaders – were increasingly envious of Jack's freedom to travel.

Of course, he was the publisher and the small newspaper chain's most visible star because of his weekly column that frequently flayed the government (at all levels) and energy corporations. In recent months, his columns about the Devil's Pipeline were starting to be reprinted in major national newspapers. And when Jack announced via a terse email that he had hired Sheode Walker – and that she would be doing some roving reporter work – it was a blow to the three editors.

Jack had been ruminating about all three newspapers' coverage the whole time he was in Iowa. He decided to make it a part of the discussion in Friday's editor videoconference.

He spent several hours in conversations with Sheode at *The Redoubt*, determining she had the right combination of reporting/writing skills, curiosity, and fearlessness that would be an asset to all three newspapers.

How and where she would fit he knew required coordination with his editors.

Jack took over an upstairs bedroom at *The Redoubt* for the videoconference, close to where the wireless box for the Internet was located, so he would get a good connection. Looking out the window, he could see the gate area where James Osmett and his friends and neighbors had been cut down by the security guards.

Caleb Osmett was walking around near the gate, picking up stones and throwing them at a tree. His juvenile court date was still up in the air.

Jack turned back to his screen when Eli's image popped up, accompanied by the sound of a clanging gong. The panes on the screen for Alexandra and Keith were empty.

"The connection might be a little slow on my end, Eli, but we'll see," Jack said. "By the way, I need you to tell me how to get rid of that damn gong sound."

"Your connection is better than it's been," Eli said. "Keith and Alexandra should link up in about 10 minutes. They're both posting stories about those militia guys being arrested in Oregon. They said they have a lot of local comments."

Jack fussed with his laptop, turning the volume up and adjusting the picture.

He could hear Eli tapping away on his keyboard. Jack had finally learned to touch type mid-career when a California editor in San Francisco complained he was breaking keyboards with his hunt-and peck-typing – even though he was extremely fast.

"Eli, before Keith and Alex come on line, can I read your mind about something? Pick your brain, you know."

Eli stopped typing.

"Well, it's not so much reading your mind as wanting to run something by you," Jack said. "I haven't figured out all the details yet, but I think I need you and Keith – and maybe Alex – to do some boots-on-the-ground reporting on the Devil's Pipeline."

Eli leaned into the camera, a suspicious look on his face.

"You know how much I am a conspiracy guy," Eli said. "Since the X-Files came back on, Alex has started calling me "Spooky," just like Fox Mulder. But the three of us have been talking about wanting to be chasing this pipeline story in the field.

"And that is *truly* spooky."

The two other boxes on Jack's screen lit up, an image of Alexandra in one, Keith in the other, each accompanied by the gong sound that grated on Jack's ears.

After a short delay, live video feeds from both newspapers came up, prompting a round of *good mornings*, coupled with a few jibes about it really being afternoon and ending with Jack calling the editors' meeting to order.

"Keith, Alex, I was just talking with your spooky colleague about our coverage of the Devil's Pipeline," Jack said. "We have a lot to talk about. There are some loose threads that I want you guys to start pulling together.

"First though, I think Keith needs to pack his bags and go out to North Dakota for a visit with his friend Harvey Wallbanger."

Keith involuntarily let out a war whoop and gave a quick fist pump.

"Thought you might like that, Keith," Jack said. "And I want you to take Sheode Walker with you."

Chapter 11

Even as Keith was packing his bags, Eli was electronically zipping around the internet like a surfer riding a huge wave, cutting across information streams, jumping from website to website, compiling bits of information about the Devil's Pipeline.

Its geographic route from east to west was a closely held secret by the company, ostensibly because DEF was quietly negotiating with land owners for leases to run the pipeline and wanted to keep prices down.

Eli didn't buy that argument. Most energy companies were on such cozy terms with the government that they could use eminent domain to take the land if people balked. He was more intrigued at the moment with the pipeline structure itself. After studying his copy of the sketch found at the site of *The Redoubt* shooting, he started looking closely at websites of pipeline manufacturers, engineering firms and anti-pipeline activists.

The only thing the sites all seemed to agree on was the pipeline's scale was so huge, it seemed more like a tunnel than a pipeline.

After an hour, Eli discovered an intriguing posting buried deep in the *National Insecurity News* website.

Eli was skeptical of most of the notions that popped up on the NIN site. It was generally considered to be way out on the lunatic fringe of conspiracy websites.

But it had published a drawing very similar to the rough sketch found at *The Redoubt* after the DEF shootings. But the one NIN published was fleshed out with more detail and came with a short piece of analysis.

One pipe, two pipes, three pipes, four...

> *National Insecurity News – The Devil's Pipeline – that wet dream of DeVille Energy Federation energy magnate Archimedes DeVille to transport Great Lakes water to California – isn't just one pipeline, NIN has concluded.*
>
> *Based on close examination of a sketch obtained by this site, it looks like the gargantuan pipeline will possibly contain at least several other pipelines inside of it, arrayed around the perimeter and with a wide flat surface at the bottom.*
>
> *We speculate that water, natural gas, propane, even gasoline (God help us!) might each have a dedicated pipeline within this monstrosity.*
>
> *It also looks like the flat surface at the bottom is big enough for vehicles – or a railway – to run through it, even considering the inclusion of large dimension pipelines, too.*

If it does contain pipelines to carry substances other than water, DeVille has been selling a bill of goods to the public by touting only the provision of water for the Southwestern U.S. and California.

It might all be a scam to get the public's goodwill, which it certainly has in the dry parts of the country.

But NIN has been puzzled by why is this getting wrapped in such a protective cloak by the federal government?

That answer, NIN believes, might be found in why the federal government is blocking attempts to get details.

The fed's involvement could just be an extension of the government's protective attitude about energy companies in general.

Could be.

After all, the Federal Energy Regulatory Commission (FERC) has never seen an energy project it didn't love.

But NIN believes there could be another reason.

It's possible that some part of this pipeline/tunnel will be used to move nuclear and other military materials around the country.

Scary.

Eli reread the NIN website posting a second time, then forwarded the link to Alexandra, Keith and Jack.
Nuclear and military materials, he thought. *It makes sense, but it's already shipped in secret by truck and train.*
He wrote a quick email to Alexandra.

> *Alex: Let's solve this puzzle while Keith is off in North Dakota freezing his butt off. I found the NIN part of it. What do you think? Can we chase this together?*

An email from Alexandra came back within minutes.

> *Yup. But you're faster than I am on web searches. Plus you know the nuts like NIN – not nuts this time, maybe. I think we need to look at railcar manufacturers. It takes time to build railcars. And engines? Shit! A year, I don't know. Maybe DEF (or a subsidiary) has put in an order. Or the Dept. of Defense.*

Eli read Alexandra's email, then sent a copy of the email thread on to Jack, who Eli was pretty sure was on an airplane on his way back to Vashon Island.

Eli was surprised to see an email from Jack pop up only minutes later.

> *Eli, Alex: My plane has wireless! I wish it had comfortable seats, too. Good work all around on this. I only have one thing to add. I think as soon as we get some ducks lined up, we have to approach DEF – and DeVille himself – directly again. I know the company is stonewalling. But maybe we can break something loose.*

Eli smiled when he read Jack's email.

Break something loose, Eli thought. *Yeah… I bet. He's going to skewer DeVille in a column to provoke him.*

Years before Jack had used his column to repeatedly pound on the CEO of Grand Energy Services. It had so enraged the man that he had dispatched a goon to threaten Jack, his son Noah and sister-in-law Cass all living in Horseheads at the time. There had even been a suspected kidnapping attempt to snatch little Noah right out of the front yard of Jack's house.

Eli made a mental note to talk to Keith about Calvin Boviné who he remembered had some connection to that incident.

Since Keith's meeting with Boviné, Boviné had dropped completely out of sight – except for his name showing up as part of an investment group buying up water rights in Nebraska.

Keith seemed convinced that Boviné was not longer working as an energy company enforcer since getting out of jail. But Keith admitted he didn't understand what connection – if any – Boviné had with DEF now.

Boviné's one of Jack's loose threads, Eli thought. *We should find him.*

Approximately 1600 miles away – in Houston, Texas – A.G. DeVille was thinking exactly the same thing.

Chapter 12

The flare stacks from the oil wells in North Dakota lit up the ground below for hundreds of miles as Keith Everlight's flight made its long descent down to Sloulin Field Airport in Williston, North Dakota.

Even from thousands of feet up the landscape was lit brightly, reminding Keith of satellite photos that showed North Dakota visible from space because of the thousands of wells of burning methane.

He made a note to do some digging into the health of the rig workers around Williston. A lot of the byproduct natural gas coming out of the oil wells was not being burned off, exposing the workers and anyone else around the area to the toxic gas.

Before leaving Rockwell Valley he had been reading up about the health issues in Porter Ranch, California – including the filing of the first wrongful death lawsuit since a natural gas storage well had started leaking badly.

People are probably getting sick from gas here, too, Keith thought, seeing the bright flares. *But if they work for the oil companies, they can't complain.*

Keith had spent time in North Dakota touring with his university's amateur boxing team. In one match he had knocked out a much heavier local boxer to the chagrin of the Williston crowd.

Keith involuntarily touched his stomach, noting that his previous *welterweight* status had slipped up to the *middleweight* division in the 10 years since he graduated. He vowed to use the exercise room at the hotel – if it had one.

The flight attendant announced they were beginning their descent and passengers should start turning off electronics in anticipation of landing.

Keith checked his email where he found a missive from Sheode.

> *Mr. Everlight: I'm on my way and will arrive tomorrow night, 9 p.m. or so. It is a bus. I will keep you posted.*

I know you and Mr. Stafford think I was crazy for taking a bus. But I have so much catching up to do. I thought it would be a good contained way to do it. Plus, I'm not keen on planes. My cell phone number is with my signature line on this. And I have yours. BTW, the bus wireless is fast. S.

Keith reread the email quickly, then looked up the aisle to see if the flight attendant was going to be doing a sweep soon to tell people they had to close things down.

From the coquettish way she was standing next to a seat in the front of the plane, Keith guessed she was flirting with a passenger and would be distracted for a few minutes.

Sheode: Thanks for the update. And please, you don't have to call me Mr. Everlight. My dad is Mr. Everlight.
I'm Keith.
Jack (who likes to be called Jack by the way) told me that you were given kind of a primer on the pipeline from our colleague Eli Gupta. Jack probably also told you, Eli's the go-to guy for any internet/web searching.
In your 24-hour enforced seclusion, would you do some searching of North Dakota government health websites? Look for anything about workers getting sick or injured. Don't obsess, but take a look, please. We'll talk about it when you get here.
I booked you a room at the same hotel where I'm staying. If you have any expectations about the hotel, you probably need to lower them.
Keith.

Keith pushed the send button just as the flight attendant began strolling down the aisle.

He tucked his computer into his carry-on bag and pulled out his notebook with the contact information for Harvey "Wally" Weilbruner, debating whether to contact Wally tonight or wait until morning.

He had sent Wally an email about his visit, receiving a fairly cool response.

A drink tonight might be good, He thought. *At least I'll invite him.*

He fussed with his bags so he could get off the plane quickly.

He felt the plane hit the tarmac with a decided bounce and his cell phone service kicked in immediately.

He keyed in Wally's cell phone number but got an odd-sounding signal loud enough that it hurt Keith's ear slightly.

He double-checked the phone number. But instead of hitting redial, he keyed it slowly as the plane taxied toward the terminal.

This time the phone rang twice. Then a recording came on: "The phone number you called is no longer in service."

Chapter 13

The last thing that Jack wanted was a tiff with Cass and Anne – or to upset Noah. His Iowa expedition had been very fruitful, both in helping Janis with Caleb and in landing Sheode Walker to work for the newspaper syndicate.

He hoped that at some point Sheode would be reporting from Nebraska where Native American tribes – already stirred up in their opposition to the Keystone XL pipeline – were angry over reports of energy companies buying up water rights.

He hoped her family background might help her get close to people who might otherwise not be interested in talking with a journalist.

One of those companies grabbing water rights was DeVille Energy Federation – not in its name, but through several shell companies which Eli had figured out in less than an hour of being alerted about the sale of water rights in the Ogalalla.

If they're going to be pulling water from the Great Lakes, why pull water from the Ogallala, Jack thought. *Why invest the money? To corner the market? Christ, how much water do they want?*

But what he really wanted was to take a trip to California to see the Porter Ranch debacle up close. There were rumors that an energy company had been drilling some injection wells that might have caused the leak.

Much as he needed to learn all he could first hand, Jack was also pretty sure his travel plan was going to cause some furor in the Stafford[1]Walsh household. He had only been back on Vashon Island for four days, much of which he had spent in the *Vashon View* office.

He was pondering the column he needed to write when Cass and Noah made a surprise entrance at noon, carrying two satchels.

"Dad," Noah said with a big smile on his face. "I brought you lunch."

He held his arms up and whispered conspiratorially in Jack's ear when Jack picked him up.

"And there's cookies, too."

Jack swung Noah around a few times and then put him down.

"It's a good thing you showed up, I'm starving. I was getting ready to go across the street to get a sandwich."

Cass walked into the conference room where she laid food out on the big table. "We made the right choice in food then," she said. "The girl at the counter across the street told us what to get for you. You're a creature of habit, Jack."

He heard his stomach growl as he sat down, grateful for Cass' concern.

He wondered why Noah was out of school but decided not to ask.

"I hope we're not bothering you, but Noah asked specifically if we could have lunch with you today," Cass said. "You've been so busy since you got back from Iowa we've barely seen you.

Jack smiled and bit into his sandwich.

When he had returned days before it was late at night and he left Noah sleeping at the big house. And because he was going into the office extra early every day, Noah stayed there with Cass and Anne feeding him breakfast and taking him to school instead of moving back in the house he and Jack shared next door.

God, I feel guilty, Jack thought. *Guilty as hell.*

He chewed his sandwich thoughtfully, stopping when Cass put her sandwich down after only two bites.

He always marveled at Cass's ability as an actress. And he learned in the past few years that the reason she was so successful was that when she was acting, she wasn't really acting. Somehow, she became the character she played.

Seeing her in a production of *Who's Afraid of Virginia Woolf* had been amazing. *And I hope I never see that character for real*, he thought.

Now in the conference room, at first her face was unreadable, but then it shifted to an expression Jack called

Cass the Wise, in which she would lay out problems and solutions – on or off stage – that were so compelling, you couldn't argue.

I'm glad I didn't make plane reservations for California yet, Jack thought. *There might be a slight delay.*

"Anne and I have been talking. Noah, too, Jack," she said. "It was after we watched an episode of Downton Abbey, two nights ago. You missed it, you were still working."

Jack winced involuntarily thinking about how quickly the days were going by.

"Anyway, Noah was the one who suggested that we should all just live in the big house. He said he thought it would be cool to have a butler like Carson, too," Cass said.

"And you know what, Jack? It does make sense. I know when we all moved here from New York you were worried about imposing. And it made sense for you and Noah to have the boys' house. But honestly, it would be easier all around if you and Noah take two of the upstairs bedrooms. You could still keep your office over in the other house."

Jack rolled the idea over, then asked what Anne thought about it.

"Anne's happy with the idea, too," Cass said.

Noah put down his sandwich and came over to Jack, motioning for his dad to pull him up into his lap. Once securely seated Noah looked up at Jack with a quizzical expression, his eyebrows arched the same way as Cass had hers.

As if I could say no, even if I wanted to, Jack thought. *But I don't want to.*

"Well, I have a question for your Aunt Cassie before I agree," Jack said.

Cass and Noah passed a look between them, both wondering what Jack would ask.

"Can we have a butler, too?

Chapter 14

The Clarion Newspaper Syndicate
Column One

The truth, national security and pipelines

By Jack Stafford

A major problem in the information age is sorting out the wildest of wild rumors and misinformation from the solid data, all published on the Internet.

Look at the Zika virus epidemic story with rumors the outbreak was actually exacerbated by the introduction of genetically modified mosquitoes in Brazil.

Another example is that the GMO mosquito story is, in fact, a cover to obfuscate the real cause of the Zika outbreak, a defective vaccine called Tdap.

So when the reporters and editors of the Clarion Newspaper Syndicate ran across an Internet report that the DeVille Energy Federation's proposed pipeline – the one dubbed The Devil's Pipeline by opponents – was actually a collection of pipelines bundled in a huge tunnel, they were skeptical. Until they had an opportunity to study a key drawing more carefully.

Looking at it now, it makes perfect sense. Kind of like one of those trick drawings in which the viewer is asked if they can see a particular image, like a horse or a child. And all of a sudden an image comes into focus.

A sketch of the pipeline, left accidentally at the site of the horrible shooting in Iowa that claimed four lives, seems to show exactly what the website National Insecurity News says it does: a tunnel that contains four discreet pipelines.

We are waiting for confirmations and more details from the DeVille Energy Federation. But as the story on the front page of this newspaper and our website says, the Devil's Pipeline is much more than a conveyance of water to thirsty states in the Southwest.

It seems to have the capability of conveying a multiplicity of liquids.

This is not to say that what DEF is planning is necessarily a bad thing. But it begs the question why DEF's founder Archimedes Gabriel DeVille has been unwilling to talk about the pipeline in more detail.

It also seems to offer a dark vision of what the federal government has in mind as it seems to have green flagged this project without even a nod to public input, public announcement or public approval.

It's past time for Mr. DeVille to speak up and explain what the Devil's Pipeline is really all about. Ditto for its federal government backers.

Jack Stafford is the publisher and editor in chief of the Clarion Newspaper Syndicate. He publishes Column One every Friday and can be reached at JJStafford@ClarionNewsSyndicate.com

Chapter 15

A.G. DeVille had never completely understood the rage other energy company presidents had toward the media in general – and Jack Stafford in particular.

When Stafford had been roasting them over scandals about illegal disposal of recovered fracking water, leaking pipelines or battles with anti-fossil fuel activists, DeVille had sat on the sidelines, amused.

His shell companies and interlocking corporations kept him well insulated and out of the media spotlight.

Until now.

Stafford was raising enough of a fuss about the pipeline project – and so intensely challenging DeVille to speak publicly about it – that DeVille knew he would have to respond especially as he was even getting pressure from Washington D.C. to counter the gravity of the anti-pipeline rhetoric.

*And I will remember **those** bastards when they're up for reelection*, DeVille thought. *Wait till they have their hands out for campaign donations.*

He looked across his desk at his vice president for special projects, certain she was as smart as most of his staff put together.

When people first heard her name – Betty Lou – they assumed that she was a Texan, or at least certainly from the South, prompting thoughts of a willowy woman with soft curls and perhaps a Georgia accent.

But *Betty Lou* was really *Betty Liu*, a petite and muscular Chinese energy expert DeVille had brought in for her knowledge of pipeline construction. She also had a long history of being able to convince Chinese government officials to see things her way.

She had been working for a Chinese DEF affiliate and had to beat a hasty retreat from China after she had been politically linked to the horrific landslide in Shenzhen that was still being sorted out by Chinese officials. When she found out her name was on a short list of Chinese officials to be sacrificed as part of a cover up to protect the real culprits, she put her name out on the energy industry telegraph and was snapped up by DeVille.

Although she had been working for only a short time with DEF, she was already a trusted staff member on the pipeline team.

Or what she thinks is the pipeline, DeVille thought.

The only thing DeVille didn't like about Betty was that he couldn't read her facial expressions to understand what she was thinking.

But she always gives me honest answers.

Betty Liu sat as motionless as a spooked deer in the woods, almost as if she was conserving her energy for when she had to speak. Her notebook was open in her lap, carefully balanced enough that a pen sat mid-page without rolling. DeVille had asked her for advice on how to publicly present details about the pipeline – without actually giving away any *important* specifics.

"Focus on water," she suddenly said, catching DeVille slightly by surprise.

"Forget politics. Forget the complaining about secrecy. Forget the internet chatter that Stafford wrote about. Just talk about the water. How important it is."

DeVille leaned back in his chair, wondering if Rod Mayenlyn would give him the same advice.

Rod was officially his vice president for public relations and normally would be sitting in on this meeting. But at the moment he was occupied in North Dakota. DeVille made a mental note to chastise Mayenlyn for not checking in with a progress report.

Rod's plugging a leak in the information pipeline, DeVille thought.

He smiled slightly, amused at himself.

"You like it?" Betty said, interpreting his smile as approval.

"Yes, I think you have a point, Betty. I need to keep focused on what *we* want and not what this Stafford wants to make a stink about," DeVille said.

Betty looked down at her notebook, then up at DeVille. "I can give you numbers about water flow that makes DEF look good, too. We haven't ever announced how much water will go west," Betty said.

DeVille smiled slightly again, nodding his head in agreement.

Then Betty cocked her head to one side and smiled – a rare occurrence. "Mr. DeVille," Betty said. "I know how to shut Mr. Stafford up."

DeVille smiled.

Good, but I know what to do if your idea doesn't work, DeVille thought.

Chapter 16

The sudden onslaught of positive media stories about the Devil's Pipeline caught Jack and the editors of The *Clarion Newspaper Syndicate* by surprise.

Sitting in the *Vashon View* office, watching a rainstorm lash downtown, Jack had to admit it was masterful public relations.

Instead of acting like DEF's corporate hand was caught in the energy cookie jar, DEF had come out with a clever rationale that said in order to make the pipeline feasible – and fiscally sound – DEF would lease out other, smaller-diameter pipelines within the large conduit known as the Devil's Pipeline.

And to announce the idea on a podunk radio station, Jack thought. *Brilliant. It made the media think they were so clever, not conned.*

Eli had spotted the first online references to the Williston, N.D. radio interview between Rod Mayenlyn and a talk-show host with named Wink Dinkerson. Jack had to check the name out himself on the station's website to be sure the name was correct.

That has to be a stage name, Jack thought. *Or maybe his parents were big Cheech and Chong fans in the sixties.*

The station had a country music and talk show format, sprinkled with occasional news. Most of the news was connected to the economy of the Williston region and the impact of the oil drilling.

A recording of the interview was going viral on the Internet.

Jack slipped on a set of headphones to listen again to a portion of it. He and Alexandra had listened to the full interview earlier.

DINKERSON: This morning I have the vice president of the DeVille Energy Federation, Rod Mayenlyn right here in our studios for a chat.
DINKERSON: Rod, welcome to KDAC, so glad to have you on air to talk about DEF's big pipeline.
MAYENLYN: Thanks Dink.
DINKERSON: You're welcome. But, ahh, it's Wink. Lot of people make that mistake.

MAYENLYN: *Sorry!* (laughing)

DINKERSON: So you said you had news for our listeners about the pipeline. It's been pretty quiet for the most part.

MAYENLYN: Yes, it sure has. But you know, there are so many wingnut environmentalists just waiting to pounce on us for everything, we have to be cautious. And in this case, we *are* working with the federal government and it's got its own set of security issues.

DINKERSON: Wingnuts is a good way to describe them.

MAYENLYN: One of those wingnuts runs a newspaper group. He started it in New York and now has papers in Pennsylvania and Washington. The state – not our nation's capital. Anyway, he wrote a column recently that pretty much made us sound like bad guys for the way we're building the pipeline, Dink. Oh *Wink!* Sorry.

DINKERSON: So, tell us about what you have planned.

MAYENLYN: Well, first, I wanted your listeners to understand we're building something important. Water from the east goes to the west. Our president A.G. DeVille is a visionary. He's an amazing guy. But the part that's most interesting – that we have kept quiet until now – is that the pipeline will have other smaller pipelines inside of it for natural gas and oil. That's how we're paying for the construction costs. And it means they'll be no taxpayer money spent on the project at all.

DINKERSON: Aha! Some people were speculating the feds were paying for the pipeline. But that's not true?

MAYENLYN: Not true at all. We did get some help from the federal government on permitting issues, of course.

DINKERSON: OK. Thanks for that. Everyone out there in Williston, I'm talking with Rod Mayenlyn vice president of the DeVille Energy Federation right here in our studios. And we'll be back after a little break and a word from Hamster Chews, the best in tobacco.

Jack pulled off the headphones and looked at his notes, laughing for a second time.

Hamster Chews. I have to tell Cass and Anne about that, he thought.

But the line "We did get some help from the federal government on permitting issues..." struck him again.

With the weight of the federal government behind you, no wonder local governments are being cooperative," he thought.

What bothered him most was the breathless way that most media were reporting the scheme, giving DEF credit for smart economic thinking.

And without asking any questions about the pipelines.

But the question foremost in Jack's mind was about the permitting process.

Initially the pipeline didn't show up anywhere on the dockets of the Federal Energy Regulatory Commission – a fact that had led Jack and the *CNS* editors to eventually figure out the pipeline would be moving water.

But now DEF had admitted it was moving products that clearly fell under the purview of FERC.

Time to start asking FERC some questions, Jack thought.

Chapter 17

The diner where Harvey Weilbruner and Keith Everlight met for coffee was mobbed with oil workers, many of whom had standing orders for food to-go to take to their rigs to eat when they got a break.

It was a mom-and-pop operation that until the oil boom was a sleepy place with only a dozen or so of the same customers at this time of the morning on a normal weekday, not the 50-plus people crammed inside with a line out the door waiting.

Most of the men did a double take when they got inside and caught a glimpse of Sheode Walker sitting in a cramped booth. She had dressed very primly in a turtleneck sweater and jeans – as per Keith's instructions. Except for the 60-year-old wife of the owner, Sheode was the only female in the restaurant.

And probably the best looking woman in the whole city, Keith thought.

The only man not paying close attention to Sheode was Harvey "Wally" Weilbruner, who scanned the crowd of oil workers in line with the intensity of a Secret Service agent on the U.S. President's detail.

Keith and Sheode both noticed that Wally's hand shook slightly when he picked up his cup of coffee.

"I guess ordering breakfast is probably not a good idea," Keith said. "What do you think, Wally?"

Wally stared at the front door for a moment, squinting.

"Yeah, forget that. We're lucky we got coffee. But it's the only decent coffee in this part of town. Your hotel serves food. I'd eat there."

Keith had suggested earlier that morning that they meet at the hotel, a move vetoed by Wally. He said he wanted to meet in a very public place.

"I think someone's watching me. But if anybody asks, you're an old friend from high school. Which you are, of course."

When Wally walked in, Keith and Sheode were already sitting down, prompting Wally to stop short, unsure whether to sit down or not.

When he did sit, he quickly asked Keith and Sheode to tell everyone they were married or dating – anything but that they were two journalists asking questions.

Keith kept his voice low enough to not be heard in the next booth – a good trick with the crowd pushing near the register all shouting orders to an overwhelmed teenager trying to write them on a paper order book.

"Wally, tell me – tell us – about what you know about the pipeline. My publisher Jack Stafford sent us after I told him the little bit we talked about. But, well, we're also going to be doing some stories about Williston and what's going on now that oil boom has tanked."

Wally's lifted his coffee cup to his lips, shaking even more than before.

"Jesus, Keith. I think I made a mistake about all this. I mean, my work is with numbers. I'm an accountant. I'm not a whistleblower or anything. You know, I just wondered. Look, I could get in trouble for giving out confidential information. And I really can't be seen with journalists."

Sheode spoke for the first time since exchanging pleasantries when Wally sat down.

"Listen, Mr. Weilbruner. Wally. I understand your concern. But I promise we will be very discreet about everything."

Wally closed his eyes for a second, then uttered a short chirping string of "sure, sure, sure."

Keith put his hand on Wally's arm when it looked like he was about to stand.

"Wally, wait a minute. What about your cell phone? It's not working."

Wally looked around again, then pushed Keith's hand away as he stood up.

"I have to get another one. I forgot it at work one night on my desk. When I went in the next morning it was gone."

He stood up quickly and pushed his way through the crowd, stopping at the door where he had to squeeze past a huge man wrapped in a fancy overcoat and wearing a dress hat, both more suited to Manhattan than North Dakota.

Christ, Keith thought. *That guy is as big as Calvin Boviné.*

Chapter 18

The small plane made its first pass over the area just south of Porter Ranch, where a gas well had blown out months before, spewing methane into the air and making residents sick.

The news media was comparing it to the massive BP Oil spill in the Gulf of Mexico in 2010.

Pilot Evanston Scott and Jack Stafford nearly gagged when they were hit with a whiff of mercaptan, the chemical added by gas companies to normally non-odorful natural gas.

"Pretty amazing that we caught that up here at 2,000 feet," Scott said. "The news reports yesterday said they had finally gotten it all stopped. Guess there's some gas still leaking."

Jack had been reading up on mercaptan's health effects for a week before he took the flight, partly for a future column and partly for his own protection.

It was added to natural gas to give it a rotten egg smell to alert people there was gas present. In homes, it was critical to warn of leaks.

Jack felt the plane bank sharply away from the ranch, then the nose went up as they gained altitude.

A former newspaper colleague of Jack's had connected him with Evanston Scott – who preferred to be called Scotty. He'd been flying since he was a teenager, starting out in a Piper Cub. Scotty also owned several gliders and an ultralight he named Millie after his mother who hated to fly – and hated even more now that her only son made a living in small planes.

Scotty was flying to Southern California every week or so, financed by a consortium of Northern California news media outlets. His job was to take video and still photos with cameras mounted on the underbody of his single-engine Mooney aircraft.

He usually did this run alone. But today he was enjoying Jack's company, chattering into his microphone nearly non-stop since leaving the Placerville, Calif. airport hours earlier.

An intercom system of microphones and headsets made conversation easy. Without them, Scotty and Jack would have to yell over the sound of the engine.

"When I first installed the cameras last year, I was reading a book about the U-2 spy planes," Scotty said. "They had amazing cameras on those rigs. But you can do the same stuff today with tiny lenses. Remind me to show you the box when we get home."

Jack nodded, then remembered to talk into his microphone.

"I bet," he said.

Jack was starting to feel a little queasy from mercaptan as well as Scotty's maneuvers. Small planes weren't Jack's favorite, but this flight was proving to be fascinating.

Flying down from east of Sacramento, Jack saw huge swathes of farmland that required irrigation. He reminded himself to talk to the editors about doing another story about the use of fracking waste water on California crops.

A season of near normal rain had people cheering that the drought was over. Plus the oil companies were selling the recovered fracking water very cheaply, diluted to make it legally clean enough for agricultural – but barely.

The farmers needed it, and selling it to them made more financial sense for the oil companies than putting it into injection wells and risking earthquakes.

"Have you heard any scuttlebutt about the cause of this leak?" Jack asked. "One of my editors thinks the company might have triggered a small quake."

Scotty shook his head noncommittally as he reached forward to wipe some dust off his instrument panel. "Nope. But it wouldn't surprise me," he said.

In addition to the occasional whiff of stray mercaptan, the air had a lot of dust in it.

Scotty maneuvered the plane high above the edge of the Porter Ranch subdivision. A screen mounted between the two men showed what the cameras could see. A small control panel sat below it with buttons for single photos, video, changing the camera angles and zooming.

"It's nice to have you doing all camera work," Scotty said. "I'm usually juggling flying and the camera."

Jack zoomed the video camera in on a cul-de-sac where what looked like a moving van was parked in a driveway. He could make out two men – maybe three – going in and out of the house.

"Respirators," Scotty said. "Look for them. That camera's good enough for you to spot them. Anybody going in that sector usually wears some kind of breathing rig. That or they'll be puking alongside the road."

Jack was feeling a little more queasy from looking closely at the computer screen while the plane dipped slightly, then rose again, then dipped. One of the men with the truck was sitting down on the curb, while the other two kept moving in and out of the house.

"No smoking breaks down there, I'll bet," Jack said.

"Not anywhere around here. Nobody's talking much about a possible big boom," Scotty said. "But we need to keep our distance when we do these flights. I don't care if they say they have it stopped."

Jack opened his laptop computer and pulled up a map most media outlets used as a stock photo to outline the area affected by the spread of the gas.

A red line showed a border where the gas cloud had been most concentrated.

Just as he compared the red line on the map with the plane's GPS display, he heard Scotty swear softly and bank the plane sharply.

A slight jerking motion made Jack think they had hit small air pocket as the plane dipped slightly.

Then Scotty swore again as the plane bucked.

"Dammit, damn it."

The next sound Jack Stafford heard was the quiet rush of wind replacing the drone of the plane's single engine.

The nose of the plane dipped sharply making Jack's stomach lurch.

Then Jack got a huge whiff of mercaptan.

Wrongful Deaths

Chapter 1

The jaunt to California was supposed to be a solo on-the-ground, energy and water reconnaissance by Jack with trips to Sacramento, Bakersfield, Porter Ranch and Los Angeles.

Only Alexandra knew Jack was planning on going up in a small plane to get an aerial look at Porter Ranch.

She was under strict orders not to mention it to Cass - or anyone else - until he was safely on the ground.

"She's worrying about me too much these days," Jack complained.

Alexandra was good at keeping secrets, but had nearly outed Jack earlier during the three-way editors' videoconference.

When Keith reported in from North Dakota, she gave a quick update on Jack's trip to California, noting that they could expect aerial photos for the three newspapers' websites as well as their print editions.

"Aerial photos?" Eli asked. "Is Jack taking them?"

Alexandra hoped that when she blushed it wasn't too obvious, as well as when she told Keith and Eli the photos were being taken by a photo service.

And that part is true, she thought.

She hated to lie to them.

Keith had checked in with Sheode sitting nearby, occasionally coming into the range of the video camera on Keith's laptop.

The four-way split screen had three panes filled in. The fourth held a cartoon caricature of Jack that had been created for his business cards.

"We've made contact with my high school friend," Keith said. "But he's as jumpy as a cat. I'm going to meet with him for coffee. Oh, for the news lineup, I think

Sheode will file a feature tonight about people stranded here. She found a couple from Pennsylvania who came for the oil boom just as they stopped drilling here. The husband had been laid off from his gas-rig job near Rockwell Valley."

When Eli and Alexandra started peppering Keith with questions about Sheode's story, photo possibilities and the likelihood of video, he slid over to let her sit down and answer herself.

Alexandra absentmindedly poked at her mop of unruly red hair. *She looks good even on a damn computer camera*, Alexandra thought.

"I spotted the Pennsylvania license plate on the couple's truck," Sheode said. "They have an old cab-over camper on it. My mom used to call those rollover specials. These people are broke and feel pretty hopeless. It's sad. It's also a good example of the boom going bust for the workers."

Keith came back into the corner of the computer frame.

"I have to run," Keith said. "Wally just texted and asked me to meet right now.

He noticed that Alexandra was looking down at something – her phone maybe? – and was laughing.

"Alex, what's up?" he asked.

"Oh, it's just Jack checking in from California," Alexandra said. "He says he's debating whether he should use the word *barf, puke* or *vomit* in his column Friday. "I'll let him tell you about it."

Chapter 2

S cotty had apologized several times on the flight back to Placerville.

The engine hiccup that forced the stall had happened once before – nothing serious, Scotty had said.

It was a problem he and his mechanic *thought* they had solved.

"When it happened the first time, I had just taken off," Scotty said. "I couldn't get it restarted. I had to land in a field. But honestly Jack, this plane glides like a dream for such a heavy bucket."

It took about 20 minutes of steady flying with the reassuring thrum of the engine in the background for Jack's heart rate to return close to normal. It also took him almost that long to clean his vomit up from the floor by his feet.

He couldn't keep his head down for very long as he tried to mop it up without feeling like another gusher was going to happen.

"I *am* sorry, Jack," Scotty said. "But like a sailor once told me after a storm nearly wrecked his boat, 'It's not an ordeal, it's an adventure.'"

Jack found that even looking at his cell phone was problematic if he stared at the screen for more than a moment or two. He hadn't been motion sick in years. But the bobbing, weaving – and mercaptan – had proven too much.

"I did a story about astronaut training once," Jack said, his stomach still churning slightly. "The guys doing the training loved it when they would get rookies in who said they had cast-iron stomachs. They made a point of spinning those guys the fastest."

Scotty laughed.

"Yeah. I hear that a lot about tough stomachs. But it's bullshit. You toss people around enough and they will *all* lose it. Guaranteed."

Jack felt his stomach settling down a little. He swallowed a sip of bottled water, then ate a salty cracker from a package Scotty had handed him.

The combination and Scotty's straight line, level flying gave him enough stability to check his phone messages.

He had several from Cass, chatty sentences about Noah's school. One message was from Eli about a potentially violent standoff in the Pennsylvania woods where a family had thrown together a blockade of cars, people and snapping dogs to stop the cutting of sugar maple trees to make way for a natural gas pipeline. The most recent email was from Janis Osmett, who had taken Jack's advice on how to help Caleb get his head straight.

The plane dipped and rocked sideways for just an instant, jolting Jack's stomach again. "How long until we land?" Jack asked, feeling his face flush.

Scotty grinned, then handed Jack another package of crackers.

Chapter 3

The meeting at *The Redoubt* had grown contentious very quickly.

Nearly all the residents – minus young children – were jammed into the main farmhouse living room where Janis was having troubling keeping order.

I wish Dad was here, she thought. *Or Jack.*

The idea up for discussion had come from Jack just before he left Iowa to head back to Washington.

After long talks with Caleb, Jack came to believe that the root of Caleb's depression wasn't just the death of his grandfather. It also came from the same sick feeling of powerlessness experienced by nearly everyone fighting against these oil and gas corporations.

Jack knew that feeling of powerlessness well, even though his columns and newspapers had made a big difference in recent years at containing the rapacious companies from taking even more land and endangering people's health.

He suggested to Janis that they turn to the courts to strike a blow and help Caleb cope.

"Can we all just quiet down for a few minutes, *please?*" Janis asked in a pleading voice, standing at one end of the room.

When the voices dipped a few decibels, she raised her arms over her head and shouted.

"Enough! Enough! Come on people! Enough!"

She crossed her arms and pursed her lips as the noise slowly dissipated.

Everyone in the room took note how red her face was.

"Until my dad died – was killed – we were always able to talk like civilized people. I'd like to get back to that. All right? Anyone object?"

She surveyed the room, her jaw set, waiting for a challenge.

The room gradually went quiet. After a moment the only sounds were people shifting in their seats or shuffling their feet.

Janis stepped off to the side to make way for the six-foot tall, solid-looking man wearing a dark suit, blue shirt and red tie standing behind her.

He stepped forward, a small smile on his face. He confidently surveyed the room letting a small murmur work its way through the crowd before he spoke.

He looks kind of like a younger version of Jack Stafford, Janis thought.

"Folks, Janis has quite deliberately kept the details of what I am going to present sketchy. That's because I asked her to do that. I didn't want people to get a lot of preconceived ideas, though I know when she told you a lawyer would be here to talk, it obviously got you thinking.

"So if you're angry at anybody, be angry at me. My name is J.W. Stone. And because you are all good people, I will tell you my full name is Jerome Wooster Stone. The Jerome came from my grandfather. The Wooster from a shirt-tail relation. The Stone from my dad. And you guessed it. My nickname in high school was Wooster the Rooster. Let's keep that a secret."

The rooster line drew a few laughs, cracking the tension in the room that had been a brooding presence nearly every time the people of *The Redoubt* had gathered since James Osmett and three other Redoubt residents had been gunned down months before.

"It's a tragedy what happened here," Stone said. "And the bullying tactics of these energy companies to force their pipelines across private and public land is going on all over the United States. You already know that. And you probably already know how much people are resisting. Your neighbors in Nebraska, particularly the Native Americans, are causing the energy companies absolute fits. Things are heating up in the northeast, too."

A man standing in the back of the group raised his hand, catching Janis' eye.

That's more like it, she thought, smiling. *A raised hand to get the floor. How civilized.*

Janis motioned to Stone then signaled to the man to stand and speak. He took a step forward, the ball cap on his head labeled with the logo of a tractor company.

"I know you are going to talk about filing some kind of lawsuit. But before that train leaves the station, can you talk about money? Sorry Janis. But you know."

Janis did know. A lot of the families were struggling. They were all land rich thanks to her father's generosity – and self-sufficient for most of their needs. But cash? That was hard to come by.

They're all scared of us taking on big legal bills, Janis thought. *Me, too.*

Stone scanned the room again, looking into the faces of people. *The Redoubt* was populated by people Stone's father would have called the *counterculture* a generation ago. Most of them were very well educated and accomplished.

He recognized one woman seated in the back from a recent photo in the *New York Times*. A book of her poems had been favorably reviewed along with a brief feature story about her national book award.

"Money is always a question," Stone said. "A good question. Before I got my law degree, my father used to tell me that if I shook hands with a lawyer to be sure to have my other hand holding my wallet. And until the day he died – just last year – when we shook hands he always clutched his wallet. Kind of a family joke."

This time a solid laugh rippled through the room.

"So let me tell you up front. This case – the legal costs – it's all going to be funded by a consortium of environmental groups. And they are doing it because they want to call attention to what happened here.

"A wrongful death lawsuit will do that. That's what we are here to talk about. We are looking at four lawsuits, in fact. We are going to sue the DeVille Energy Federation to get justice. It won't be easy. But I'm in this to win."

This time the rising murmur was less hostile and had edges of surprise.

The man who had asked the question about money raised his hand again then spoke.

"Well, I can't speak for everyone in this room, but I support this. The sheriff and the local judges swept this under the rug. If you can kick out that damn oil company. I'm with you."

Stone's entire face lit up with a smile.

"You may all need to talk about this some. Janis has details of how I think we should proceed. But the first step if you agree is for all of you who were there the day of the shooting to let my office do a video of your recollections of what happened," Stone said. "We're going to court. But we're going to make a movie, too, that will inspire people all over the country who are fighting big oil."

Chapter 4

The Clarion Newspaper Syndicate
Column One

More pipeline follies

By Jack Stafford

Activists across the U.S. – even the globe – might seem to have backed off on their efforts to stop hydrofracking.

They have. But only slightly. And only temporarily.

Some of it is in response to the slowdown in the energy industry, suffering (if suffering is the right word) from the amazing worldwide glut of oil and natural gas.

That glut has encouraged gluttony in fossil fuel consumption.

But the main reason for the change in activist strategy is that activists are battling the most pressing environmental issue the slithering, snaking pipelines energy companies are attempting to build to bring oil and gas products to markets, both domestic and international.

The scope of what these companies have planned is breathtaking, all documented in recent newspaper stories and on the websites of the Clarion Newspaper Syndicate, as well as most other media outlets.

Also breathtaking is the barely disguised collusion between regulators and energy companies to trample property rights of private citizens and the public in allowing pipelines where residents clearly don't want them.

It was heartening to see the federal government recently turn down a request to run a pipeline through national forest land in West Virginia and Virginia. The company proposing that pipeline howled over having to reroute, but wisely chose not to sue the federal government over the decision.

The pipeline mania is understandable from the industry's standpoint. But from the environmental end of the telescope the pipelines will provide far more headaches than benefits.

In Pennsylvania, one energy company that successfully used eminent domain to seize private property to run its pipeline, last week sent detailed instructions to property owners on whose land the pipeline will be constructed sometime in the next 18 months.

Here's an excerpt:

"Property owners will be responsible for checking the pipeline for any natural gas or oil leaks where it runs through their property. We recommend that the property owner do so at least once a week and call our toll free number in Houston, Texas to report any problems. Failure to report any leaks may result in assessments levied by the company."

Those assessments are part of the agreement property owners are being forced to sign as part of the eminent domain/sale proceedings.

It's bad enough to be forced to give up your land for a natural gas or oil pipeline. But to be legally requiring people to act as sentry for the company that forced the pipeline onto them is so incredible, it's hard to believe. Even though it's in black and white.

Most recently a family in Pennsylvania stood up both in person and in court to block a pipeline from running through their farm. In their case, they wanted to protect long-established trees, some of which were integral to a maple syrup operation.

They lost the argument.

Dramas like this will be playing out repeatedly. It's clearly part of the activist playbook to bring attention to the notion that the destruction caused by fossil fuel folly isn't limited to what

happens at the wellhead or when the fuel makes it to its destination to be burned.
What happens in between is just as devastating.

Jack Stafford is the publisher and editor in chief of the Clarion Newspaper Syndicate. He publishes Column One every Friday and can be reached at JJStafford@ClarionNewsSyndicate.com

Chapter 5

The sun had just set, plunging Williston, North Dakota into a gloomy darkness, broken only slightly by poorly powered streetlights and a glow on the horizon of flare stacks from oil wells burning off natural gas.

The gloom outside the trailer made the 10-by-30 foot office space seem even smaller to Harvey Weilbruner, sitting at his corner desk.

But Weilbruner was feeling more claustrophobic – and inches away from panic – because of the presence of Rod Mayenlyn sitting in a chair right in front of him and Marsden Weesley standing behind him just out his line of sight.

Weilbruner could see Mars' huge shadow stretching over his desk.

Weilbruner had waited to go into the office until late in the day, just as the other two people he shared the space with were leaving. He cursed that he hadn't locked the trailer door the minute they left.

"So, *Wally* – that's what they call you, isn't it?" Mayenlyn asked. "We were asked to have a little chat with you. To remind you about that confidentiality agreement you signed when you went to work to here. Do you remember, Wally?"

Mayenlyn dragged out the two syllables of Wally's name, making it sound like *Wall – E*.

Wally had read several internal memos with Mayenlyn's name on them in the six months since he came to Williston. He also remembered that Mayenlyn was one of the survivors of the huge natural gas and propane explosions that nearly leveled Rockwell Valley, Pennsylvania several years before.

"Yessir. Yessir, I do remember that agreement. I have a copy in my files right in my top desk drawer," Wally said.

As he pulled the drawer open and reached in, Mars' huge hand reached down and slammed Wally's hand in the drawer. He did it with such force that the desk slid forward towards Mayenlyn.

His immediate scream was stifled by Mars' other hand.

Mars clamped his hand so tightly over Wally's mouth and nose that he could barely breathe.

Then Mars released it along with his hand in the desk drawer, letting a whimpering Wally pull his rapidly swelling wrist out of the drawer.

He tried to stand, but felt Mars huge hand holding him down, then spinning his chair around so it faced the wall – and Mars.

"My associate is *very* protective of our company and our company's privacy," Mayenlyn said. "Very protective. *Wall-E*... It would be good for you to remember that."

Tears ran down Wally's cheeks from the pain. He saw his wrist had already ballooned up like a snake with a rat in its gullet.

"Listen, I don't know what you're talking about. I just do the numbers, man. I don't know anything about your pipeline."

As Wally finished saying *pipeline*, he felt the weight of Mars hand lift off his shoulder.

He stood up, holding his damaged wrist with his other hand, when he heard Mayenlyn's voice.

"Perhaps give *Wall-E* one more little reminder how protective we are of our privacy."

This time Mars didn't bother to stifle Wally's scream, until Mayenlyn shouted at Mars to stop.

Chapter 6

Sheode Walker found Wally the next morning, on the floor behind his desk.

Unable to sleep, she left the hotel at first light. The continuous rumble of trucks all night with workers coming and going from the oil fields had kept her awake.

She had promised Keith she would be vigilant walking alone in Williston. The number of assaults against women was high enough to even concern *her* – despite her self-defense skills.

But she figured this early in the morning most men would be working or sleeping off drinks from the night before.

The trailer where Keith said Wally worked was only a half-dozen blocks from the hotel in a cluster of similar units, obviously brought in hurriedly to provide office space for the booming oil industry

Sheode tested the door to the trailer and found it was unlocked an hour before the posted time of opening for the day.

She pushed the door open slowly, calling out Wally's name.

Then she saw that his feet were sticking out at an odd angle from behind the desk.

Just like movies, she thought, panicking. *My God!*

She raced to the desk and knelt down. Wally was lying on his stomach, his right hand and wrist stretched out, swollen so big they were almost unrecognizable. But there was no blood on the floor around him. And the left side of his face – even though his mouth was etched in a grimace – looked unmarked.

Sheode touched his shoulder, eliciting a groan.

Alive, she thought, her heart racing. *Thank God.*

She saw that his left hand was underneath him and that any attempt to push or move him, made him wince.

She pulled out her cell phone. "I'm going to get you some help right way," Sheode said.

Before she could dial 911, Wally spoke. "Don't call the police." His voice was low enough it was almost a whisper. "Please. Don't."

She hesitated, then decided she would call either 911 – or Keith – in a minute.

Wally slowly rolled over onto his back, a move he accomplished with Sheode's help.

His right arm was still extended over his head, his left hand cupped his crotch.

"I just need a doctor. Please. No cops. I just fell, that's all. It was a stupid accident. I fell." He groaned loudly again.

Sheode knew that Wally was certainly lying. "Do you want an ambulance?" she asked. "Can I call them?"

Wally groaned and slowly removed his hand from his crotch, groaning as he did so. "I think that's a good idea," he said. "But I fell. Remember? I fell."

Sheode put away her cell phone and used the office phone on Wally's desk to call.

The ambulance crew came through the door within 15 minutes to find Wally alone, sitting up in his office chair, his badly swollen hand and wrist on top of his desk, his left hand in his lap.

The woman who had called had left, Wally told the ambulance crew.

Chapter 7

The news that a wrongful death lawsuit was going to be filed against the DeVille Energy Federation got a huge news media boost when one of the security guards involved in the shooting deaths of James Osmett and three other residents of *The Redoubt* pulled the trigger on his own .40 caliber handgun, the barrel of which he had stuck in his mouth.

He had pointed the gun more horizontal than vertical and blew the back of his head all over the rear window of his pickup truck parked on the road not far from *The Redoubt*'s main gate.

The news media began swarming the farm as soon as the Boyette County Sheriff's Dept. announced the guard had killed himself.

It wasn't long until the media learned Caleb found the security guard's body. He had walked out to see why the truck was parked there for so long.

In Horseheads, Eli and his staff at *The Clarion* were pulling together the story with some on-the-ground assistance from two freelance photographers in Iowa. The story would be running in all three newspapers – plus their websites. And because the three newspapers had more background – and access – to the people of *The Redoubt*, Eli knew other media would be republishing and reposting their work.

It took Eli nearly an hour to track down Jack, who was taking a tour of Porter Ranch in California where a few families were moving back into their homes now that the company had announced the massive natural gas leak had been stopped.

But the majority of the families doubted there wouldn't be another leak – and weren't budging from their temporary living quarters far away from the Aliso Canyon gas storage area.

"It still stinks around here, Eli," Jack said. "I'm sitting in a nice air-conditioned van with some reporters. It's actually a gas company van with fancy filters keeping the air breathable. Where are we with the suicide story?"

Eli checked his computer screen for the latest update from his staff writer.

"We're about a half-hour from publishing a solid report," Eli said. "It's really a matter of getting to talk to Caleb now if we can. He found the guy in the truck. But somehow it's getting tangled up with Caleb and that gun charge he's still facing. We need to get our story out fast before someone reports that *he* shot the guy in the truck."

There was a long pause on Jack's end.

"Jesus, Eli. Police have ruled that out, right? God!"

Before Eli could answer, Jack saw he had an incoming phone call.

"I'll call you right back. I have to step out of the van to take this call. It's personal."

Eli laughed aloud.

Personal probably meant Jack didn't want the other reporters in the van to hear his conversation, otherwise he would have simply said who it was.

Ten minutes later, Eli's story about the guard's suicide was published online, a much more complete story than any published in other media.

The phone call had been from Janis Osmett who put Caleb on the phone to talk to Jack.

Caleb said he only would talk to Jack about what happened.

Chapter 8

The pimply-faced male desk clerk at the Williston, North Dakota rental car agency mispronounced Calvin Boviné's name.

In the years before he went to prison, Boviné would have – at a *minimum* – reached over the counter and grabbed the front of the young man's shirt, threatening him with bodily harm if he didn't pronounce his name correctly.

More than a few times, he would have skipped the *threatening* step and give someone a beating.

But today, Boviné simply corrected the clerk.

"It's French," he said, forcing a smile. "Three syllables? Bo-Vin-Ay."

The desk clerk was about to make a snotty comment until he took notice that the man standing in front of him was huge and obviously powerful.

Like most airport workers, the clerk rarely looked at customers, so many came through and would never been seen again.

"Um, sure, Mr. Bovine. Oh shit! Sorry! I mean Bo-vin-ay," the clerk said, giving a little chuckle.

He noticed Boviné didn't join in his laugh and that the big man's already frowning face was sporting a slight tint of red.

"We'll get you right out of here in a minute," he said. "We're pretty short on cars right now. All these oil people coming and going. And speculators, you know."

Boviné did know.

For months, he had been living in a retreat house/monastery in Northern Minnesota, studying eastern meditation in the morning. Afternoons he was learning an Asian self-defense regimen developed before the birth of Christ.

The meditation helped him control his temper. The self-defense work gave him the exercise he needed and the knowledge of how to protect himself without doing much damage to others as had been his habit.

In prison he had mangled more than a few inmates before they started leaving him alone. But his cellmate – a mixed martial arts expert and a devout Buddhist – showed him how it was possible to protect himself without ending up in solitary confinement.

Boviné picked up his suitcase and took the car keys with his other hand from the clerk.

He stalked away, fighting down the feeling of his rising anger.

As he walked through the airport terminal towards the rental car exit, he had to push through a surging crowd coming from the opposite direction. The crowd was nearly exclusively male, business types with briefcases or oil field roughnecks, likely headed to some other oil field jobs now that North Dakota oil production was slowing down.

When he was squarely slammed into a third time, in this instance by a man wearing a not-too-clean oil company work shirt, he lost his temper.

The man who ran into him was beefy looking, but nowhere near Boviné's height or weight.

Boviné put his hand on the man's chest, holding him in place while the crowd surged past them like a moving river of water.

"Watch where you're going buddy. You could get *hurt*," Boviné said.

The roughneck looked at Boviné, dressed like a businessman in a suit. The roughneck calculated that no apology – or even acknowledgement – was necessary.

He grabbed Boviné's hand and squeezed it, simultaneously attempting to push Boviné's arm aside so he could pass.

But before he could even get a solid push in, Boviné dropped his suitcase, used his other hand to grab the man's arm and slipped his leg behind the roughneck, dropping him flat on his back onto the terminal floor.

The roughneck let out a gasp of air when he hit the floor, banging his head on the concrete.

The streaming crowd gave the two men a wide berth, unsure of what was going on and not wanting to get involved.

Boviné stared at the roughneck on the floor. He could see that man was debating whether to get up and start a brawl.

After a moment, the roughneck rolled onto his side and pushed himself up onto all fours. Then he stood and moved sideways around Boviné, keeping eye contact until he turned and disappeared in the crowd headed to the departure area.

Boviné picked up his suitcase and walked towards the exit sign. He could feel the anger slowly draining away.

He felt the phone in his pocket vibrate and answered.

"Any trouble with your flight, Calvin?" Keith Everlight asked.

"Just one small bump," Boviné said. "Nothing to worry about. So where is this guy named Wally?"

Chapter 9

Sheode was glad that Keith had arranged for them to meet Calvin Boviné at the same diner where they had met Wally before.

He nearly filled the entire opposite side of the booth from where she and Keith were sitting, the same booth they had sat in when they talked with Wally.

He wouldn't fit in any of the chairs at the hotel restaurant for sure, she thought.

Keith had told her how big Boviné was – and about Boviné's involvement with Grand Energy Services, his time in jail, and his newfound enlightenment about problems caused by the energy industry.

Still, she was a little unnerved by his bulk and a scowl that seemed to be his default facial expression.

"Thanks for coming to North Dakota, Calvin," Keith said. "You were hard to track down. Then I remembered the name of that retreat center you mentioned. They did not want to give you up easily though."

Boviné wrapped his hand around his coffee mug obscuring it.

"It's so peaceful there," Boviné said. "So quiet. But you must have been persuasive."

Boviné eyed the legal-looking file folders on the table between them, some of which had notes on the front with Calvin's name displayed.

"I pulled them from the files in Wally's office," Sheode said. "Harvey Weilbruner? I went in the afternoon after Keith talked to him at the hospital. The other people in the office barely even said a word to me while I rifled through everything."

Boviné pushed the top file with his index finger, eyeing it very suspiciously. Then he opened it and saw that the letterhead belonged to an investment group based in Houston that had links to a DEF subsidiary.

He read the cover sheet, then flipped a few pages before closing the file.

"I thought you wanted me here because of your friend," Boviné said looking at Keith. "You said you thought he needed some protection."

Keith took the top file folder that Boviné had just looked at and reopened it. He flipped through to a list of people on the third page, where highlighted in yellow marker was Mr. Calvin Boviné, investor.

"Calvin, my friend Wally does need somebody to protect him," Keith said. "But we're also trying to figure out why this company is buying water rights in Nebraska. And, what the hell your name is doing on this."

Sheode saw the redness creeping up Boviné's neck into his face and wished she had sat on the outside of the booth. She had no doubt that if Boviné stood up he could probably easily bowl over the table between them.

"Calvin!" Keith said. "We're not making any accusations here. But did you know about your name being used? Can you tell us anything about what's going on?"

Boviné put his hands flat on the table, exerting enough pressure that Sheode could see from the level of coffee in their cups was tipping slightly. He breathed in and out, as the redness in his face and neck slowly disappeared.

A meditation-anger management technique, Sheode thought. *Thank God.*

After a moment more of controlled breathing, Boviné reached over and pulled the file in front of Keith back to his side of the table. He thumbed through it again. This time he grunted occasionally.

"I can't tell you too much about it," he finally said. "When I first got out of jail, I met with Mr. DeVille and Rod Mayenlyn. They offered me a job. Kind of like my old job. You remember, Keith. Odd jobs convincing people to do things. I needed some money so I took it. I should have told you when I saw you in Rockwell Valley. But they said they would use my name to help out with investing."

Keith nodded and motioned to the waitress for more coffee.

"So you have no idea about these contracts, what's going on," Keith said. "Other than the obvious, that they're trying to corner the market on water?"

Boviné waited for the waitress to fill their coffee mugs.

"All I remember is that Mr. DeVille said he was making me some kind of a corporate officer maybe – of that company you have there. And it was part of the new pipeline. The one you call the Devil's Pipeline."

Boviné leaned down conspiratorially to say something else to Keith, giving Sheode a view of the restaurant lobby area that had been blocked by Bovine's bulk.

A man leaning on a cane was on his cell phone, staring at the three of them in the booth. Sheode poked Keith, then pointed to the man.

It took Keith a moment to figure out who it was she was pointing at, then he grinned.

"Hey Calvin, seems we have an old friend visiting North Dakota," Keith said. "Rod Mayenlyn."

Sheode watched the redness run up in Calvin Boviné's neck to his face as he struggled to quickly extract himself from the booth.

Chapter 10

The crowd in the diner provided Rod Mayenlyn enough time to make his escape.

As he hustled across the parking lot to his car – using his cane occasionally to be sure he didn't slip – he wasn't sure why he was running away.

Christ, he's the one meeting with the reporter, Mayenlyn thought. *DeVille is going to be furious.*

Still, Mayenlyn knew he needed to let A.G. DeVille know right away that he had found Boviné – and that he was chatting with Keith Everlight and some young woman. Mayenlyn also knew he would likely now have to change his just-made travel plans to head back to Texas to meet with DeVille.

He and Mars had delivered the message they had been sent to give to Harvey Weilbruner. It had been delivered way too brutally for Mayenlyn's taste. But it was unlikely Weilbruner would ever tell company tales out of school again.

Mayenlyn was used to firing off nasty letters and using public relations dirty tricks to advance the company's position. *But this rough stuff is getting out of hand*, he thought. *Just like it did at Grand Energy Services.*

Mayenlyn talked briefly on the company's secure cell phone to DeVille, who was concerned about the wrongful death lawsuit and the increasing activist activity in Nebraska.

Mayenlyn had expected a wrongful death lawsuit in the Iowa shootings and was surprised it took the family so long to file it. He suspected it was going to be a public relations nightmare because of the Kent State shooting connection.

DeVille and Mayenlyn had talked through how to fight the lawsuit, and how quickly the company should settle it. If they offered to settle too early, it would send a bad PR signal, admitting guilt. If they dragged it out right to the brink of going to trial in a civil suit, public opinion might get inflamed – again – making further pipeline planning problematic.

But Mayenlyn didn't offer up what he was really afraid the lawsuit might do: force DEF to make documents public about the company plans for the pipeline.

He started his rental car to get the heater working, pushing the buttons on the dashboard so he could use his telephone through the car's speaker system.

Mayenlyn had just connected to DeVille's office when he glanced in his rear view mirror. Boviné was standing behind the car, blocking his exit.

Chapter 11

Keith Everlight was just coming out the diner's front door when he saw a car driven by Rod Mayenlyn skid out of the parking lot.

He and Sheode had to push their way through the crowd in the diner to catch up with Boviné, who had plowed through the people like a professional football player through a team of junior high school kids.

Boviné was sitting on the parking lot pavement, holding his leg.

"That son of a bitch," Boviné roared. "Damn him! That son of a bitch."

The big man gingerly tried to stand, eventually coming upright, favoring his right knee. His pants were torn slightly. His hands were dirty from the parking lot.

"I came behind the car and the son of a bitch hit the gas and backed up right into me," Boviné said. "Right into me. What a stupid fuck."

He limped a few steps, shaking his leg.

"Any chance he didn't see you?" Keith asked.

Boviné stared at Keith for a long moment, then shook his head.

"I saw his eyes in the rear view mirror. He saw me all right," Boviné said. "And I pounded on the trunk! What an asshole. I'm going to *kill* him when I find him. Just wring his chicken neck."

Keith offered to drive Boviné to the hospital, but he was waved off.

"No, I think it's okay. I'll walk around a bit. Damn it."

Keith and Sheode watched Boviné limp off down the sidewalk back towards the center of town likely to the same hotel where Keith and Sheode were staying.

They pushed their way back into the diner where their booth was now occupied by four men, busy ordering.

The file folders with the documents Keith and Sheode had been looking at with Boviné were gone.

Chapter 12

Jack, Eli and Alexandra were having a short videoconference – called at Eli's request – to discuss the plethora of energy company pipeline proposals and how various companies were talking about piggybacking their applications to build on the concept used by the DEF pipeline.

Jack was still in Southern California where a court had just ordered the company involved in the Porter

Ranch natural gas leak to continue to pay for the temporary housing of people it has displaced.

Alexandra was in the office of the *Vashon View*.

"Eli, you have always had those double computer screens, but what's that I see behind you?" Jack asked. "It looks like a computer showroom."

Eli scrunched his face into the same sort of innocent look that Jack's son Noah used when he did something he knew Jack might not approve.

Noah might have even picked up that expression from Eli the last time he visited us in Washington, Jack thought. Thinking about Noah caused Jack to miss the first part of Eli's explanation.

"Come again on that, Eli? Did you say *virtual reality?*" Jack asked.

Jack and Alexandra both heard some fast clicking of keys and suddenly the image of Eli shifted to an overview of the newsroom of the *Horseheads Clarion*.

Jack recognized the view from a security camera mounted in a corner of the newsroom.

"I added four screens on the desks around me," Eli explained. "The virtual reality comment was a joke. But I have to say, if you play video games, using all six screens is wild," Eli said.

"But, besides video games?" Jack asked.

Jack and Alexandra's screen went dark and then popped alive again, this time with all four windows showing the displays from the four screens that Eli had on the desks behind him.

"I was trying to get a handle on pipeline projects here in the east, although we could do it for any location," Eli said. "There are a lot of pipelines concentrated here and there. But this helps give some idea of the scope."

Jack could hear Eli fussing with his keyboard, muttering slightly to himself.

And then the screens all came alive with graphics overlaid on a set of maps that showed the routes of current – and planned – pipelines.

But what made the display so amazing was that the display at first showed static images, then evolved to illustrate the proposed pipelines being built, ultimately revealing a snarled, twisted tangle of pipelines all over the Northeast.

"Eli, that's an amazing thing you done. Amazing," Jack said.

"Can you adapt it for other regions? I know it's the Northeast, but I think the interest in this is going to be huge nationally."

Eli typed for a moment. Then the pipelines disappeared and the four-panel computer screen with Jack, Alexandra and Eli replaced it. The fourth panel had a picture of Keith.

"It's almost ready for the website. But we need to talk about coordinating coverage of the pipelines in all three papers," Eli said. "They are *all* talking about water now. The DeVille pipeline started it. But some of these pipeline companies are saying they can fix problems like Flint, Michigan. They just need more right of ways to run gas and water pipelines side by side."

Eli flipped the four-screen pipeline model back up. But this time he added a graphic with a headline in the corner of each screen.

The graphic was the head of Medusa.

But instead of snakes, there were pipelines on top of her head – writhing pipelines that moved.

Chapter 13

It seemed very unlikely. But A.G. DeVille was certain. Betty Liu, his vice president for special projects, was drunk. Not fall down, slobbering, driving-under-the-influence drunk. But she was tipsy enough that her normally flawless English was fraying. Plus, she hiccupped several times – a tiny "urp" sound.

He had called Liu in because he was fuming over the threat of the wrongful death lawsuit linked to the shootings of James Osmett and three other people at *The Redoubt*.

He was so angry that he thought briefly about having Rod Mayenlyn postpone his trip back to Houston and fly to Iowa to have a talk with a DEF-friendly judge DeVille's lawyers hoped would hear the case.

But Betty Liu – hiccups and all – was talking him out of it.

"Mr. DeVille, you no need. You *don't* need to do that. Not now. If DEF got caught trying to influence the judge, it would be huge mess. It would be *a* huge mess," she corrected herself.

"Plus, you want the case, to focus only on the shooting and stay away from our pipeline plans. You are much more exposed there."

DeVille rocked back in his chair and stared at Liu. Her facial expression gave away very little. Plus, she was wearing thick reading glasses today that made her eyes difficult to see.

Goddamn Coke-bottle lenses, DeVille thought. *Just like the ones Stanley Erbermeir was wearing the day he raped me.* He shook that dark thought off and concentrated on Liu. She had paused in talking, waiting for DeVille to respond.

It's like talking to a computer, DeVille thought.

With Mayenlyn out of town, DeVille had gradually started letting Liu in on more of the plans for the pipeline. In conversation, they had even started calling it "the Devil's Pipeline" as an in-house slap in the face to the environmentalists who opposed it. "They want a devil, they'll get a devil," he had said one afternoon.

He had no illusion that Liu was loyal because she liked him.

What she *liked* was the H1B visa that he had sponsored to get her out of China, just one step ahead of the Chinese authorities.

Still, she was fearless in talking with DeVille and thus was an excellent sounding board. Almost everyone else – Mayenlyn included – was frightened of him, he knew.

Christ, she even showed up a little drunk today, DeVille thought. *That took balls.*

DeVille broke the silence. "Betty, have you been drinking?" he asked.

He tried to mask his near amusement with a frown.

Betty broke into a grin – the first time he had ever seen her actually smile.

"Yes, I drink," she said. "I had two drinks. Wine. With the head of purchasing at lunch. He's from China. The north. He's an H1 baby, too."

DeVille leaned forward, making a mental note to have human resources give him a full rundown on how many H1B visas the company had, in case it came up somehow as the press ramped up its scrutiny of the company.

We don't need any illegals floating around either, he thought.

"So, Betty, was the lunch just social? I don't approve of drinking on the job. You knew that when I hired you. And you know I don't drink."

The smile disappeared off her face even more quickly than it had shown up, replaced by something that looked faintly like a frown.

"Mr. DeVille, you forget. I *don't* drink. Except today. It was only way. The only way to get him to talk. He's a smart man and he said things. He has said things to me and I needed to find out."

DeVille leaned back, his respect for his vice president for special projects growing. "And what did you find out?" he asked.

Betty Liu stifled a hiccup before speaking.

"He wonders why we are ordering just replacement pipeline and supplies for what we have. He doesn't see how we can build the Devil's Pipeline. There's no orders for pipes or new equipment. Nothing."

DeVille reached in his desk drawer and pulled out a bottle of pain relievers. He put in on the desk where Betty Liu could reach it.

"Betty, take two of these. No, take the whole bottle with you. And take the afternoon off, too. We'll talk in the morning, first thing. You did good work today."

DeVille waited for her to grab the pills and make her exit from his office before he had his secretary return a phone call to Rod Mayenlyn who had left DeVille a two-word message.

Found Calvin.

Chapter 14

The Clarion Newspaper Syndicate
Column One

Maple syrup, pipelines and water

By Jack Stafford

Two years ago a Pennsylvania family lost a long struggle to protect their maple tree farm, dubbed by many people as the Maple Tree Massacre.

An energy company using eminent domain – and eventually the brute force of armed guards – cut a huge swath through the middle of the family farm to make way for a natural gas pipeline.

The heartbreaking anti-environmental symbolism of cutting down these aged but very-productive trees to make way for a snaking metal monster pipeline was not lost on activists.

The family – supported by environmentalists from several states – threw up blockades and used the courts in an attempt to stop the chain saws. But eventually they were forced to stand aside or face arrest.

The actions of the family and the activists continue to be mirrored across the nation as natural gas and oil companies fight against local land owners to construct of these monstrous pipelines.

The vast majority of the pipelines are used to get private corporation products to market, especially international markets. The pipelines are sending natural gas, liquid propane gas and oil to U.S. ports to ship overseas where they fetch higher prices and where there is a great demand.

U.S. citizens, like the family that saw a major portion of its longstanding business wiped out, receive no benefit other than a token payment in exchange for their property being taken.

Dramas like the one in Pennsylvania are demonstrating just how firm the fix is. Energy corporations have local governments, the courts and often even law enforcement in their pockets.

In the Maple Tree Massacre, U.S. Marshals toting semi-automatic weapons provided security for the men wielding chainsaws.

U.S. Marshals? Really?

The limited successes activists have had in slowing pipeline construction and occasionally forcing a shift in pipeline routes are few and far between.

And for most of these woes you can blame the DeVille Energy Federation. DEF has grand plans for building what activists have dubbed The Devil's Pipeline, a huge tunnel affair that will run from the shores of Lake Michigan in Wisconsin across the entire United States, though its exact route and terminus are still being kept secret.

At first, DEF led the public to believe that only water for the thirsty Southwestern U.S. and California would be shipped through the mammoth pipeline. But then solid digging by investigative reporters – including ones working for the Clarion Newspaper Syndicate – found out that was a lie of epic proportions.

The Devil's Pipeline will carry water, we believe. But it will also carry natural gas, oil and whatever else the DeVille Energy Federation chooses to shoot through its privately owned pipelines enclosed in the larger structure.

And it will do so with the blessing of the federal government that has clapped a tight security lid on much of the project, in part because the federal government has itself some controversial connection to the project.

Activists now speculate the government might be planning to use the giant tunnel to ship nuclear waste to some Western desert state – or even weapons.

In the last two weeks two major pipeline construction companies that had been struggling to get approvals for their pipelines have suddenly been given the federal go-ahead.

What changed?

They announced they would be constructing not one, but two pipelines parallel to the routes they seek.

You guessed it – one will carry natural gas or oil. The second will carry fresh water.

Jack Stafford is the publisher and editor in chief of the Clarion Newspaper Syndicate. He publishes Column One every Friday and can be reached at JJStafford@ClarionNewsSyndicate.com

Chapter 15

The doctor attending Harvey Weilbruner was overworked and bone-weary when Weilbruner showed up in the emergency room.

Dr. Eamon McCartty had been lured to North Dakota to work in the hospital by a huge salary – more than twice what he had been paid in Elmira, NY, where he had spent several years in a medical group practice doing family care. He was one of four out-of-state doctors brought to handle the rush of patients that had boomed along with the oil industry.

Now that the oil boom has gone bust. I might get laid off, he brooded.

McCartty had brushed off Keith Everlight's request for information about Weilbruner's case several times. He relented when Weilbruner came out of his deep painkiller-induced fog long enough to say Keith was to be told anything he wanted to know.

Sitting in his tiny hospital office, McCartty hesitated for a moment while Keith and Sheode sat waiting to hear his assessment.

"Well, I'm way too tired to put this very gently, I'm afraid," McCartty said.

He looked down at the medical chart on his desk, reading slowly before speaking. "OK. Your friend? Mr. Weilbruner? He suffered a badly smashed right hand. He took a really solid knock on the head. Maybe a couple. One hard enough to turn into a nasty shiner."

McCartty paused again, biting his lip slightly. "And… And it appears that someone nearly crushed one of his testicles. Sorry."

McCartty looked up and saw Sheode's eyes were showing signs of tears.

When he shifted his gaze to Keith, he saw Keith's face turning crimson.

"So, this wasn't any accident," Keith said, looking at Sheode. "It sounds like he was beaten – an out-and-out assault. Have you called the police on this? Has Wally – has your *patient* – told you *anything* about what happened?"

McCartty tipped back in his chair and wondered how much to say.

In his orientation he and the other new doctors had been given strict instructions to keep quiet about rig accidents, chemical poisonings, illnesses caused by bad water, barroom fights – even rapes. The community was already getting plenty of negative ink about the crime rate, he and the other doctors had been told. The hospital didn't want to add to the stories drawing national attention.

"Well, to be honest, I called the police and they said they would talk to Mr. Weilbruner when he was more, well, *coherent*. We get a lot of fight injuries here. In fact, that's the majority of my cases. The police are pretty overwhelmed."

Keith leaned back in his chair, a dozen questions whizzing through his mind.

"You said *someone* crushed his testicle. How do you know he didn't fall like he said?"

McCartty looked down at the report again.

"The broken blood vessels and marks around his groin area," McCartty said. "If he had fallen – like he claims – there would have likely been a single point of trauma. The trauma and broken vessels were widespread, in a pattern. It was almost like someone put his balls in a vise."

He looked at Sheode. "Sorry, Miss Walker."

Sheode wiped at her eyes while she asked how long Wally would be in the hospital.

"Oh, well, today's Friday. I would think over the weekend, and probably until Monday or Tuesday," McCartty said. "I neglected to say that we had to operate to relieve the pressure. His other testicle is badly swollen, too. But the surgeon and I agreed they *will* heal."

McCartty didn't mention that Weilbruner would probably be in pain for months.

Keith and Sheode stood up, thanked McCartty and started for the door before Keith turned around. "Oh. Doctor. A friend of ours is going to stay with Wally until he gets out of the hospital. Kind of really big guy. Wally knows about him. We want to be sure Wally's safe."

McCartty smiled for the first time.

"Already met him. I had to put a couple of stitches in his knee. He said he fell down in a parking lot. Kinda touchy about his name, isn't he?"

Chapter 16

When Jack walked in through the front door of the *Vashon View* office Monday morning, it startled Alexandra so much she nearly dropped her full coffee mug onto her computer keyboard.

"Geez boss, you scared the crap out of me! Nice to see you again though. Eli said we should plant a locator on you. I thought you were still flying around California, looking at that gas leak mess."

Jack put his laptop computer on his desk and then plunked down in the chair next to Alexandra's desk. She noted dark rings under his eyes.

But she was more than a little jealous of the raccoon-like tan lines he had from wearing sunglasses in sunny Southern California.

"Sorry to keep you all in the dark," he said. "But I wasn't sure how long I would stay south. That gas leak is *supposedly* stopped. But a lot of people aren't buying it. And the people who want to get out of there are stuck. Who wants to buy a house downwind of that place now? And for a million dollars or more."

Ten minutes of professional chit-chat later, Jack was up to speed on all the local news that Alexandra was already putting into the Tuesday paper, a pastiche of events and reports.

There were two letters to the editor about his maple syrup/pipeline column. One complained that he was picking on the energy companies. The other raged about the federal marshals protecting the tree cutters.

Jack made a note to follow up on the federal marshal angle.

When did the federal government get in the business of providing security for corporations, he wondered?

The balance of Tuesday's newspaper was devoted to various environmental and energy issues, including a front-page piece about the wrongful death lawsuit in Iowa.

It looked like the case was going to land in the court of Judge Roy Bean, a move Jack thought would give *The Redoubt* residents hope for a fair hearing.

He and Alexandra were debating two possible headlines for that story when images of Eli and Keith popped up on Alexandra's computer for their daily editor's conference.

"Oh my God," Eli said, "Is that the *elusive* Jack Stafford, world traveler, I see in Washington?"

Jack made a face into the computer camera.

"Eli, *don't* even start. I had to listen to that same song last night for an hour when I got home from Cass, Anne *and* Noah."

"Keith. You're still in North Dakota, right?" Jack asked. "With Sheode? That was an excellent piece you two wrote about that Rockwell Valley couple stuck there because of the oil price crash."

Alexandra looked carefully at Keith and realized that he looked even more tired than Jack.

"Thanks, Jack," Keith said. "We could stay here and write dozens of stories, to be honest. That is not an offer to stay, by the way. I'd like to get out of here. It's kind of creepy. It's like the wild west but *not* the romantic version."

Jack let the editors wrestle with what stories would be running in all three newspapers and how they would be promoting Eli's new pipeline graphic scheduled to debut Tuesday on all three websites.

Even though it would not officially go live until Tuesday morning, numerous media outlets across the nation had been given a sneak peek in case they wanted to link directly to it and offer it to readers.

A simplified version was scheduled for the open, public portion of the websites. But for readers to dig down and find detail – the kind of detail that would show if a pipeline was going to run through a backyard – they needed to subscribe.

That graphic could pay Sheode's salary all by itself, Jack thought.

As they began to wrap up, Jack asked Keith about Wally.

"I read your email about wanting his assault to be kept quiet. I agree. But how is he?"

Keith shifted over, letting Sheode's face slide into the frame.

She looks tired, too, Alexandra thought.

"He's going to be okay," Sheode said.

"He had to have surgery on his ... on his groin area. And he's drugged up pretty much. But I talked with him over the weekend and I think he's willing to talk to us now about DEF. We do have a problem though." Sheode slide off to the side and Keith popped up again.

"Sheode's has a gift for understatement – except in her stories," Keith said.

"We actually have two problems. One is the documents. They're gone. It's my fault. I left them on the table at the diner when Calvin chased Rod Mayenlyn outside and we went, too. When we came back in, the file folders were gone. The waitress said she didn't see anybody take them."

Jack closed his eyes for a moment, then sighed. "OK, what's the second problem?"

"Well, it's Calvin. We had him standing watch at Wally's hospital room. Kind of on bodyguard duty, you know? "He's disappeared, too."

Chapter 17

The news that Sioux City, Iowa Judge Roy Bean would preside over the wrongful death lawsuit of James Osmett and three other residents of *The Redoubt* sent A.G. DeVille into a rage. Bean was the same judge who had issued an injunction to stop DEF from surveying *The Redoubt* property, an injunction he eventually reluctantly lifted.

It's like pulling a thread on a sweater, DeVille thought. *That goddamn judge will let them pull and pull.*

DeVille was angry at Betty Liu, too, for convincing him not to interfere with the judicial process in Iowa.

We needed a friendly judge to limit testimony and evidence, not that liberal asshole, DeVille thought.

The DeVille Energy Federation had a small army of attorneys on contract specializing in energy litigation. Earlier that morning he had nearly fired the law firm that handled most DEF work when the managing partner told him his firm didn't have a good attorney to handle the wrongful death suit. That meant DEF would have to go outside to get a hired gun – or guns – to handle it.

DeVille was upset about shelling out even more in legal fees. But he was even more torqued about giving another law firm access to sensitive documents about the pipeline.

Legally, we have no problems, DeVille thought. *But this will be a press nightmare. Especially because the case is in Iowa.*

A message from DeVille's secretary popped up on his desk, saying Rod Mayenlyn had returned his call and was waiting on the secure company phone.

When the call connected, it sounded to DeVille like Mayenlyn was in a car.

"Rod, I want you and Mars back here," DeVille said. This Iowa court case is going to require your touch. But first you need to contact someone named Ellie Sue Linter. You'll get her contact information in a text. "She says she has some DEF documents we might want. And we do want them. They were stolen."

"Is Mars with you?"

The connection faded in and out for a moment.

"A.G. I heard you say *documents*," Mayenlyn said. "And *stolen*. That right? And Mars is at the hotel."

DeVille double-checked to ensure they were talking on the DEF encrypted line.

"Just contact her and bring the papers back here. She'll ask you for some money, I imagine. Use your judgment. And Rod? Take Mars with you to talk to her."

Chapter 18

Ellie Sue Linter blamed her dilemma on a legal-thriller movie she had watched the weekend before.

In the film, a smart aleck secretary steals some sensitive documents from a law firm that connected the company to a notorious Mafia Don. The secretary hooks up with a dashingly handsome attorney and ends up with a boodle of money, sailing off into the sunset on a yacht.

She had loved the movie and dreamed of seeing herself whisked away from her waitressing gig in Williston.

Then the very next day, sitting on an empty table in the diner she found a stack of file folders full of documents that only minutes earlier a newspaper reporter had been looking at with a young woman and a big, well-dressed guy.

The well-dressed guy she remembered the most vividly. He made most of the oil-rig roustabouts look like skinny teenagers.

When she saw the three of them dashed out of the diner, she picked up the folders and stashed them in the diner's silverware cupboard, thinking she would return them.

Then she remembered that the same reporter had been in and out of the diner all week, sometimes talking with an accountant named Wally who had bragged to her one afternoon about how his work was very hush-hush.

Her romantic notions about sailing off to paradise evaporated when two men pushed their way into her studio apartment as she returned home from work.

They ordered her to sit on a kitchen chair while they stood.

One man was average height, normal-sized and leaned on a cane.

The one standing behind her – whose massive hand was pushing down on her shoulder to keep her from standing – was huge and with a misshapen head and ugly face. She remembered seeing him at the diner once, briefly.

"So, the thing is, Miss Linter, those documents you contacted the DEF office about are very sensitive. *Very*," Rod Mayenlen said.

"And because they were stolen from our offices here. Well, we could involve the police in recovering them. You could be an accessory to the theft for all we know. It would be a felony. You could go to jail, Miss Linter."

Her dreams of trading the documents for cash faded.

When she tried to stand, the grip on her shoulder from the big man kept her from rising even an inch.

"Look. I found them," she said. "There were on a table. In the diner where I work? Nobody was around. They were just, you know, sitting there. We have sometimes maybe a thousand people a day come through to eat. No shit. I just wanted to, you know, to see if there was a reward or something? I didn't steal anything."

She saw the man with the cane processing her story, his eyes darting around the room. Her heart was pounding so hard she wondered if the gorilla holding her down could feel her pulse through her uniform.

"Well, here's the thing, Ellie Sue. Can I call you Ellie Sue?" he asked.

"I'm authorized to pay you a finder's fee, but *not* until we check the documents. We need to authenticate. Do you have them here?

She put her hand on the big man's hand behind her to push it away. *Ewwww*, she thought. *Even his skin feels creepy.*

She watched the man with the cane look behind her and nod slightly. The pressure on her shoulder lightened, then was gone.

The documents were in her microwave – she had seen that in the movie, too.

In the climactic scene of the film the secretary heroine turns on the microwave and the documents catch fire, causing a huge panic, allowing her to escape.

She weighed that option as she shakily walked across the kitchen.

The two men moved to stand in front of her door, the only exit.

When popped open the microwave door and pulled out the file folders she wondered if she was about to become a crime statistic.

She handed them over

"Ellie Sue, I'm sure the company will be generous in its thanks," Mayenlyn said. "We'll let ourselves out."

As they walked out, she double locked the door then raced to her bedroom where she reached into the closet and pulled a small Barbie suitcase she had been given when she was 10 years old.

An envelope containing photocopies of the documents were in there, tucked underneath an impressive collection of Barbie dolls and accessories.

Brilliant, she thought. *Or suicidal.*

Chapter 19

The Medusa pipeline graphic was a huge success with media and anti-pipeline activists, drawing hits so fast that the counter on Eli's computer was spinning like a slot machine.

The static image showing the pipeline map of the U.S. was making its way into print publications quickly. But it was the video of the projected growth of nearly 5,000 *more* miles of interstate pipelines over the next decade – and showing their exact locations – that was the real mind blower.

Plus, thanks to the work of an activist in Pennsylvania, Eli's pipeline charts showed many of the smaller, previously unchartered pipelines that ran from gas or oil wells to the larger pipelines.

All across the U.S., normally sanguine citizens were checking to see if their backyard was in the path of one of these energy-industry Golems.

Some clever Silicon Valley programmers had put together a short video spoof using the premise of the popular *Tremor* horror movies and television series, but using gas and oil pipelines bursting through the ground up into the air instead of rampaging creatures.

In the video, a suburban couple enjoying a barbecue suddenly has a natural gas pipeline heave up out of the ground right in the middle of their concrete patio. That scene is quickly followed by a truck crashing through their backyard fence with a crew of hard-hatted workers who attempt to wrestle with the writhing tube.

The workers are all sporting shirts with the name Eminent Domain Pipeline Co., Inc.

It was grabbing as much Internet traffic as the trailer for the latest Home Box Office series about a new Star Wars film.

As a journalist, Jack was very happy to see the impact of the video. The programmers had been kind enough to link back to Eli's work.

As a publisher, Jack was pleased to see advertising revenue had taken a big bounce upward, both in print and online.

These kinds of graphics have so much punch with our audience, he thought. *Probably more than my column.*

He and Alexandra sorted through a barrage of negative emails, letters and proposed opinion articles penned by the public relations departments of a dozen energy corporations.

They were trying to decide which to publish – and which to simply toss out – when the newspaper received a phone call from someone claiming to be from the National Security Agency.

The call came in through the main phone line of the *Vashon View* picked up by a newly hired receptionist/advertising sales person who had just graduated from college.

"Mr. Stafford, um, it's the National Security Agency? On line one?" she said. "Should I put the call through to your desk?"

Jack and Alexandra looked at each and spiked their eyebrows simultaneously.

"How do you know it's the NSA?" Jack asked.

"Well," the receptionist said, "that's what he said? And he sounds well, pretty official?"

Jack made a note to himself to tell the new receptionist to please stop ending every sentence as if it was a question.

"Did he give you a name?" Jack asked.

"No."

Jack looked at Alexandra then back at the receptionist.

"Okay. Ask for his name and a phone number for me to call him back."

The receptionist fussed with the desk phone and began to talk, suddenly snapping her head back.

"He *hung up* on me!" she said. "As soon as I asked him his name. What an *asshole*. Oops, sorry, Mr. Stafford."

Jack smiled at Alex and the receptionist. "Don't worry about it, I agree with your assessment," he said.

"And what does your phone log say about the number?"

She punched a button. A disgusted look blossomed across her face.

"No caller I.D. Of course," she said.

Chapter 20

The flight from Williston to Houston was packed with energy-company related travelers.

Most were briefcase-toting business types. But a few looked like they could be field workers, maybe headed home to families.

They weren't laid off, Rod Mayenlyn thought. *If they were, they would be driving their vehicles out of this wasteland.*

He smiled to himself about his bit of clever deductive reasoning. Then he frowned when he looked at the pile of file folders on the tray table in front of him.

Some detective I'd make, he thought, angry at himself. Mars was sound asleep in his first class seat next to Mayenlyn, snoring slightly, his huge mouth open.

Mayenlyn had waited until Mars was asleep to look at the documents again to avoid Mars saying anything about what might be in them. Mars' deep voice was often way too loud. And it was quiet in the first class cabin, even with the sound of the engines.

Mayenlyn flipped open the top file and scanned the accounting reports on purchases of things likes piping for transmission lines that had been part of a series of such pieces done by Harvey Weilbruner. It was all such pedestrian crap. Mayenlyn winced when he thought about Mars assault on Weilbruner.

That's really why I fucked up, he thought. *Five more minutes and I would have seen it. But I had to get Mars out of there before he hurt the girl.*

He flipped through another few pages of numbers that showed land purchases and sales with some references to leases. The leases and purchases of water rights were the part that Mayenlyn knew could pose a problem if it all became public. But the documents were all easily defensible.

To Mayenlyn, they just looked like business as usual, except that it did draw a straight line to the DeVille Energy Federation, not the subsidiaries that were set up to keep the public in the dark.

But even so, Mayenlyn didn't think these documents provided any kind of smoking gun – even the ones showing where DeVille was considering using eminent domain.

Most of the nation was so happy to have cheap gasoline and cheap natural gas that negative data about the energy industry were a hard sell with most media.

Except Jack Stafford and his *mob*, Mayenlyn thought.

He saw the flight attendant coming down the aisle with a sack to collect trash.

He flipped to the last page of the top folder where a receipt was attached neatly with a paper clip.

He checked to be sure Mars was still asleep.

He was, snoring again, his chasm of a mouth wide open, revealing rows of silver fillings.

Mayenlyn plucked the cash register receipt from a Williston UPS store from under the paper clip as the flight attendant held out the bag for him to deposit any trash.

He read it one more time before crushing it into a ball and handing it to the attendant.

Fifty copies, he thought. *Probably every goddamn piece of paper in these file folders.*

Chapter 21

The Clarion Newspaper Syndicate
Column One

Playing Where's Waldo – but with energy pipelines

By Jack Stafford

The word breathtaking doesn't come close to covering the plans of the energy firms or the extent of the pipeline system and infrastructure we have lurking underground already, all detailed in the Medusa pipeline project published in Clarion Newspaper Syndicate newspapers and linked on the CNS websites.

The use of the word "lurking" is quite deliberate. Pipelines – even new ones – frequently leak product, be it natural gas or oil. But the vast majority are buried underground and are accidents waiting to happen.

The energy companies always downplay these toxic leaks, which poison the ground and water. Some leaks are quite small. Some are spectacularly large.

And sometimes there are explosions, like the one in San Bruno, California in 2010 that killed eight people and leveled 35 houses, causing incredible damage to the neighborhood.

A year later, there was a similar blast in Woodside, California only 20 miles away while the energy company was testing the strength of its gas lines in the wake of the San Bruno blast.

In that case, the only damage was a mudslide that closed an interstate highway.

People were lucky.

The San Bruno explosion prompted calls for energy companies to have large buffer areas around their pipelines, safety buffers in case of leaks and explosions.

As it is, major transmission pipelines – 30 inches in diameter and larger – are currently buried in residential and city neighborhoods. And in rural areas, pipelines are placed way too close to homes, school, and businesses.

That's one of the major reasons the Clarion Newspaper Syndicate put together the Medusa graphic that allows you to see what's in your backyard now – or planned.

In the same spirit, the editors and graphic artists of the CNS are putting together a video and graphic compendium of pipeline accidents and incidents, with plenty of detail.

Collectively there is a national problem that deserves full public scrutiny. One small accident in West Virginia is, well, one small accident. But collectively? All the accidents combined are a huge problem.

Which brings us to the National Security Agency.

Since the tragedy on 9-11, national security concerns have been in the driver's seat of many fields, including energy and energy transmission – such as the location of oil and natural gas pipelines.

Often the exact locations have been kept secret, part of an anti-terrorist strategy thought up in some Washington, D.C. office.

The problem, of course, is that the locations are secret to you – but generally not to the energy companies. I say generally because many of the pipeline accidents and incidents have occurred because the companies themselves are often unsure exactly where particular pipelines might be.

The CNS has received unofficial word that our graphic showing the exact locations and GPS coordinates of these pipelines – like the one perhaps running near your home – may violate some federal statute.

We say keeping those locations secret violates common decency and safety.

Jack Stafford is the publisher and editor in chief of the Clarion Newspaper Syndicate. He publishes Column One every Friday and can be reached at JJStafford@ClarionNewsSyndicate.com

Chapter 22

The news that two families in Dimock, Pennsylvania had won a federal court judgment of more than $4 million was welcomed in Rockwell Valley where several families had been involved in similar civil lawsuits themselves with the bankrupt remnants of Grand Energy Services.

Like Dimock, the wells of dozens of families were suddenly contaminated with methane – and at times, toxic chemicals.

Like Dimock, GES said its drilling was not responsible and that the methane that mysteriously appeared about the same time as the drilling started was "naturally occurring."

But unlike Dimock, Rockwell Valley residents were still fighting in federal court to get a payout from the financial sliver of what remained of the assets of GES.

"It's played out exactly the way we predicted," Eli told Jack, Alexandra and Keith in their morning editors' videoconference.

"Remember when you wrote that column about requiring GES to post a bond?" Eli asked Jack. Jack laughed.

"I sure do. I remember especially because I had to do a lot of research about companies that said they were self-insured. Most of them all went down in flames, too, when they had accidents."

The Dimock decision had charged up anti-pipeline activists.

In the weeks leading up to the decision, several major pipeline applications before the federal government were put on hold by the companies.

The delays were a combination of the free-fall of energy prices and regulatory agencies that were suddenly much less likely to rubberstamp everything that crossed their desks.

"It kind of feels like the good guys are starting to win," Eli said. "I would hate to jinx it. But, that brings us to the DeVille project and the Iowa lawsuit. Keith, you want to go first? I think Jack has the Iowa update."

Keith disappeared from the screen for moment, then came back, holding a stack of papers and wearing a grin.

"These are the missing Harvey Weilbruner documents," Keith said. "A very unhappy waitress from the diner where we lost them gave them back to us two days ago. She tracked us down through the hotel where we stayed. And she told us a fascinating story about two guys from DEF who paid her a visit."

Jack jumped in before anyone else.

"So are there any revelations in the papers? You weren't sure before," Jack said.

Keith shook his head, but kept the grin firmly in place.

"No. The more we look at them, the less valuable they seem. Wally is still recovering and not all that coherent because of the painkillers. And it was Rod Mayenlyn and some goon of a guy, we know now. The waitress described Mayenlyn perfectly."

The editors noticed Jack looked troubled.

"Mayenlyn is a creep and willing to say anything to smear people or save his boss and the energy company," Jack said. "But violence?"

Keith held up a photo of Wally he had taken the day after he was taken to the hospital. He was sporting a shiner that looked like he had been in a boxing ring with a heavyweight prizefighter or slugged with a baseball bat.

"I don't think Mayenlyn did anything physical," Keith said. "But the guy with him? The waitress said he was the ugliest man she'd ever seen. And huge."

Eli agreed to try to find out who the mystery giant was.

"But we do have some good news," Keith said. He moved over while Sheode slipped in front of the computer camera.

She offered a cheery "good morning" then held up a barely palm-sized turtle that looked like child's toy.

"When I took some file folders the day I found Wally on the floor, I grabbed a small sack of things from his middle desk drawer," Sheode said. "Even lying there in pain, he told me to take it. He said it had personal things he didn't want to lose.

"I had almost forgotten it until yesterday when I was going to visit him. I wanted to take it along."

Jack sighed loud enough that everyone one understood Sheode needed to make her point quickly.

"So," she said, "I found this turtle in the sack. My people are from the Turtle Clan – in case anybody cares. When I looked at it I realized it isn't toy, it's a data stick. Wally was keeping a backup of sensitive stuff on it. Including information about DEF and the pipeline."

Jack gave a quick fist pump.

"Yes!!! I want you to make a backup of whatever is on that stick and send copies to Eli, Alexandra and me," Jack said. "I'll give you all a full update on Iowa later. But subpoenas are about to start flying."

Chapter 23

Janis had to admit it was nice having a handsome young attorney hanging out at their house nearly round the clock.

Even Caleb had mentioned that her mood improved – and that she had switched from wearing farmer coveralls all the time to occasionally wearing skirts – clothes Caleb always had called his mom's "go-to-town" clothes.

Jerome Wooster Stone had take over a small bedroom on the second floor as an office to mount their wrongful death lawsuit. At Janis's insistence, he let her call him Jerome, not his preferred J.W.

"J.W. just sounds *too* much like that awful character from the *Dallas* TV show," she said.

Jerome had only seen a few episodes of *Dallas* on a classic TV channel. But he knew who J.R. Ewing was. And he understood why Janis wouldn't want to make *that* connection.

The legal planning for presenting the civil suit was moving right along, in tandem with a burst of positive public support.

Jerome had been in court just once so far.

Days after he filed the lawsuit, attorneys for DeVille Energy Federation filed a motion with Judge Roy Bean to dismiss the case.

The four DEF attorneys who flew in for the hearing – all members of a high-priced New York City law firm – didn't get an ounce of sympathy from the judge when they argued that the lawsuit was without merit.

"A man's dead, shot by employees hired by the company that is paying you handsomely to be here in the Hawkeye state," Bean said. "I am not sure why it took four of you to come all the way from the Big Apple for this hearing. And I am certainly *not* going to short circuit the legal process of deciding about how wrongful Mr. James Osmett and his neighbors' deaths might have been. I'll let an Iowa jury do that.

"Motion to dismiss *denied*."

The sound of his gavel cut off any further argument.

The judge's ruling to let the wrongful death suit proceed prompted a tsunami of national publicity along with a spate of stories about the original National Guard shooting on the Kent State campus.

Anti-pipeline activists suddenly found themselves in communication with former Kent State students from the 1970s who wanted to help with the lawsuit.

Headlines in major metropolitan newspapers echoed the Kent State connection.

Kent State shooting casts long shadow in lawsuit

Wrongful death lawsuit eerily echoes 1970 shooting

Ohio National Guard may be dragged into lawsuit

Jerome had even been in communication with one of the editors of the website *NIS*, the fringe outfit that had tipped *CNS* that the DeVille pipeline wasn't just a water conduit.

NIS said it had information it was holding back for the time being that might be very useful to Jerome's case.

Jack had been pushing Jerome to put together a large team to level the legal playing field. But Jerome was used to working alone, with just a few paralegals and support staff. Plus, he relished being cast David to DEF's Goliath as the national media were framing the battle.

At *The Redoubt*, Janis and Caleb were taking on research tasks with the tenacity of first-year law students studying for class presentations.

And he was getting plenty of off-the-record research assistance from Eli and Alexandra.

Jerome's farmhouse office gave him a commanding view of the front gate where the shooting had taken place. There were small stone cairns placed approximately where each person had fallen after being shot.

Sometimes he would see Janis or Caleb out walking in that area. *Hallowed ground*, he thought.

He grabbed his legal pad to make a note of this thought, then logged onto the website for the county library, located in Boyette, where the trial would be held. After the initial court hearing, Janis and Caleb had taken Jerome into the library and convinced the librarians to give him lending privileges.

He smiled when he saw the book was on the shelf. A few keystrokes later he had put it on hold.

Jack Stafford will like the irony of my using a journalist's book in my research, he thought.

An email notice came through from the Boyette County Library.

A copy of 'The Killing Fields' is on the patron shelf ready for you to pick up.

The Fire This Time

Chapter 1

The rubber bullet had caught Keith Everlight just above his right kidney, hitting hard enough that he had blood in his urine that night back at the motel.

He'd been hit while observing a DEF protest that turned violent.

When he told Sheode about the blood, she loaded him into their rental car and drove him straight to the hospital where several dozen Native Americans were already in the emergency room, complaining of maladies ranging from severely burning eyes, pepper spray burns, breathing problems from tear gas, and rubber bullet-related injuries similar to Keith's.

Keith observed that the nurses and ER doctors seemed much more interested in treating the handful of DeVille Energy Federation pipeline workers than any of the Sioux needing help.

"These hospital people seem to have the same low opinion of Native Americans as the DEF workers," Keith said, wincing from the pain. "This is going to be part of my story tomorrow."

Keith and Sheode had been south of Williston where DEF had started construction on an oil pipeline crossing land a tribe claimed was sacred and part of land stolen by the U.S. government when it abrogated a treaty in the late 1800s.

The pipeline was to be buried underneath several creeks used as water sources for the nearby reservation.

"You would think with all the chaos over the Dakota Access Pipeline that DEF would be, more... I don't know," Sheode said.

"Don't bother to say *sympathetic*," Keith said, wincing at the pain in his back. These DEF guys only know timetables and corporate profits. What's a little pollution or stepping on native toes to them?"

The protesters – who like their tribal brothers and sisters near Cannonball – used the title Water Protector, *not* protester, had been praying, chanting and blocking the road so DEF trucks could not enter the construction site.

When a contingent of security guards arrived, dressed in full body armor, they shouted for everyone to move out of the way and followed within moments with a hail of rubber bullets, a quick dousing with a powerful water cannon, pepper spray and tear gas.

Some of the Water Protectors were veterans of the Cannonball standoff at the Dakota Access pipeline construction site and were prepared. But Keith learned from one Water Protector being treated for a badly injured eye that of the 100 or so Native Americans at this site, only half were ready for the level of aggression they encountered.

Keith was sure the guard who shot him knew he was there as a reporter. And he was also sure the guard might have let off another round or two at him except for the intervention of a Water Protector named Hector Round Mountain.

Hector broke ranks with the Water Protectors who were standing arms linked and rushed the DEF security guard, knocking the barrel of his rifle up in the air and forcing the rubber bullet to go nearly straight up.

It would be several weeks before Keith and the rest of the world found out that Hector's wife Sally Two Goats had been hit in the belly by a rubber bullet from the same rifle, causing her to lose her six-month old fetus.

Chapter 2

Judge Bean stared at his wall calendar, the top half showing a fisherman landing a trout, the bottom the month of October.

Fishing, Bean thought. *How nice that would be.*

His eyes hovered on the following Monday's date circled in red by his secretary. It was the anniversary of what the media had started calling *The Redoubt Massacre.* It was also the day that the wrongful death lawsuit trial would begin.

The timing guaranteed that an already volatile situation would heat up even more.

All I need is O.J. Simpson to make an appearance to cap it all off, Bean thought.

The number of requests for media interviews had grown so large that Bean's secretary had created a database that sorted the requests by date, media, and circulation of newspaper (or viewership of TV station).

So far, he had turned down all requests for even cursory comments on how the trial would proceed. But he was intrigued by a request from Jack Stafford, the publisher/owner of the *Clarion Newspaper Syndicate.*

Bean had read Stafford's two books on the environment and politics. He liked Stafford's take-no-prisoners attitude when it came to dealing with the powerful energy companies.

He thought Stafford's reporting and columns from Iowa right after the shooting had been fair, if a bit overwrought at times. *I probably should talk to him before my name shows up in his column anyway,* Bean thought.

He opened a file of press clippings his secretary had collected from the last few days. They ranged from dry Associated Press reports to wild alternative newspaper predictions to even international coverage. He smiled at a Toronto report that compared his judicial style to that of a character named Judge Bone from a 1990s American television program "Picket Fences."

> *"Judge Roy Bean has the same common sense – and no-nonsense – demeanor that the late actor Ray Walston displayed playing Judge Henry Bone,"* the Toronto Ledger said.
> *"Look for Bone, er, Bean to slap down the attorneys for the DeVille Energy Federation if they get out of line.*
> *And anybody else if they act out during the trial."*

Concerns about courtroom security were being openly discussed in the press, though Bean thought any ruckuses would be outside the courthouse, possibly between pro-pipeline forces and those supporting the wrongful death lawsuit.

Boyette hotels were already overbooked with people from out of state coming for the trial. *Just what Iowans hate*, Bean thought.

He shuffled through some of the briefs already filed by lawyers for the DeVille Energy Federation and the young attorney who had filed the lawsuit, Jerome Wooster Stone. Bean liked the young man's spunkiness. *Spunky without being arrogant*, Bean thought.

The DEF attorneys however, made his stomach go sour. They reminded him of too many of his law school classmates from Fordham three decades before, most of whom joined huge corporate law outfits with big salaries, low morals and imperceptible ethics.

The thought darkened his already dark mood.

"Damn it," he said aloud. "Goddamn it."

He pushed the intercom button to connect to his secretary. "Janine, can you contact that journalist Jack Stafford? I think I would like to have a chat with him… But do it quietly. Please? I don't want anyone to get wind of it for the moment."

Bean heard Janine chuckle.

"Will do, judge. I wish you buzzed earlier. I overheard that cute attorney for the Osmetts talking to him on the phone on the courthouse steps."

Chapter 3

The Clarion Newspaper Syndicate
Column One

Echoes of Kent State in Iowa shooting case

By Jack Stafford

A trial began this week in a wrongful death lawsuit – exactly a year since security guards shot and killed four people on a farm called The Redoubt in Iowa, an intentional community dedicated to non-violence.

The main thrust of the lawsuit against the DeVille Energy Federation holds the company is responsible for the shooting of the farm residents, including James Albert Osmett, a witness to the brutal slaying of four people at Ohio's Kent State University in the infamous shooting on that campus in 1970.

The district attorney of the county where The Redoubt is located determined that the shooting was accidental – a mistake.

It certainly was.

But it was no accident that DEF sent armed men to the farm that morning. DEF wanted the men to intimidate the residents so that surveyors could cross the land without interference, laying out a path for a giant steel tube/tunnel now known as The Devil's Pipeline.

DEF lawyers have been arguing since the lawsuit was first filed that because it was an "unfortunate" accident DEF really bears no responsibility in the case.

Preposterous.

Even in a no-injury, fender-bender automobile accident, the person who caused the crash has some culpability. And in this case the shooters were working as agents of DEF when they let loose a hail of bullets and killed four unarmed people.

While claiming publicly the company has no responsibility, outside of court, these same slick attorneys have been desperately making settlement offers – offers of eye-popping dollar amounts. The offers have been rejected out-of-hand by the Osmett family – and the families of the three other people killed that day.

"This trial isn't about money, it's about responsibility," plaintiff attorney Jerome Wooster Stone said. "It's about an out-of-control energy conglomerate that has been playing hide-and-seek with the law. We're going to make sure that the public sees the corporation for what it is, where it is, and what it has done. And not just to the Osmetts and the residents of The Redoubt."

Stone's requests for documents and his demonstrated aggressive legal strategy are why DEF attorneys are so desperate to quash these legal proceedings quickly. Decades of DEF business dealings – plus the ongoing path, construction and contractual details about The Devil's Pipeline – are likely to be prominently featured in testimony and evidentiary items brought before the court.

A motion to limit such discovery and the evidence it will bring forward has already been denied by Judge Roy Bean.

"Four people are dead and the DEF armed guards weren't at the farm scouting out a place for a picnic," the judge said on the first day of the trial. "They were there because DEF has plans for that land. A pipeline, I believe. The court would like to hear about what's so special that the company was willing to risk a shooting."

Only moments after Bean made that ruling he also denied a motion offered by DEF attorneys to keep all references to the 1970 shootings on the Kent State University campus out of the court case.

The Redoubt founder James Albert Osmett, killed by the DEF guards, was a witness to the university shootings and a lifelong pacifist. The Kent State shootings were what prompted Osmett to move to Iowa and create a non-violent community.

If the DEF attorneys have done their homework, they are aware the Judge Roy

Bean knows all about what happened May 4, 1970 on the Kent State campus. He earned his undergraduate degree from Kent State in the 1980s before getting his law degree from Fordham University in New York City.

Jack Stafford is the publisher and editor in chief of the Clarion Newspaper Syndicate. He publishes Column One every Friday and can be reached at JJStafford@ClarionNewsSyndicate.com

Chapter 4

The picture of the wolverine sprinting across an open field was dramatic, Jack had to admit.

Eli had sent the photo to him via email, with a note that the feisty animals were still being considered for protection under the Endangered Species Act. There were only about 300 left in all of the 48 contiguous states in the U.S.

Jack's fondness for the wolverines had grown out reading several books about the critters years before when a shadowy group of people bent on harassing energy companies adopted the name Wolverines.

They had most likely pulled the moniker from the mid-1980s movie *Red Dawn* about a scrappy group of teenagers that wage a guerilla war in the U.S. against an invading army.

The Wolverines tactics had caused such significant ruckus for a company called Grand Energy Services that the federal government eventually labeled the group a terrorist organization.

Most of the Wolverine's activity was more prank than destructive, though there were lingering suspicions the group had a part in a natural gas explosion that killed the GES company president.

I wonder why they just disappeared? Jack thought, sitting in his *Vashon View* newspaper office. ***Maybe they did*** *blow up old Grayson Oliver Delacroix.*

He shook off the thought and made a note to ask Eli to have one of the reporters in Pennsylvania work on a follow-up story about the Wolverines. Some of the vandalism incidents happening to DEF equipment there and in Iowa bore similarities.

But just like other energy companies, DEF did its best to cover up incidents of vandalism or destruction, partly to avoid embarrassment and partly to deter copycats.

For the Devil's Pipeline, DEF's federal support brought along with it a level of security – *taxpayer-funded*, Jack thought – that kept any Wolverine-like groups from doing much serious damage to anything.

Jack tried to concentrate on a story about California where record rainfall and snow suddenly provided hope that the state would get relief from the ongoing drought. But he gave up after a few minutes and turned back to reading a wire service account about the first two days of the trial in Iowa. The *Clarion Newspaper Syndicate* was using the wire reports, supplementing them with local comments until the news group could get Keith and Sheode to Iowa.

Keith and Sheode had missed the early rounds of jury selection because of his injury, but were expected to be at the courthouse in the next day or two when proceedings resumed and selection of the jury continued.

Jack had told them to be sure Keith was okay to travel. DEF attorneys kept asking for recesses, in-chamber discussions, and objecting to almost anything that the Osmett's attorney said.

The delay tactics were puzzling to all and causing Judge Roy Bean to grow more irritated.

All of it should make for a more interesting interview, Jack thought. He was just trying to figure out how to break it to Cass that he was leaving Vashon Island again to head to Iowa when a text from Sheode popped up on his phone.

> *Jack: Delay of plans. Keith was just arrested by county sheriffs and charged with rioting. They grabbed him at the hospital. It's the same charge as some of the water protectors got hit with. He's headed to the jail for processing. I'll let you know as soon as I know what's going on. Crap! S.*

Chapter 5

The nightmares had started again after a decade of peaceful sleep. The scene was always the same – a barracks-like room similar to where A.G. DeVille had slept as a child at the Iowa orphanage where he was raised.

He would be in his bed, awakened by noises around him, but unable to move.

Then suddenly he would be able to see himself, surrounded by older boys, all moving in towards him like sharks. Sometimes they were sharks.

Always he would wake up with a start, often having sweated through his nightshirt.

But last night's had been worse. He had felt the boys pulling at his clothes and putting their hands on him. *Again.*

The nightmare was still on DeVille's mind that morning as he walked into his office, past his secretary who knew better than to offer even a subdued "good morning."

Since the Iowa trial got underway, DeVille had been perpetually angry and threatened to fire so many people in the executive offices that nearly everyone from secretary to vice president did an office version of *duck-and-cover* when he was anywhere nearby.

His secretary screwed up her courage and spoke at the last second as he tapped the keypad to unlock his door although she was careful to keep her eyes down towards the floor when she stood to speak. "Mr. DeVille? I am *sorry* to bother you. But you have a message from Rod Mayenlyn. He says it is really urgent."

She felt his eyes on her. She carefully looked up just in time to catch a glimpse of him as he slammed the door to his office without speaking.

She jumped when he jerked the door open a moment later and glared straight at her.

"Get Mayenlyn on the phone, the secure phone," he barked.

She hesitated, his stare holding her in place.

"**Now**," DeVille yelled, turning back to his office door.

She had just taken a breath when he turned around again, this time his face desperately trying to approximate a smile. "Please," he said, his teeth locked so tightly it was like his jaw was wired shut.

He turned and went into his office again, this time closing the door excruciatingly slowly.

That's it, she thought. *I have to get another job.*

Chapter 6

The targeting of journalists by police had become almost a sport all over the country. But it had reached near epidemic levels in North Dakota at the Native American protests against the Dakota Access Pipeline.

North Dakota law enforcement especially targeted small independent media operations that didn't have the backing of some major corporation.

And even though the area where Keith happened to be was many miles from Standing Rock and major protest activity, the police had adopted the same tactics. If journalists happened to be standing with people where the police didn't want people to be, they would be swept up and arrested, too.

Or as was often the case, hit with water cannons, tear gas, pepper spray or rubber bullets.

"Shoot the messenger," Jack muttered, looking out the window of the airplane that was taking him to Iowa.

"What's that?" a sleepy Cass asked.

They had been sitting on the tarmac at the Seattle Airport for nearly an hour, waiting for clearance to leave the gate and wing their way east to Iowa.

The Republican candidate for U.S. president was visiting Seattle to meet with aircraft manufacturing officials, so security was keeping planes on the ground for an extra long time.

"I'm sorry. Did I say 'shoot the messenger' aloud?" Jack asked. "Jaysus."

Cass closed her eyes again, exhausted from packing late into the night.

When Keith was arrested, it was clear right away he would spend a day or more in jail – and likely have travel restrictions placed on him that would prevent him from leaving town.

Rioting, Jack thought. *Rioting*! He was watching a bunch of people being mistreated by the police. He shook his head and glared out the window.

As soon as he learned about Keith's arrest, he decided that covering the wrongful death trial in Iowa would be really above Sheode's pay grade, even as quickly as she was developing into a first-class journalist.

He really wanted Keith at the trial. His legal training and experience covering courts were needed.

Plus, Jack had set up an interview with the judge, which presented problems if he had to write stories about the trial itself.

He decided to get Sheode to Iowa quickly to write the basic stories while he would edit. *Once more into the breech*, Jack thought.

Cass shifted in her seat and put her head on his shoulder.

When he had come home the night before – all flaps up over the arrest of Keith – Cass said firmly she was going with him back to Iowa. On their last visit together, she had helped smooth his rougher edges in his dealings with some of the more difficult members of The Redoubt community – people who were suspicious of media in general.

Cass shook awake as the plane lurched back away from the gate.

She looked over and saw that Jack was staring intently at his cell phone.

"Jack, you need to break the trance," Cass said. "We're moving and one of these flight attendants is going to slap your hand."

Jack glanced at Cass and gave her a half-smile that usually meant he was thinking really hard about something.

"Sir, SIR! You need to close down all electronic devices," the female flight attendant said sternly. "Now please?"

Jack nodded and slipped the phone into his pocket, still turned on, Cass noted.

"I want to read the text again more carefully when we're airborne," Jack said. "Those DEF bastards are working with the District Attorney's office and putting pressure on Janis to settle the lawsuit before the jury is even seated."

Cass shook her head. "The DA? What does a DA have to do with a civil suit?"

Jack looked over his shoulder and saw the flight attendant had made it to the front of the plane where she was strapping herself into her seat for takeoff.

"Here, you can read it now," he said, pulling out the phone. "It's about Caleb and that gun charge. If she plays ball and settles, the DA will drop the charges. If not? Then the DA is going to try to get the court to sentence him to a stretch in a very nasty juvenile detention center near Des Moines.".

Cass glanced at the message from Janis. She imagined her crying as she typed it.

"Did you respond to her?" Cass asked glancing at the phone. "Wait, I see you did."

Jack took the phone back and powered it off.

He watched the words "Hang on – we'll get those bastards" disappear as the plane swung onto the runway and picked up speed.

In the distance, Jack could see presidential candidate Donald Trump's plane in the distance. He shook his head.

Chapter 7

It was a relief for Rod Mayenlyn to be away from Mars – even if it was because he had to meet A.G. DeVille in DeVille's office.

Mayenlyn didn't even mind that it was 7 a.m., an hour when he was usually just rousing himself.

He sat admiring DeVille's new secretary, *Sally? Susan? Sarah?* Who had just come onboard a few days before. Mayenlyn made a mental note to talk with the former executive secretary to DeVille to find out why she left suddenly.

The cover story Mayenlyn had been told – which he would have to pass along to the press if anyone really cared – was that her husband was ill and she needed to be home to care for him.

Except that bitch hated her husband, Mayenlyn thought. *If he had dropped dead she would have danced a jig in front of her house. Naked.*

DeVille's anxiety over the Iowa trial was puzzling to Mayenlyn. Certainly the company had some exposure legally – and might even end up paying a whopping amount of money to settle the case eventually. But money was hardly an issue for DEF, given profits and the generous hidden subsidies it was getting from the federal government.

And since the details about the pipeline had leaked out – in good part because DEF let them leak – there weren't really dark secrets left that he and DeVille needed to keep out of the press.

Shit, everyone's happy the goddamn thing is going to be built, Mayenlyn thought.

The only thing Mayenlyn could imagine was that A.G. DeVille didn't like all the background stories that were starting to pop up here and there related to the case, some of which included a recounting of DeVille's upbringing in the orphanage.

Mayenlyn shifted in his chair, thinking uneasily about the conversation months before when DeVille explained about the gang of boys at the orphanage attacking him.

"Mr. Mayenlyn? Mr. Mayenlyn," DeVille's secretary said. "Mr. Mayenlyn!"

He looked up at DeVille's new secretary, standing behind her desk.

"I'm sorry," she said. "But Mr. DeVille said it will be another few minutes before he can see you. He's on the phone with the attorneys in Iowa right now."

Mayenlyn smiled while the secretary turned back to her computer screen.

She thinks I'm smiling at her, Mayenlyn thought. *Ha! If she tells everyone who comes in this office who DeVille's talking to on the phone, she won't last a week.*

The cell phone in Mayenlyn's pocket vibrated, a text message coming in, likely from some media outlet.

Mayenlyn had started fielding most calls from the major news outlets instead of letting them fight their way through the labyrinth of the public relations department.

The chummy relationship worked well with most of the reporters. *Except for those assholes that work for Jack Stafford,* Mayenlyn thought.

He had finally blocked all of Stafford's reporters and editors – and Stafford – from calling him directly.

He pulled out his phone and saw the text was from one of his staff members in the PR office. It was a screen shot of a front page from a long-shuttered Iowa weekly newspaper. The story was about the fire that had destroyed the orphanage where DeVille grew up. It had broken out just a few months after he left.

Mayenlyn remembered the fire faintly, barely mentioned in one of the published profile pieces about DeVille.

"Mr. Mayenlyn?" the secretary said. "You can go in now. He's off the phone."

Mayenlyn read the headline again as he stood up and headed into DeVille's office.

"Arson suspected in orphanage blaze"

Shit, he thought.

Chapter 8

Keith was still nursing the bruise from the rubber bullet that had hit him when he was near the DEF construction site.

Sheode had left North Dakota and was in Iowa covering the wrongful death trial, thrilled and terrified at the responsibility.

But Keith knew Jack had gotten there, too. *It will kill Jack not to just jump in and write the court stories*, he thought.

Keith had spent one night in jail on the rioting charges before he appeared in front of a local magistrate who said he would let Keith out without bail, but only on the condition that Keith not write a word about his arrest, the incarceration or anything related to the incident.

When Keith refused he was quickly dispatched back to jail, then suddenly released a day later, without any explanation from anyone.

"Just pack up and make your way to Iowa," Jack said on the phone. "And don't worry about things back in Rockwell Valley at the newspaper. Eli is covering all the editing duties at both newspapers."

Eli and Alexandra were providing background research for Jack and Sheode. The volume of historical material about the shootings at Kent State was staggering. And as Jerome Wooster Stone prepared his case, he started relying heavily on Alexandra and Eli's unofficial help, too.

When they said they were uneasy providing him with the background information, Jack told them not to worry about it. "There's no conflict of interest here," he said. "What we are doing is simply sifting data that is likely to show up in our stories and columns. We're not building his case for him."

A bigger problem for Jack was the conversation he had had with Judge Roy Bean, a talk Jack was trying to shape into a column about common-sense law in an age of hair-splitting legalities that rarely ended in justice for any parties involved.

Most of what they had talked about had to be off-the-record while the trial was ongoing, a caveat that Jack agreed to reluctantly. And during their interview/conversation, Bean and Jack stayed away from talking directly about the wrongful death lawsuit.

Jack was going over his notes when he got a text from Eli:

> There's some connection between Judge Bean's family and the orphanage in Iowa where DeVille grew up. Alexandra is trying to track it down.

Chapter 9

The Clarion Newspaper Syndicate
Column One

Pipelines, candidates & hydrofracking
By Jack Stafford

The national press has been paying most of its attention in this presidential campaign to the slurs and insults shot back and forth between Democratic Party candidate Hillary Clinton and Republican nominee Donald Trump.

Secretary Clinton has been by far the more polite of the two.

But both candidates seem hell bent on promoting hydrofracking for oil and natural gas – and the construction of more pipelines to carry crude oil and natural gas away to shipping sites. That's no doubt because the sites are where oil and gas can be processed and sent to foreign nations where they are sold at a hefty profit for the energy companies.

Whoever is elected in November is likely going to continue down the path of approving even the on-hold Keystone XL and the Dakota Access pipelines. Both are disastrous mistakes.

The environmental drawbacks and dangers of Keystone's proposed shipping of tar sands oil from Canada was documented so sufficiently that President Barack Obama put the project on hold in the U.S., effectively killing the project in 2014.

The Dakota Access situation is different in that the pipeline to bring crude oil from the North Dakota oil fields is almost complete except for a short stretch of pipeline under a lake made from damming the Missouri River.

The protests, mostly by Native Americans, to stop that last bit of pipeline have been effective so far.

The most pressing environmental danger is the possibility of a break in the pipeline – similar to what happened in Kalamazoo, Michigan. If it did break, the waters of the Missouri could be polluted for hundreds of miles, perhaps even all the way down the Mississippi to the Gulf of Mexico. Anyone living downstream of the DAPL could lose their only water source.

News accounts about the DAPL have made the connections between the pipeline company and many big-time financial backers. But as noted in the newspapers in the Clarion News Syndicate, DeVille Energy Federation's pipeline project (known colloquially as The Devil's Pipeline) may be somehow linked to the DAPL – and even the Keystone XL pipeline – if either (or both) are approved by the next president.

DEF, as noted in the story, says the pipeline it's constructing is mostly dedicated to getting water to thirsty California. But the plans made public by DEF months ago are clear.

If the company wants to shift the entire capacity of the various pipelines contained inside the larger structure to other uses – like transiting crude oil, tar sands oil or other petroleum products, it can easily do so.

And The Devil's Pipeline would potentially have more carrying capacity than the Keystone XL and the DAPL combined – by a factor of four or five.

Although DEF is keeping most of its pipeline plans secret, the wrongful death trial just started in Iowa promises to put DeVille Energy Federation – and its president and founder Archimedes Gabriel DeVille – under an oath-sworn microscope.

Let's hope both presidential candidates are paying attention, too.

Jack Stafford is the publisher and editor in chief of the Clarion Newspaper Syndicate. He publishes Column One every Friday and can be reached at JJStafford@ClarionNewsSyndicate.com

Chapter 10

Three's a charm, Rod Mayenlyn thought, waiting in a coffee shop for Marsden Weesley to lurch in.

First I worked for that maniac Delacroix, then Burnside and now DeVille. If I get out of this alive, I'm retiring.

Retiring *now* was out of the question for Mayenlyn, even though he had stashed money here and there through his years working for GES. *DeVille will want me closer than ever now*, he thought.

Mayenlyn's stomach started roiling as if he had filled it with under-cooked, oily fish.

I don't even know what burning flesh smells like, he thought. But it didn't matter. The odor of anything being cooked took him back to DeVille's long gruesome and graphic tale about the deaths in the orphanage fire that burned the structure to the ground.

"We can't have Stafford and his group digging up things about that," DeVille had said. "You and Mars need to shut him down on this. And I mean *now*."

Mayenlyn smiled at the waitress who brought his coffee. As she put down the cup, she was looking over his shoulder, her mouth hanging slightly open.

Mars must be here, Mayenlyn thought. Then he heard the slight wheezing sound that usually preceded Mars' arrival.

Now I know why he wheezes, even after all these years, Mayenlyn thought.

Lung damage from smoke inhalation.

Chapter 11

The editors' meeting was getting more contentious than normal, Jack thought.

Keith had arrived in Iowa at *The Redoubt* exhausted, but insisted on sitting in on the videoconference with Eli and Alexandra.

Keith said his time in the North Dakota jail had given him some time to think, unfettered by non-stop electronics and news. A half-dozen local Pennsylvania stories that needed chasing had come to mind, he said.

Eli – normally quite placid in these meetings – was staunchly advocating for more coverage of the presidential election in all three newspapers, a shift that meant backing off on some local reporting.

"There is something wrong with the polls," Eli insisted. "Everyone is so goddamn sure Clinton is going to coast to a win they have blinders on. Make that blindfolds. They're wrong. Trump may win."

As he spoke his voice jumped an octave, too.

That's a sure sign how upset he is, Jack thought. *And how sure he is of his research.*

The Redoubt side of the three-way video conference was in Jack's just-reclaimed bedroom office upstairs in the rambling Osmett farmhouse filled with Jack, Cass, Sheode, Janis Osmett, Caleb, attorney Jerome Wooster Stone – and now Keith, all working on some aspect of the wrongful death suit.

Jack leaned forward to listen more closely as Alexandra and Keith tried unsuccessfully to argue with Eli against the need to pay more attention to the national politics.

"Eli, I'm seeing the same things and hearing the same paranoia," Alexandra said. "But honestly, Donald Trump? I think we need to stick with our local stories and keep focused on the energy issues and pipeline stuff. I mean, Jesus, Eli, look at what's going on at Standing Rock!"

Often when the editors started banging this hard on one another about coverage, Jack would step in to referee. As owner/publisher of all three newspapers, he could veto – or order – anything he wanted. But preferred to let them sort it out.

Today however, the more he listened, the more concerned he got – not about the increasing level of vitriol – "Don't be an ass," Keith had just barked at Eli – but about Eli's stubbornness.

The slight time delays and minor technical glitches were probably exacerbating the tension, Jack thought. "OK! OK! That's it! Time out!" he said.

The editors all stopped talking.

"We have a lot on our respective plates. And especially with Eli running both the *Clarion* and the *Tribune*. So we all need to dial it back a notch. OK?

"Here's what I want. I want to stay the course with our coverage patterns and stories. With this wrongful death suit and the pipeline stuff, we are stretched. I get it. But I've known Eli longer than you two. And if he says there's something going on here, well, he could be right."

None of the editors spoke.

"Eli, you didn't pluck this Trump winning idea out of the sky. I've seen some stuff on it, too. But it all seems to be sketchy without much evidence. Pull together a case about this, so we have something more concrete to work with."

Eli was already typing as Jack finished.

"That's fair," Eli said. "I should have done that first. It's just, well, you're right about being swamped."

Eli hit the keys a few more times. Suddenly, where his image had been a document with a cover that said "Election 2016 Upset" popped up in its place.

"Jack, remember that old 1960s-era movie *The Graduate*?" Eli said. "And the line about how the future could be summed up in one word? Plastics? I'll send this to everybody so you can all read it. But I have just one word about this election.

"Psychographics."

Chapter 12

Alexandra was puzzled as she stared at her computer screen.

The Medusa graphic that Eli had created months before was swirling in front of her.

How does he find the time to do this stuff? she thought.

What grabbed her attention at the moment were the planned segments of The Devil's Pipeline, represented by a bold blue line from Michigan to the southwestern U.S. and California.

It also had tentacles running north and south mid-nation at various spots where Alexandra was pretty sure the DeVille Energy Federation – or one of its subsidiaries – had negotiated to take over water rights.

Bastards, she thought. *They say they are going to take Great Lakes water for California but they're going to suck the middle of America dry, if it's more convenient. Or more profitable.*

She clicked on the icon to show bright yellow "Construction in Progress" projects that quickly illuminated pipelines large and small across the nation.

But The Devil's Pipeline route showed up in a light gray, without a single hint of yellow anywhere along its possible tortuous national route.

At first Alexandra thought it was likely Eli hadn't updated the graphic, until she remembered that he had linked it to public agencies and their databases, all required by law to keep track of energy project progress.

The graphic automatically picked up on their online reports, updating the information. If they were up to date, so was the interactive graphic.

It was possible they were holding back on updating their databases, she thought – perhaps even part of the national security paranoia that she and Jack had talked about.

But it was equally possible that there wasn't any actual construction going on yet, just ongoing right-of-way purchases (or property being seized through the eminent domain process).

She made a note to have someone contact DEF directly to ask about the lack of progress.

As if they would talk to us, she thought. She had burned her bridge with DEF on her last contact with Rod Mayenlyn, asking about Judge Roy Bean's connection to the orphanage where A.G. DeVille had grown up.

The conversation had gone fine until Amanda asked what Mayenlyn knew about the fire that destroyed the orphanage weeks after DeVille had left for college.

Mayenlyn said DeVille knew nothing about the fire or the arsonist who set it.

Who said it was arson? she thought. *Did I miss something?*

Chapter 13

A.G. DeVille was having trouble breathing again, particularly when he first woke up each morning.

For nearly a week, he'd been having dreams again of boys approaching his bed at night, mixed up with his inability to move, prompting a helpless dread and nightmarish struggle. In the background, he would see big people, all men.

And it felt as if they were sitting on his chest crushing him. And when he awoke he was in a full sweat. Sometimes there were flames in his dreams, too, flames so real he would get out of bed half-asleep to look around to see if his bedroom was on fire.

His new secretary, way too chipper and familiar for DeVille's taste, had commented this morning that he looked, well, a little tired as she inquired about how well he slept.

Had A.G. DeVille been the kind of man who would talk with a psychologist, he would have known his dreams and breathing troubles were all tied up with forces outside of his control, slowly drawing a political and legal noose around his life, present and past.

But DeVille had no intention of talking to anyone about his dreams, the breathing difficulty or the federal government's increasing questions about the pipeline project.

Instead, he brooded about Jack Stafford and Stafford's newspapers that were ramping up their coverage and criticism of the pipeline while most other media were too busy chasing the national elections to pay anything but passing attention to DEF.

A wire service story prompted a call from a federal energy official, asking for an update on the DEF pipeline's progress.

The official's arrogant tone angered him more than the questions.

The story also ran in all three Clarion News Syndicate newspapers.

Extremely wet winter ahead for California and west

The story detailed an analysis by a well-known national weather prognosticator who predicted California and the West Coast of the U.S. were going to get a record – or near-record – amount of rainfall in the winter, raising questions about the need for the DeVille project as envisioned.

It quoted several environmental groups and water providers saying that less-expensive, less-intrusive projects could provide the same volume of water, particularly considering how much water DeVille proposed taking from sources in the Midwest, especially the Ogallala Aquifer.

The story also included information DeVille thought had been hidden about the water rights DEF had secured in Nebraska and other more western states and quoted experts saying the water DEF had rights to in the Midwest was more than enough to keep the proposed pipeline running at full capacity without drawing a drop of Great Lakes water.

But what angered DeVille the most was the breathless revelation that the actual *construction* of the pipeline had not started anywhere along the entire route.

His anger was compounded as newspapers and other media across the country picked up the story. He sat steaming in his office, then took a deep breath and called Mayenlyn on the secure phone.

Chapter 14

The Iowa courtroom of Judge Bean was packed again, a fact that Bean didn't mind, except each time the audience gasped so loudly he had bang his gavel to maintain order.

Plus, it was a little unnerving having television cameras trained on him so much.

But he had been convinced by Jack Stafford it was a good idea to allow video media access – at least for limited parts of the proceedings.

The early testimony so far – much of it talking about the 1970 Kent State shootings – had been historically fascinating. But Bean was getting tired of listening to the near-constant objections of the DEF attorneys.

The morning newspapers had reported that he snapped sharply at one DEF attorney the day before, calling the him "Counselor Jack-In-the-Box" after he stood to object for the third time in less than five minutes.

Mercifully the television cameras missed that moment – or simply chose not to air it in their short evening news summaries.

Today when Bean had arrived at the courthouse, he told the bailiff to summon the DEF attorneys as well as Jerome Wooster Stone into his chambers the minute they showed up.

Bean had noted the nine jurors (eight seated on the panel plus one alternate) had arrived just as he did, including one white-haired woman who gaily waved at him as she shouted "Mornin' yer honor! Let's hand out some justice today."

Stone had arrived a full 40 minutes early before court for the third day in a row, a trait which Bean admired.

The DEF attorneys dragged in only a few minutes before it was time to convene court, all looking slightly bleary eyed, no doubt from pounding down drinks at their hotel bar.

The hotel owner, a fly-fishing pal of Bean's, had offered up that bit of intel along with the fact that the DEF attorneys drank the most expensive vodka he carried.

Russian, Bean remembered.

Bean hated delaying the start of the trial mostly because the media would speculate on why there was a pre-hearing conference and, in all likelihood, get it flat wrong, speculating about a mistrial or some other notion.

He decided to let his secretary leak the reason – maybe to the young Native American-looking woman who worked for Jack Stafford. She had been as aggressive – but also professional – as many of the major media players who were sitting in on the trial. *Plus she gets it right*, Bean thought.

*****

"Counselors, we need to move ahead here today," Bean said, looking at the lawyers. He was seated at his in-chambers desk adjacent to the court, while Wooster was seated in the comfortable chair Bean like to perch in to read.

When the DEF team straggled in, they gasped when they realized that Stone and judge had been talking.

"Don't worry gentlemen. Mr. Stone and I were swapping tales about fly fishing, not your case," Bean said.

After some preliminaries, Bean stood up and put on his robe. The DEF attorneys had come in without even stopping at their table and were still toting massive binders they had been bringing into court each day.

"Mr. Stone has to start wrapping up his Kent State history lesson and the tie-in to this case. And you on the DeVille Energy Federation team need to stay in your seats unless it's an absolutely major issue," Bean said. "These objections are not endearing you to the jury and *certainly* not me. I know DEF doesn't want to be connected even *existentially* to the Kent State massacre. But it's a fact of life. Or in this case, a fact of death because of who your security guards killed. Are we clear on this?"

The DEF attorneys all nodded uneasily. But Bean noticed several sideways smirks as they filed out blocking the doorway so that Jerome Wooster Stone had to be last out into the courtroom,

Smug bastards, Bean thought. *Wait until they find out Stone is going to subpoena A.G. DeVille to testify.*

Chapter 15

When Eli analyzed data of any kind, his mental image was often a funnel.

The various bits of information would swirl around the rim, gradually going down, intermixing until they reached the bottom, spilling out in a concentrated form. It was a good way to envision computer searches, political events and even history.

And Iowa is drawing everyone and everything in like a swirling black hole in space, he thought.

Since convincing the other two *Clarion Newspaper Syndicate* editors to run a daily "Trump Watch" section on their websites – and devote at least a half-page to polling data and reports – Eli had shifted more of his attention to The Devil's Pipeline, the wrongful death lawsuit, and the early life story of A.G. DeVille.

The revelation that construction hadn't started on the pipeline was news, but got mostly lost in amid the national election coverage. Plus, even if the water transit element was removed from the pipeline, the carrying capacity for oil, gas, propane, gasoline – and even defense material – remained.

The wrongful death suit was moving along and looked like a slam dunk.

The most perplexing part of that case for Eli was why DEF had made a wildly high settlement offer. Equally perplexing was Jack's information that the county DA was using Caleb's gun arrest as leverage, trying to get Janis and the other *Redoubt* plaintiffs to *agree* to a settlement.

The county can't care if DEF's case moves forward, Eli thought. *Or even if the jury turned in some historic dollar judgment. It's not the county's money.*

He flipped to the email Alexandra had sent about Judge Bean and how his grandparents had donated the property and building that had been used as an orphanage and was A.G. DeVille's childhood home.

They had donated it years before Bean had been born.

Alex had done an excellent job of pulling every thread on DeVille's official bio.

Except for his quick rise through the ranks of the energy industry, his life was pretty unremarkable. His bio detailed a classic workaholic financial genius who was devoted to his work building DEF into a world energy powerhouse. It also mentioned that he never married.

Eli noted that Alexandra hadn't found any speculation that DeVille might be gay, even on websites that trolled the energy industry, often making wild, hurtful accusations just to take a mean shot at the rich and powerful.

Among Alex's online documents were some digital copies of photos that had been published of the fire at the orphanage. She had contacted the owner of the long-shuttered newspaper that ran them and was able to get copies of nearly two dozen photos that had not been published.

She also got a copy of the one story the newspaper ran in which authorities speculated the blaze might have been arson.

The owner had also been the editor of the paper and that night had run out to shoot the photos while the newspaper's only photographer was sleeping off an afternoon of too much beer at a hops festival.

The night shots – taken while the structure still blazed – were the most graphic. But the photos taken the next morning showed the skeleton of the wood structure in the center, a huge building (for Iowa) that a century before had been a hospital.

The building – what was left of it anyway – grabbed the eye. But years of shooting photos himself had taught Eli to look carefully around the edges of any photo for details that might not be as dramatic as what the photographer was trying to illustrate.

Off to the right, well away from the fireman, blaze survivors, police and a small knot of rubberneckers, Eli saw someone standing alongside some kind of outbuilding – like a garden shed.

He zoomed in, enhancing the photo as much as possible.

Then he blew it up to full screen size on his biggest monitor.

The photo was grainy. But Eli could make out the images of a gasoline-powered lawn mower and fuel can next to the shed.

It also showed a very large person facing away from the camera and towards the smoldering ruin.

Eli dashed off a quick group message to Jack, Keith and Alexandra.

I think I found Lurch.

Chapter 16

Calvin Boviné wasn't particularly pleased to find out he was going to get subpoenaed to testify in the wrongful death trial in Iowa.

But Keith had convinced him – in a long telephone conversation – to leave his retreat house/monastery to testify. "And the subpoena makes it look like you are doing it under duress," Keith said. "Otherwise the attorneys for DeVille will paint you as some kind of traitor or disgruntled former employee."

Boviné pointed out that in fact he was technically *still* part of DEF with his name on various documents, mostly dealing with the acquisition of water rights. "But you're right. I *am* disgruntled," he said.

Keith tried not to laugh, not so much because of the disgruntled comment, but because Calvin actually *growled* the word disgruntled.

After his brief stay in Williston, protecting Keith's friend Wally, the security guards at the hospital said they would watch Wally's room allowing Calvin to retreat to the monastery where he had taken up residence before. It helped him center himself and keep his explosive temper in check. He knew that if he ran into Mayenlyn again in Williston – after Mayenlyn had backed into him with the car – he would probably snap Mayenlyn's neck.

While Calvin was willing to testify about all the DEF dealings – many of them illegal and unethical – just thinking about doing so raised his blood pressure and started adrenalin surging in uncomfortable ways.

He also dreaded telling the head of the monastery he was leaving again. The man exuded calm and patience but made it clear when Calvin had arrived this time that he needed to make a commitment to the place and the spirit of what the monastery meant. "This is not a motel you check in and out of," he had said with uncharacteristic sternness. "Buddha understands. But many people would like to seek him here. You must make a decision."

As he packed his few belongings for the trip, he knew he wouldn't be coming back.

That realization made him feel sad and angry, just the way it had before his prison cellmate had gifted him with the notions of Buddhism and meditation.

His primal howl was heard all through the building.

Chapter 17

The Clarion Newspaper Syndicate
Column One

Justice and a dropped charge

By Jack Stafford

A few days ago criminal charges against 17-year-old Caleb Osmett were dropped in Iowa. If Caleb's name seems familiar, it should be.

He is the grandson of the late James Albert Osmett, gunned down at his rural Iowa homestead a little more than a year ago.

The name Osmett has been all over the news because of the wrongful death lawsuit filed by the family over James' death and the death of three other people at the farm and sanctuary known as The Redoubt in ultra-rural Iowa.

Caleb witnessed his grandfather's shooting death at the hands of agents working for the DeVille Energy Federation.

In the ensuing weeks and months afterwards, Caleb made a bad judgment call that resulted in his being arrested. When security guards came to The Redoubt some time after the shooting, Caleb stole a backpack containing a gun belonging to a security guard and at one point he had it – loaded – in his hand when he saw another DEF employee on The Redoubt property.

After a long bit of deliberation and reviewing a counselor's report on Caleb's state of mind, District Attorney Gil Understipe opted to drop the charges "in the interest of justice."

Understipe said he was convinced that Caleb's actions were simply the result of the awful trauma he had suffered. And the fact that he had grown up in a totally weapon-free environment added to the decision to simply close the case.

It is as good – and just – an ending to this small part of the saga as could be expected.

Understipe is the same district attorney who ruled more than a year ago that there was no basis for criminal charges against the DEF security guards who opened fire on a group of Redoubt residents when the people stood – on their private property – in protest of DEF's wanting to survey the land.

The DA ruled that the shooting – while tragic – was an accident, a result of poorly trained security guards who were spooked by concerns that The Redoubt residents might be armed.

That ruling seemed eminently unjust to young Caleb – as well as many to other residents of The Redoubt.

The dropping of the charges removes a distraction for jurors as the wrongful death civil lawsuit continues under the eye of Judge Roy Bean.

Attorneys for DEF had made it clear they were going subpoena Caleb to testify. Their aim was to show that there was a reasonable expectation by security guards they might have been met with force on the day of the shooting.

They withdrew the subpoena, realizing that Caleb and his youthful mistake might actually add fuel to their contention about how distressing the entire episode has been to the peaceful people of The Redoubt.

The DEF attorneys will still get to hear Caleb's take on that October day.

He is now scheduled to testify – but as a witness for the plaintiffs, his family and the other residents of The Redoubt.

Jack Stafford is the publisher and editor in chief of the Clarion Newspaper Syndicate. He publishes Column One every Friday and can be reached at JJStafford@ClarionNewsSyndicate.com

Chapter 18

The expression on Archimedes Gabriel DeVille's face was so contorted Rod Mayenlyn hesitated to even blink, in case any movement on his part would send DeVille into another paroxysm of rage.

DeVille was staring at the center of his desk where a subpoena – requiring his presence in an Iowa courtroom in just a few days – sat like a grenade.

DeVille's recently hired secretary had been escorted out of the building earlier that morning – *a little roughly* Mayenlyn thought – after she had ushered a well-dressed man into DeVille's office who had charmed the secretary and presented himself as an old friend of DeVille's from the orphanage where DeVille had grown up.

He said wanted to surprise DeVille, which he did – by slapping the subpoena on his desk.

Frantic phone calls to several of the dozens of DEF attorneys on retainer in New York, Houston – and even the lawyers on the ground in Iowa – all came back with the same legal advice. DeVille needed to show up in Iowa and be ready to testify. And even a short delay was highly unlikely.

"The Iowa boys said the judge won't let me out of this. Given how little sway they seem to have, appealing probably won't work either," DeVille said, still staring at the subpoena.

Christ, he's actually hissing when he talks, Mayenlyn thought. *Sounds like a snake ready to strike.*

DeVille's eyes seemed sunk back in his head and his face drooped. To Mayenlyn's eye, DeVille's slender frame seemed to have grown nearly skeletal since the trial started and the media had started poking around into the fire at the orphanage.

And in the last week Jack Stafford's newspapers had run several stories about The Devil's Pipeline, all opining that it was in serious trouble and hinting that there was something odd about the financing, too. An anonymous federal government source said there were questions being raised in Congress about apparent off-the-books appropriations.

Several sources claimed that the federal government was actually withdrawing its support *entirely*.

DeVille looked from side to side, up and down, twisting his neck like someone with a bad cramp. He began to shift his jaws from side to side, too, in between bouts of clamping them tightly shut.

He looks like a dog about to attack, Mayenlyn thought.

"I want you to go to Iowa with me," DeVille said. Mayenlyn shifted in his chair. "What should I tell Mars?" Mayenlyn asked.

The look on DeVille's face told Mayenlyn to stop talking.

Chapter 19

The cellphone in the plastic bag sat in the center of the dining room table where Jerome Wooster Stone, Jack Stafford and Sheode Walker sat surrounded by stacks of legal files around them.

Only a single light was on over the table while several kerosene lamps dimly lit the rest of the room.

It was late enough that the rest of the house had been tucked in bed for several hours. The house was filled to overflowing now, including two young female paralegals sleeping in a tiny top-floor room just below the cupola.

Jack had convinced Stone to hire the legal help the week before as the paper burden mounted in the case.

Cass had left early that morning to catch a flight back to Vashon Island and Noah. She was replaced at lunchtime by Calvin Boviné who showed up in anticipation of his court appearance.

Calvin's occasional snores from his upstairs room were loud enough to draw laughs around the table.

"The key to winning the case is right there," Stone said, pointing his finger at the cellphone.

Jack reached over and slid the phone out of the plastic bag, touching it gingerly like someone holding an antique.

"The data is all backed up from this, right?" Jack asked. "I'm sorry, I've asked you that three times already today probably. I'm just spooked something will happen to it."

Stone smiled and shook his head, holding up a shiny silver digital recorder. "Jack, I told you before I made a quick digital copy as soon as I heard the recording on the phone. Then I had a second, professional audio copy made at the county seat with two witnesses and a notary listening.

"Like I said before, the notary said she doesn't like the DeVille Energy Federation's tactics around here. I asked her to keep this confidential. The witnesses were from here at *The Redoubt*. And the sound engineer who did the transfer in front of the notary seems like a standup guy, too.

"But you're right to handle the phone gently. That's the *actual* evidence. And I need it to work in court."

Sheode reached over and took the phone from Jack's hand, turning it over gently. It still had tiny smudges of mud on it, remnants from the day that it was in the hand of the 25-year old victim killed in the hail of bullets that had also killed James Osmett and two women.

The phone had had the video recording function turned on. But the two-minute recording only showed the ground and sometimes the legs of other people out that morning in front of *The Redoubt*.

"You think he had it turned on accidentally, right?" Sheode asked. "Maybe he meant to take still photos and turned on video by mistake."

Jerome reached over and took the phone from Sheode's hand.

"We'll probably never know. But it doesn't matter. The phone was new, bought just a week before in Boyette. It's always puzzled me that none of the other people here had any electronic recording of that morning."

Jack laughed. "No puzzle there. Cell phone service is so bad out here most people don't have them. There's a little anti-tech thinking, too. James Osmett wasn't keen on much that the 21st century had to offer when it came to technology."

Sheode yawned, prompting Jack and Stone to both blink back their fatigue but she pointed at Stone's digital recorder and put her hands together as if to say *please*.

"OK, *one* more time," Stone said. "But I have to get some sleep. I'm going to give DEF a heads up tomorrow and enter this into evidence."

The already quiet dining room seemed to get even quieter as Stone pushed the play button.

The sound recording was from the telephone of one of October 2015 shooting victims at *The Redoubt* and had been mistakenly locked in an evidence locker at the county sheriff's department until discovered a week ago. Because the victim had no local family, no one had thought to recover the few belongings the sheriff's department had picked up that day. When it was returned to the *The Redoubt*, Janis had discovered the data.

At the beginning of the recording, the voices of *The Redoubt* residents shouting at the DEF survey team and guards, telling them to stay off the property were loud, overshadowed after a minute or so by an amplified voice.

"Enough of your shouting, you people. Enough! We have the legal right to come on this property. Move it now. All of you. God damn it. I said move it. Move it right NOW."

The voices of *The Redoubt* residents receded to just a few low voices, saying "watch out… they're pointing their guns… They've cut through the fence. They're coming in… God!!! …"

In quick succession a voice Jerome Wooster Stone would say in court belonged to James Osmett could be clearly heard saying "Back up everyone. Back up, now."

Then another voice came across at a slightly lower volume, as if the person was standing farther away.

Stone would argue in court that the voice belonged to the person who had used a bullhorn a moment before.

"Goddamn them," the voice said. "Goddamn them. Fire over their heads and scatter them."

Chapter 20

The notary Jerome Wooster Stone thought was a solid citizen unfortunately was also one of the biggest gossips in Boyette County.

And knowing that the plaintiffs in the wrongful death lawsuit had obtained a piece of evidence *so* damning was just too delicious for her not to tell her sister, though she made her sister promise she wouldn't say a *word* until after it showed up in the local newspaper.

That gossipy-sibling pact might have been sufficient, except that her sister's husband whom her sister just *had* to tell had a hunting-fishing-drinking buddy who worked as a line supervisor for DeVille Energy Federation and was likely to be dragged in to testify in court in the lawsuit.

When the DEF supervisor-buddy heard the news over a beer, he was pretty sure giving his boss a heads-up about the recording would mean a promotion, pay hike and maybe a new company truck to sport around in.

Chapter 21

For such a big man, it was surprising how catlike Mars moved across the field approaching the old farmhouse of *The Redoubt* even hefting two containers – one filled with gasoline, the other with diesel fuel he siphoned from a tractor.

He had driven all day from Chicago in a 10-year-old, well-worn sedan a DEF employee left for him in a parking garage at the airport. He'd made it a point to ask the parking attendant for directions to Milwaukee where he said he had business.

The drive had been uneventful with successful diversions in small towns along the way to collect what he needed. An abandoned farm just across the Iowa border from Indiana provided two fuel containers. He found a baseball cap with the logo of a tractor company in the bathroom at a rest area. It shielded much of his face when he went through fast-food restaurant drive-up windows – his only food stops.

Mars couldn't believe his luck when he spied a clothesline at a remote house only 100 miles from *The Redoubt* that sported a pair of huge workman's coveralls and some other clothing in his size.

Arriving near *The Redoubt*, he had walked several miles from a copse of trees where he parked the car in a pullout hidden from the main road, well away from *The Redoubt's* main gate. He still tasted gasoline and diesel, spitting quietly every few minutes. Siphoning had proven difficult. *Out of practice*, he thought.

He put down the cans for moment while he scratched his face. His month's worth of beard growth was really itchy, but he knew it would help camouflage his very recognizable visage, though not his size.

The Iowa license plates on the car were a trophy from a dust-covered sedan in a run-down section of Des Moines. It looked like no one had touched the vehicle in months.

In a final maneuver to deflect attention, Mars let some of the air out of a rear tire and leaned a jack next to it in case anyone drove by. He knew the electric air canister in the trunk would get him back on the road quickly if needed when he was finished.

It had been five years since A.G. DeVille had last asked Mars to do him one of their shared *big-secret* favors like this.

Mars didn't count going to Williston to rough up the little weasel that was giving away company secrets or the waitress who had documents she found in the restaurant as *big-secret* favors. He was still unhappy Mayenlyn wouldn't let him do anything more to the woman than frighten her.

But this! This is a real favor, Mars thought.

As he approached the house, Mars checked the wind, shifting his path to ensure that he was coming from downwind. He had been told there were no dogs living at the main house on the property but he didn't want to take any chances. Mars hated dogs, a feeling that was usually mutual.

The wind was strong and gusty enough that any sound he made walking towards the large wood-frame house was unlikely to be heard, he thought. And the tiny sliver of moon moving across the sky wasn't enough to give him away, either.

Mars stopped 200 yards from the house and knelt down to look around. The house was dark. No lights were showing. He spotted a barbecue next to the side porch with two propane tanks – filled he hoped – sitting on the ground next to it. *Perfect*, he thought.

He was ready, except for one final detail. *Where should I watch from?* he wondered.

Chapter 22

The first wisp of smoke tickled Calvin Boviné's nose enough to elicit a long snort that sounded more buffalo than human.

It was just loud enough to rouse Jack, sleeping fitfully in a second-story bedroom across the hall. It also pulled Keith Everlight out of dream in which he was winning a welterweight boxing match, as he had often done a decade before.

Keith was bunking with Jerome Wooster Stone across the hall from Jack.

On the third floor, Sheode, Janis, and Caleb were conked out in different rooms. Everyone – except Calvin – had closed their doors and windows tightly to cut down on drafts from the late fall winds.

Keith shook awake, groggy and grumpy. When he was a high school student, his mother had sometimes used a broom handle to poke him from a safe distance to wake him so as to avoid the half-awake punches he would sometimes throw.

The dream about boxing had left him in a combative and defensive state of mind.

As the haze of sleep lifted, his combativeness kicked in intensely as he sniffed the air.

A floor above, Caleb rolled over at the same moment, thinking he smelled a trace of smoke.

Tiny wafts of smoke odors were not unusual around *The Redoubt*, particularly in the fall when brush was burned and fireplaces and woodstoves were put into service for heat.

Caleb could see out his window, remembering there had been a pile of burning brush earlier that day across the field. *Crap, I hope it's not flaring up,* he thought.

He had just swung his legs over the side of the bed when he heard simultaneous *whooshing* sounds from several directions followed by shouting.

"Fire, fire!" Janis Osmett shrieked. "Fire! Everyone out. Fire, fire!"

Chapter 23

As Keith Everlight ran down the staircase to the first floor, he saw that the front door and porch were engulfed in flames.

He turned and looked through to the kitchen where flames were already framing the door leading to the back porch – the other exit from the downstairs.

The heat was already intense.

Flames were visible through nearly every window as half-clad people came tumbling down the stairs.

Jerome Wooster Stone and Jack stopped Keith just as he was about to open a window on the side of house where it looked like the flames were less intense.

"Wait until everyone is here," Jack said. When you open that window it might fan the flames. Get towels, blankets, and wet everything – quick!"

Within moments everyone downstairs was dousing themselves with water and wrapping themselves in something soaked before they made a break to escape through a window.

The flames were building quickly, prompting Keith to declare they had to go *now!*

Jack and Jerome readied a thoroughly soaked quilt to throw over the window ledge – hopefully to dampen the flames as people piled out the only safe exit.

"We're going to pop the window and go out as fast as we can," Jack said. "Tie those wet towels over your faces so you don't inhale the smoke. And when you hit the ground, roll and then run away from the house fast. Don't stop."

Janis pushed the two young female paralegals to the front of the group. She stopped and looked around wildly. "Caleb!" she shouted. "Caleb. Oh my God! Where is Caleb?"

Jack grabbed Janis to keep her from running back up the stairs just as they heard *The Redoubt's* alarm bell ringing loudly from the cupola at the top the house.

A moment later two explosions rocked the house – front then back – as the strategically placed propane canisters blew up.

Chapter 24

In the days after the fire at *The Redoubt*, the survivors credited quick thinking on the part of Jack, Keith and Jerome Wooster Stone for getting everyone out of house.

They were also very thankful to Calvin Boviné for carrying out the two terrified paralegals out through the window.

And they all thanked the late James Albert Osmett for his lifelong dislike of plastic and fear of conflagration.

When Osmett had finally been convinced to replace the century-old wood siding on the farmhouse several decades before he died, he opted to sheath the house from the ground to the roof in long-past state-of-the-art aluminum siding, with a high-tech fire-retardant insulation sandwiched between the siding and the wood framing.

"My dad saved our lives with that choice," Janis was quoted in news reports.

The remains of the house had finally stopped smoking two days later as state arson investigators packed up their gear and ended their on-site investigation.

The arson team gave Janis, Jack and Caleb permission to cautiously sift through the remains of the rubble.

Caleb had rung the bell repeatedly the night of the blaze until he saw people streaming towards the farmhouse from every direction. Then as the flames grew, he grabbed a coil of rope he and his grandfather had tied off to a sturdy rooftop post years before and slid down to the ground below.

"He called it an 'Indian fire escape rope'," Caleb told investigators. He had hit the ground hard, banging his head in the process after he pushed himself out away from the house and then dropped the last 10 feet to the ground.

When he was taken to the hospital doctors said he had probably suffered a mild concussion in the fall.

He told the police he couldn't remember much.

The arson investigators had found the bell that had stood atop the farmhouse that Caleb had rung to bring the community running. It was blackened from the fire but repairable.

They had put the bell in a wheelbarrow, so Caleb could to move the bell farther away from the wreckage. He had gone about 100 feet when he stopped suddenly.

"Bigfoot," Caleb said. Then he said it again.

"Bigfoot."

He put down the wheelbarrow handles and pointed across to a grove of trees near the gate where James Albert Osmett had been gunned down with three other people.

"That night. When I was ringing the bell. I saw someone standing there. Everyone else was running towards the house. But he was like a shadow. He didn't move. I remember thinking *Bigfoot*," Caleb said.

He leaned on his mother for support.

"Caleb, let's find a place for you to sit down," Jack said. "You need to tell that to the arson investigators."

While Caleb and Janis walked towards a downed tree for Caleb sit down and recover, Jack looked off into the distance where Caleb had pointed.

Not Bigfoot, Caleb, Jack thought. *More like* Lurch.

Chapter 25

A motion by DEF attorneys to reconvene the wrongful death civil trial – after a four-day delay – was quickly dismissed by Judge Bean.

"I understand the defendant corporation's position in this. But given that the lead attorney and several of the plaintiffs were the target of what appears to be an attack designed to kill them, I'm inclined to let the case simmer for another week," Bean said.

"Sorry, that was an inconsiderate verb, given the circumstances."

He made his announcement in open court with the jury seated in the jury box, after listening to brief oral arguments made by DEF attorneys and by Jerome Wooster Stone.

The DEF attorneys objected to the jury being seated, an objection that Bean quickly overruled. "In this case, these good people need to understand why we are going to delay resuming the trial and keep them waiting," Bean said.

The well-coiffed DEF attorneys were a stark contrast to Stone, who had picked up a less-than-fashionable, off-the-rack suit at Boyette's only menswear store. His whole traveling wardrobe had gone up in farmhouse flames. Bean noted that Jack Stafford looked like he had shopped at the same place.

The courtroom was packed with a mélange of local residents, media and a smattering of law enforcement officials, including District Attorney Gil Understipe.

When Understipe had slipped into the back of the courtroom shortly after Bean took the bench, he shot the judge a smile and raised his eyebrows.

Well, well, Bean thought.

Chapter 26

Eli smiled as he read Jack's email. Eli had laid out the disaster-in-waiting that was lurking in the presidential race – and what it would mean for environmental politics.

> *ELI: Sorry that I haven't been attentive. But are you kidding? Trump? Jaysus. Really?*
> *I know some polls show him close. But they're on the fringe. I read your emails about psychographics and that analysis. I'm not too sure what to do exactly. I suppose we should do some more stories about what a disaster he would be for the environment – and a shill for the energy companies. That's already being covered, though nobody really thinks he'll win.*
> *Of course, nobody thought he would be nominated either. Kee-rist!*

> *Let's talk. Maybe a column might be in order. And thanks for keeping the whole outfit going through all this. You and Alexandra deserve raises. (And this email will destruct in five seconds! Hahahahaha*
> *JACK*

Eli started to draft a quick reply, then decided to hold off until he had a chance to check the off-the-books polling data he was being fed by someone close to the Trump campaign, a former contributor to the conservative Breitbart News website.

With only a week before the election, the letter to Congress about Clinton's emails from the director of the FBI had tipped the *off-the-radar* polling scales firmly over to Trump – though mainstream media reports on polls *still* weren't showing it as that close a race.

Eli was also getting information about a long-suspected Russian connection – and even interference – with the election.

That stuff is going to be written about for years, he thought.

After reviewing the polls one more time, he tapped out a quick response to Jack knowing he was probably still hunched over a keyboard, doing a draft of his next column.

> *Jack, I've been tracking the data more carefully since the FBI director threw his stink bomb. It's way worse than anyone thinks. There's also a big problem in all the down ticket races for any GOP opponents. A column is a great idea… Alexandra agrees. And yes, we both want raises! Eli*

Chapter 27

In his years on the bench, Judge Roy Bean had never had a conversation quite like this one. He, DA Gil Understipe and Jack Stafford were gathered in the judge's chambers early on a Saturday morning with the wrongful death civil trial set to resume Monday, the day before the nation would go to the polls and select the 45th President of the United States.

This feels like we are choreographing a stage play, Bean thought. *Maybe that's* exactly *what we* are *doing.*

"Judge, I just wanted you to have a heads up about everything that's going on in the background of all this," Understipe said. "And Jack and his people have done a lot of the research." Understipe looked over at Jack. "Okay. That's an understatement. If his editors and reporters hadn't dug so hard, we wouldn't be reopening this arson cold case."

Bean shifted in his chair, his mind fast-forwarding to the future when the wrongful death lawsuit and the criminal cases Understipe was laying out might come back to haunt him in some judicial review.

In Understipe's case, the DA was looking at using this to his political advantage in his upcoming re-election campaign.

If this all goes right, he could even run for governor, Bean thought. He laughed aloud at the thought.

"Um, Judge? What's funny?" Jack asked.

"Nothing Jack. Just politics. You either want to laugh or cry."

The trio talked for an hour about Monday's court hearing and the likely resumption of intense media coverage.

"With the fire declared an official arson and attempted murder, the courtroom will be packed to overflowing," Jack said.

"Agreed. But let's be clear. I'm happy to know the subplots that might be going on Monday – in and out of my courtroom," Bean said. "But we are going by the book while court is in session. Understood? What happens outside the doors is up to you gentlemen."

Chapter 28

The DeVille Energy Corporation's jet was waiting for A.G. DeVille and Rod Mayenlyn for the short flight from Houston to Iowa.

DeVille was beyond unhappy about having to testify. And the idea of a night in a Boyette, Iowa hotel made him cringe.

Mayenlyn knew that no excuse – short of dying – was going to keep him off the plane.

The two men were sitting in a DEF company limo, waiting for the flight staff to signal them to come aboard.

Since the fire Mayenlyn's stomach had blown out completely. And the last place on earth he wanted to go was anywhere near *The Redoubt*. *I've outlived two energy company maniacs*, he thought.

The fire at *The Redoubt* had Mars' fingerprints all over it as far as Mayenlyn was concerned. But Mayenlyn hadn't had any contact with Mars – not even a phone message – since before DeVille got the subpoena.

DeVille hadn't mentioned Mars since the subpoena came either. In fact, he calmly discussed *The Redoubt* as if it had nothing to do with, well, anything.

"I suspect this whole case might go away now," DeVille had said.

Jaysus, Mayenlyn thought. *We're flying right into a hurricane and he can't see it.*

Mayenlyn regretted not giving in to an urge earlier that day to grab his passport and leave the country. *I have enough money stashed. I should have done it.*

"Rod, are you ill?" DeVille asked. "You look like you have a touch of the flu or something?"

Mayenlyn looked over at DeVille and was even more terrified than before. DeVille never asked questions like that. *Ever.*

And suddenly Mayenlyn had the horrible thought that DeVille was going to throw him under the bus, for everything. There could be a record of the string of telephone calls – all on the secure DEF phones – between himself and Mars over the last few months.

"We need you healthy in Iowa," DeVille said.

Mayenlyn tried to smile as he wondered who the "we" was DeVille referred to.

Chapter 29

The atmosphere outside the courtroom wasn't nearly as crazy as expected.

A handful of national reporters *were* in a frenzy – but not about the wrongful death lawsuit about to reconvene with A.G. DeVille on the stand.

Instead, they were spending most of their time quizzing the Iowa residents about which presidential candidate they would be voting for the next day.

On his way into the building Jack Stafford heard several reporters muttering among themselves. "Have you found *anybody* voting for Clinton?"

Jack could tell from their expressions – and the preponderance of red baseball caps in the crowd emblazoned with "Make America Great Again" – that they had an uphill battle.

Two classically overweight deputies stood by the open courtroom doors, eyeballing people as they streamed in to grab a seat in the small room.

A third college-aged looking male deputy wearing stylish horn-rimmed eyeglasses sat at a security table down the hallway where he was looking at a large screen computer with a three-way split-screen video display. He was toggling back and forth, zooming in among images of the hallways, Judge Roy Bean's courtroom and a large auditorium where the county legislature held its meetings.

At Bean's order, it had been opened to the public. The proceedings were being streamed on two big-screen televisions in front.

At the moment, the young male deputy was far more interested in talking with Sheode Walker than what was happening on the screens in front of him as the courtroom doors were closing in anticipation of the judge exiting his chambers.

"So you actually worked in the tech industry in California, then, Deputy... *Ralf* is it?" Sheode said, straining to read his name badge.

"Actually, it's *Rolf*," the deputy said, grinning. "Old family name. And yeah, I went to college there and then worked. Came home when my dad died two years ago. The sheriff hired me to do this stuff."

With only the slightest of smiles and encouragement from Sheode, Deputy Rolf quickly found himself demonstrating the video system's bells and whistles.

"OK, there, see? That's the DeVille guy sitting with his attorneys up front," Rolf said, zooming in. "And there's the DA sitting right behind him. And next to him, isn't that your boss, Jack Stafford?"

Rolf turned slightly to look at Sheode.

"Hey, you're looking at the wrong part of the screen," he said. "This one is the courtroom. That one you're looking at is the overflow in the auditorium."

He shivered when Sheode put her hand on top of his hand holding the mouse, double clicking directly on the auditorium feed so it would fill the big monitor.

"Oh my God, I am sooooo sorry… I'm so embarrassed," she said removing her hand. "But could you zoom in towards the back of the auditorium? That row near the exit?

A blushing Deputy Rolf took a deep breath. "*Sure*. You see somebody you know?"

A moment later an image loomed up of a big man wearing coveralls slouched down in the end-of-the-row seat. He had on a ball cap with the logo of a tractor company shading much his face.

Sheode tried to mask her excitement but felt the blood rushing to her cheeks.

"You know that guy?" Rolf asked.

"Um, maybe," Sheode said. "Are there recordings or tapes from when he walked in I could see?"

She could tell she was pushing Rolf beyond his comfort zone.

"Deputy Rolf, I'm asking too much here. I'm sorry. I better be getting into court. Thanks for your help."

I'll go look myself, Sheode thought. *Then I'll tell Jack.*

Deputy Rolf watched Sheode walk off then took a close look at the row Sheode was so interested in, zooming in on the big guy with the ball cap.

Oh my God, he thought as he grabbed the phone to alert the Sheriff.

Chapter 30

Sitting at the front of the auditorium, Keith Everlight watched one of the big screens intently as Jerome Wooster Stone skillfully shifted from asking softball questions of A.G. DeVille to a rapid-fire series of questions, all accusations related to the fire at the orphanage where DeVille had grown up.

His performance drew an immediate volley of objections from the bank of DeVille Energy Federation attorneys packed in behind the DEF table.

Stone mostly spoke directly to the jury as he tried to present the connection between the orphanage fire and one that burned *The Redoubt* main farmhouse.

"Odd to have a second historical coincidence," Stone said, looking at the jury. "Isn't it, Mr. DeVille? First your employees are responsible for a shooting reminiscent of the Kent State massacre, then an arson so similar to the one that burned the orphanage where you grew up."

Bean banged his gavel hard as the objections continued to fly.

"All right Mr. Stone," Bean said. "All right. I've been giving you plenty of latitude here. But you're abusing it. Objection *sustained*. This case is to consider the deaths of four people in a shooting. The fire at *The Redoubt* and the one at the orphanage are *not* relevant.

"We listened patiently to your history lesson about Kent State. And I am distressed by the recent fire, too. But to draw a line between a fire from decades ago to this case is out of order."

Bean motioned for all the attorneys to approach the bench.

Keith watched the camera swivel away from Stone and the judge to pan the jury and the packed courtroom.

The camera stopped and hovered on Jack Stafford and District Attorney Gil Understipe who were pulling out their cell phones almost simultaneously.

Although cell phones were not normally allowed in court, Bean let them in them provided they didn't ring or disrupt the proceedings.

Keith cursed under his breath as the camera shifted away from the two men who were heading toward the courtroom's doors.

What's that all about? Keith wondered.

Just as he was getting ready to text Jack, he saw a message pop up from Sheode.

Look behind you. By the fire exit.

Chapter 31

People in the courtroom hallway later reported that when District Attorney Gil Understipe and Jack Stafford got to the courtroom door, they tried to squeeze through it at the same time, making them look like Black Friday shoppers battling to get to after-Thanksgiving Day bargains.

The image was reinforced as three broad-shouldered plainclothes sheriff's deputies pushed their way behind Understipe and Stafford. The deputies had received a text from Deputy Rolf at the same time as Understipe and Jack.

In the auditorium barely 100 yards away, Keith pushed himself up out of his seat so he could turn around to look for Sheode. He paused for a second to look at the television screen. The camera had panned back to the judge who was waving a finger at the attorneys.

Wish I could listen in on that *ass-kicking*, Keith thought, smiling. He was still smiling at that thought as he shifted his line of sight away from the courtroom scene to Sheode standing at the back of the auditorium. She was pointing to the far corner of the room where a bright red emergency exit sign hung above an equally brightly painted door with a panic bar affixed to it.

Keith remembered later thinking how his mother *always* said it was impolite to point.

He followed Sheode's extended arm and locked eyes with Marsden Weesley sitting in the outside seat in the row. His baseball cap was pulled down. His coveralls made him look like an oversized Iowa auto mechanic.

When Keith looked away and towards Sheode, Mars swiveled his head following Keith's.

He spotted Sheode pointing at him, recognizing her from the diner in Williston months before.

Sheode later told Jack the malevolent expression on Mars' face frightened her enough that she wanted to run. But instead she froze, even as she saw Mars rise up out of his seat.

She watched him burst through the emergency exit door to the outside, moving so fast she didn't even see him reach over and pull the courthouse complex fire alarm.

Chapter 32

In the hallway halfway between the courtroom of Judge Roy Bean and the auditorium, Calvin Boviné was perched alone on a bench, waiting to be called in to testify.

He had seen A.G. DeVille and Rod Mayenlyn walk in earlier that morning through the first floor entrance doors in front of where he was sitting.

Both men pretended not to see him as they marched by, surrounded by a phalanx of DEF attorneys.

As it was, Boviné was pretty sure that he might not have to testify at all.

Jack Stafford had told him that if things went according to the district attorney's plan, A.G. DeVille would be leaving the courthouse in handcuffs right after he testified.

Boviné closed his eyes and tried to meditate, suppressing the rage he'd felt when DeVille and Mayenlyn had walked by.

That's the old Calvin, he thought, remembering his lessons from the monastery.

He was just getting close to a familiar, almost-dream state when a shrill honking sound intruded, pulling him out of his reverie. An alarm, he thought, his eyes snapping open. Shit!

As he turned to his left, he saw Jack, three deputies and the district attorney headed towards him, followed by a flood of people pouring out of courtroom.

To his right, the auditorium's back doors had burst open with an equally impressive flood of people coming out, anxiously looking for an exit from the building.

The fire at the farmhouse has everybody spooked, he thought.

Boviné watched Stafford, the DA and the three deputies blow past him – barely noticing him sitting there.

As they reached the auditorium doors, they tried unsuccessfully to force their way past the mob of people streaming out. The two groups who were converging in front of Boviné all headed out the main doors.

He nearly missed seeing A.G. DeVille and Rod Mayenlyn sliding out. surrounded by their attorneys amid the dozens of people pushing and shoving.

Boviné smiled to himself as he stood up, watching DeVille's bobbing head as it went down the steps.

He's not going far without having a chat with me, he thought.

Chapter 33

The sidewalks around the county courthouse complex were overflowing. The crowd from the courtroom and the 150 or so people who had been in the auditorium accounted for about half the people who surged out of the building onto the sidewalk.

The rest were building inspectors, clerks, public health staff, unsworn sheriff's department employees, secretaries, probation officers and cleaning staff, most of whom took the fire alarm as nice break from their daily routines.

There were also a handful of volunteer election staff who had been getting their instructions on what to do the next day.

Mars had made it to the parking lot behind the courthouse, where he was able to stand out of sight behind a large county dump truck. As soon as he got outside, he had pushed a heavy dumpster in front of the emergency door, blocking that exit, funneling the auditorium crowd away from himself.

He had shed the coveralls and baseball cap, throwing them in the back of the dump truck. He now sported the dark business suit he had on underneath. And except for the scruffy beard, he could *almost* pass for an attorney. *I should leave now*, he thought.

But decades of dedication to DeVille made his feet feel like they were encased in cement. He had been worried about DeVille having to testify. He didn't like DeVille being in Iowa *at all*. Too many bad things had happened here. Too many bad people had hurt DeVille.

Then he felt that something was just *wrong*. He peered over the hood of the truck so he could see the edge of the crowd spilling on the street on the other side of the building, the fire alarm still sounding loudly.

They never can figure out how to shut those off quick, he thought. *Never.*

When he had done his last big favor for DeVille, a fire alarm was still ringing when the apartment house collapsed in a fiery tumult killing the last surviving DeVille tormenter from the orphanage.

A dozen innocent people died that night, too.

Mars' mind drifted from the courthouse scene in front of him to remembering *that* blaze. The fire made national headlines because of the natural gas explosion in the basement of the apartment house that had preceded the fire that swept the structure.

He snapped out of his reverie when he heard sirens.

Idiots, he thought. *There's no real fire.*

Then he listened more intently.

The sirens were police units, not just fire trucks.

And he saw several people on the sidewalk in front were pointing his direction.

Chapter 34

The attorneys for A.G. DeVille flanked him and Rod Mayenlyn like a protective wedge on a football field as they headed towards the limousine in the county courthouse parking lot that had brought DeVille and Mayenlyn in earlier that morning.

Given the half dozen police cruisers and fire trucks rolling up in front of the courthouse, the attorneys were pretty sure court would be adjourned for the balance of the day. Regardless, it might take an hour – or longer – to clear the building for people to go back in.

As they made their way to the limo, Calvin Boviné was trailing them about 100 yards back.

Boviné wasn't entirely sure what he was going to do. He knew he wanted to have DeVille and Mayenlyn look him in the face. He felt anger rising and tried to stifle it.

He knew the attorneys surrounding DeVille would give way in a heartbeat if he confronted them so he could face down DeVille and Mayenlyn.

Pencil necks, he thought. *They look like they're pretending they're the goddamn Secret Service.*

The fire alarm suddenly went still as the sounds of the crowd in front of the courthouse burbled into the parking lot. He heard a bullhorn voice order people to move away from the front doors to allow the fire department to go inside.

From across the parking lot, Mars spotted DeVille, Mayenlyn and the attorneys beginning to cluster around the limousine.

I have to go now. This second, he thought. *This second.*

But just as the mental cement holding his feet started to crack, he spotted Boviné.

Boviné's hands were shaped into fists. He was leaning forward and quickly closing the distance between himself and the DeVille entourage.

Not far behind him Mars could see the young girl reporter who had spotted him in the auditorium. And just behind her, he recognized the reporter he had seen with her in Williston, the one who had been sitting down in the front of the legislative chamber.

The reporter was having trouble keeping up with the girl as he struggled to run in a pair of pointy-toed cowboy boots.

Everything *screamed* to Mars to simply walk away, to get to where he had stashed a full change of clothes and a car.

Now! I need to go now, he thought.

Now! he thought again. Except Boviné looked like he posed a real threat to DeVille – to the man Mars had been protecting since they were children.

He felt a roaring sound in his head. His vision blurred as he launched himself from behind the dump truck and started walking quickly towards the limousine on the opposite side of the parking lot.

Then he broke into a loping run towards DeVille, his mind sliding back to the day when he came upon DeVille, pants around his knees, being attacked by the boys at the orphanage.

Mars barely noticed that the two overweight sheriff's deputies who had been standing guard in front of the courtroom door had rounded the corner behind Keith and Sheode.

Run away Archimedes! Mars thought as he quickly closed the gap between himself and DeVille.

Archimedes! Run away! Run! Run! Run!!!!! Tears streamed down his face as he ran faster to intercept Calvin Boviné before he got to his only friend.

Chapter 35

Later that week Jack Stafford's column about the brawl and arrests in the parking lot of the Boyette County Courthouse called it "an ugly human, emotional, and legal convergence."

> It was as if everyone was trapped in a funnel, swirling around, forced together in a wild melee with A.G. DeVille, head of the DeVille Energy Federation, at the epicenter of the downward pull.
>
> It will take time – maybe weeks – to sort out all the threads.
>
> But suspected arsonist Marsden Weesley – who authorities believe set the recent fire at The Redoubt in Iowa – is in custody in a Boyette, Iowa hospital listed in critical condition with a serious head injury.
>
> Energy magnate A.G. DeVille is in custody at the same hospital with a gunshot wound to his arm. He faces charges of conspiracy relating to the fire – as well as charges in connection to a decades' old arson cold-case from a fire that destroyed the orphanage where he and Weesley grew up.
>
> Officials also say they have opened an investigation into nearly a dozen of what they are calling 'revenge murders' of former orphanage residents. DeVille and Weesley are considered persons of interest in the case.
>
> At the same time, federal government officials – speaking on condition of anonymity – say the DEF project known as "The Devil's Pipeline" will now be the

subject of an investigation over issues relating to suspected misuse of funds.

The officials say the DEF project has been on the political skids – and regulators' radar – for months since officials discovered that federal funds were not being used to make forward progress on the pipeline as required, but leveraging more DEF purchases of water rights around the nation.

Chapter 36

The cast that ran from Keith Everlight's right elbow to his wrist sported signatures from Jack, Sheode, Calvin Boviné, and the two sheriff's deputies whose noses had been broken by Marsden Weesley.

Even one of the DEF attorneys signed it when he thanked Keith.

"I like your funnel analogy," Keith told Jack, reading the column.

"When I hit that Weesley guy it was like my fist was kissing a freight train going 100 miles an hour. The doctor says I actually splintered by forearm."

Keith arrived at the melee in the courthouse parking lot just as Calvin Boviné and Marsden Weesley collided like two comic book "Transformer" characters, immensely powerful and seemingly invulnerable to any pain from the roundhouse punches and kicks they were throwing at each other.

Mars was slightly taller than Calvin but had much longer arms. He was in a maniacal state, swinging wildly at Calvin and the DEF attorneys who couldn't move out of the way fast enough. He was trying to keep Calvin away from DeVille, while DeVille was scrambling to get the door open to the limo.

As Calvin expected, the attorneys had tried to scatter as he approached. But Mars reached them from the opposite side at the same time, stepping in front of DeVille.

Amid the wild punching and kicking, Mars kept trying to grab Calvin long enough to get an arm around his bull-like neck to choke him.

Keith – a full foot shorter than either man – slid in underneath the two men, throwing his best punch at Mars' jaw, sending a shooting pain from Keith's fist to his shoulder.

The punch only succeeded in diverting Mars long enough for Mars to grab Keith with one hand and toss him onto the hood of the limousine like he was a sack of oranges.

One of the badly huffing sheriff's deputies – whose duties since joining the force had been mostly limited to acting as a bailiff and looking menacing – pulled out his service weapon when he saw Mars had gotten his hands around a struggling Calvin Boviné's throat.

The deputy shouted "Halt!" but quickly realized the ape-like attacker was not going to stop. His equally winded deputy colleague – whose field experience was also almost nil, too – used a two-handed grip as he swung his heavy baton at the back of Mars' head.

Mars loosened his grip on Boviné and calmly swung a backhand solidly across the deputy's face, snapping the deputy's nose to one side.

At that point, the deputy with the drawn weapon yelled "Halt" in a shaking voice one more time, almost simultaneously pulling the trigger. His shot missed Mars huge body entirely but managed to put a .40 caliber round through the shoulder of one of the DEF attorneys. The bullet passed neatly into the arm of A.G. DeVille, who fell into the limousine.

*****

The roar of the gunshot startled nearly everyone enough that it stopped almost all motion.

The exception was Keith, who despite the pain in his arm had slowly crawled up on the top of the limousine. He crabbed his way along the roof towards the back door where A.G. DeVille had fallen into the limo after being shot.

The gunshot ended Marsden Weesley's assault on the now-unconscious Calvin Boviné sprawled on the ground. Mars was reaching into the limo with both arms to get to DeVille who was screaming in pain.

This better work or that fat deputy will shoot me, too, Keith thought. For a moment he wondered if he should back off and wait. He could see deputies running across the parking lot toward the limo.

But then he saw Mars' contorted face as his head popped up at the level of the limo roof where Keith was.

He'll kill someone, Keith thought.

Mars roared at Keith, opening his mouth like an animal about to use his powerful jaws to attack. His hands were still below, inside the door of the car, where he was trying to cradle and comfort the still-howling DeVille.

Keith leaned on his right side on the roof of the limo and swung his left cowboy boot as hard as could, taking aim at Mars' head.

Police later said it was a very lucky kick for Keith, less so for Mars.

A moment after the point of Keith's boot connected with Mars' temple, the big man dropped to the pavement in one swift motion like a marionette whose strings have been cut.

For a sickening moment, Keith thought he might have killed him.

Epilog

January 20, 2017

VASHON ISLAND, Washington State – All three houses at the Walsh-Stafford compound were full of journalists from the *Clarion Newspaper Syndicate* and their families concluding a weeklong staff meeting.

The main event this last day was watching the inauguration of the 45th President of the United States.

The DeVille Energy Federation's Devil's Pipeline project was officially shut down, partly by the uncovering of A.G. DeVille's machinations, coupled with the ongoing, drenching wet winter that was making California's drought problems less urgent by the day. Jack proudly told the staff that DEF's project was doomed also "by dogged reporting by all of you."

The outgoing federal administration announced withdrawal of all support for the pipeline on the same early January day A.G. DeVille was indicted on conspiracy-to-commit murder charges with co-defendant Marsden Weesley.

Numerous staff changes at the three newspapers and realignments were announced during the week, including hiring reporter Sergei Lakanovich, a Russian native who had graduated three years before with twin M.A.s in journalism and environmental studies from a Southern California university. He earned his media spurs by writing dispatches for Agencé-France Presse and as a science correspondent for magazines.

A deeply blushing Keith Everlight used the occasion to announce his engagement to Sheode Walker. That bit of joyful news added to the glow of an announcement by Jack that a consortium of Kent State alums had put together sufficient funding to build and operate the James Albert Osmett Peace Center at *The Redoubt* on the site of the burned-out farmhouse.

Perhaps the happiest person was 7-year-old Noah Walter Stafford.

Since Thanksgiving his father and two aunts had been living fulltime in the main house at Vashon Island, no longer jetting off to Iowa or California.

And he was thrilled to have the estate overflowing with other people like Uncle Eli from Pennsylvania, who Noah knew wasn't his real uncle.

Everyone had gathered in the main house to watch Donald Trump take the oath of office, a stunned silence replacing a raft of smart-aleck comments that preceded it. The reality of what they faced seemed so unreal. The journalists sat uncharacteristically silent listening to the pundits dissect the event.

When it was over, Jack took Noah outside onto the large patio that faced Seattle where the two of them often sat. Noah vaulted up onto his father's lap.

The days of listening to the editor-reporter-media conversations had accelerated Noah's already precocious interest in the news. "Somebody said the president's really mean," Noah said. "And Uncle Eli said Russia made him president."

Jack let Noah's words hang in space as he watched pleasure boats move across the wide channel along with ever-present Seattle ferries.

He knew that Noah would persist with his questions as his late mother Devon always had when they worked together as journalists – and his two aunts still did. *A Walsh family trait*, he thought. Persistence with a touch of relentlessness, even at 7-years-old.

Jack caught a whiff of cigarette smoke from the other end of the patio.

Sergei, he thought.

"Dad," Noah said. "When you were talking to everybody you thanked them for protecting people from bad people. Is the president bad?"

Jack shifted Noah's weight slightly. "We can't say that yet. You know we try to be fair. Right?" Jack said. "But you asked about what Uncle Eli said? About Russia? Maybe that's a good question to ask Sergei."

Noah gave Jack a hug and slid off his lap, immediately breaking into a half-run, half-walk towards Sergei. Then he stopped and came back, whispering conspiratorially.

"I'm going to tell him he should stop smoking cigarettes."

Jack smiled and gave Noah a thumbs-up as he watched his son trot again towards Sergei.

He heard the double doors to the patio pop open behind him, followed by the chatter of the reporters and editors who had continued to watch the inauguration coverage and anti-Trump demonstrations.

He braced himself to hear news about some foul political bombshell or more anti-Trump violence. Instead he heard the word "whale" spoken by several voices almost like a chant. He turned to see several people scanning the channel with field glasses. Then he spotted the breaching whales, too, majestic orcas, now visible with the naked eye, quickly moving closer to the Vashon shoreline. He watched his excited news staff chattering like children, pointing out each whale, straining their eyes to make the next sighting. The inauguration, the demonstrations and all the violence had been left behind.

Jack could see Noah was holding Sergei's hand, pulling on it to ensure he looked in the right direction where Noah spotted a whale.

Now the whales were breaching wildly, putting on one of those displays that Jack felt were good for the soul.

After an often-glum morning and conversations about the future, the leaping whales were providing a magnificent living reminder about nature, balance and above all, the simple joy of life. *I need to hang onto this moment*, Jack thought. *I need to remember it.*

He was surprised to feel tears welling up, dabbing quickly at his eyes before anyone noticed.

Happy tears are the best, he thought. *I need to remember to tell Noah that.*

#####

Author's Note

The initial inspiration for *The Devil's Pipeline* came as my wife Sylvia Fox and I were driving through Kent, Ohio several years ago, traveling west to California to visit our children and friends.

It wasn't until the novel was near publication that I realized I had been a refugee of sorts from the violence that occurred on the Kent State University campus May 4, 1970, similar to one of the main characters introduced in this novel's first pages. It was the spring of 1970 and the nation was in turmoil. Much like today, people were divided and politicized.

Almost three months to the day after the Kent State massacre, I left my Lakewood, New York home – fled might be more accurate – and drove west in a Volkswagen van on a long, looping trip around America, ending up in California.

A steaming cauldron of hate spilled over after the Kent State shootings. Hateful people – including some where I worked – said the college students mowed down in a hail of Ohio National Guard gunfire "had it coming," for protesting the Vietnam War.

That hateful, ignorant attitude was on my mind as I drafted *The Devil's Pipeline*.

It is mirrored today by the blatant contempt by oil and gas corporations for anyone who dares attempt to thwart plans for building pipelines.

That contempt has help spark violent confrontations as some communities try to protect themselves from the many dangers posed by oil and gas pipelines.

The Devil's Pipeline joins predecessor novels *The Fracking War* and *Fracking Justice* in a series of books chronicling the fictional journalistic efforts of Jack Stafford and his staff.

Their efforts will continue.

Point Richmond, California
November 1, 2018

Praise for THE DEVIL'S PIPELINE

The Devil's Pipeline takes us to the front lines of an escalating war between environmentalists' resistance and the fossil fuel industry. Michael J. Fitzgerald's novel may be fiction, but the conflict between big energy companies and grassroots defenders of land, water, and a livable planet is very real. In this tale of crusading journalism and activism, readers will discover what it takes to keep the 'devil's work' at bay."
— **Steve Early**, labor activist & author of *Refinery Town: Big Oil, Big Money, and the Remaking of an American City.*

This is a page-turning eco-thriller served up with a dose of humor. It is a cautionary tale about unbridled corporate greed and those who battle, David-like, against our earth's devastation.
— **Rita M. Gardner**, author of the award-winning memoir of *The Coconut Latitudes.*

A handful of dedicated journalists do battle with a titan of the petrochemical industry, and, amazingly, heroically, win, though not without tragic losses along the way. This is Michael J. Fitzgerald's third eco-thriller novel, and perhaps his best.
— **Elizabeth Claman**, author of *The Prodigal Wife* and other novels, poems and art.

ALSO BY MICHAEL J. FITZGERALD

The Jack Stafford Series

Praise for *The Fracking War (2014)*
First Place, General Fiction, Green Book Festival, New York 2015

"It was *Uncle Tom's Cabin*, not economic data, that turned the page on slavery. It was *The Grapes of Wrath*, not demographic reports that opened a nation's eyes to Dust Bowl relocation. Out of that tradition comes Michael J. Fitzgerald's *The Fracking War*. Here within a smoldering crucible of social crisis, is a tale of power, money, fateful choice and consciences around. If you like your drill rigs served up within the context of a fast-moving plot line, you've got what you want right in your hands."

— Sandra Steingraber, author, *Living Downstream* and *Raising Elijah*

"If you thought the debate over energy policy was a tad dry, this novel might change your mind. God hope it never comes to this!"

— Bill McKibben, author, *The End of Nature* and co-founder of 350.org

Praise for *Fracking Justice (2015)*

Named Top 100 Indy Books of 2015 by *Kirkus Book Reviews*

"This isn't just a good read — it's grounded in a very real ecological crisis, and a backlash against those who dare to speak up. *Fracking Justice* captures exactly what is at stake, both for the planet and for our freedoms."
— Will Potter, author, *Green is the New Red*

"It maybe fiction but it shows how the fossil fuel industry is fracturing not only our land but our communities. Read this page-turner than pass it on."
— Josh Fox, director of *Gasland* and *Gasland 2*

"*Fracking Justice* is a smart, powerful page-turner, leading the way into a genre we need more of — environmental thriller. It's exciting, edge-of-your-seat writing and all the more scary because it's so timely."
— Ellie Ashe, author, *Chasing the Dollar*

"This is a must-read whether you want to learn more about fracking or are simply a fan of good writing."
— Mike Cutillo, Executive Editor, *Finger Lakes Times*

Watch for more books by this author at
http://michaeljfitzgerald.blogspot.com/

Made in the USA
San Bernardino, CA
27 March 2019